C000184818

Ethel Carnie Holdsworth

Helen of Four Gates

To Anne,

Enjoy!

All best,

Nicola

x.

The Ethel Carnie Holdsworth Series
General Editor: Nicola Wilson

Pamela Fox is Professor of English at Georgetown University specialising in working-class literature and culture as well as feminist and cultural theory. She is the author of *Class Fictions: Shame and Resistance in the British Working-Class Novel, 1890-1945* (Duke U.P., 1994) and *Natural Acts: Gender, Race, And Rusticity in Country Music* (Univ. of Michigan Press, 2009). She is also co-editor of *Old Roots, New Routes: The Cultural Politics of Alt.Country Music,* with Barbara Ching (Univ. of Michigan Press, 2008).

Nicola Wilson is a lecturer in the English Literature department at the University of Reading. She is the author of *Home in British Working-Class Fiction* (Ashgate, 2015) and has published on working-class writing in *Key Words; The Oxford History of the Novel in English, vol. 7* (Oxford U.P., 2015); and *A History of British Working Class Literature* (Cambridge U.P., 2016). In 2011 she introduced and edited Ethel Carnie Holdsworth's 1925 novel, *This Slavery* (Trent).

Ethel Carnie Holdsworth

Helen of Four Gates

WITH AN INTRODUCTION BY PAMELA FOX

Edited by Nicola Wilson

Kennedy & Boyd

2016

Kennedy & Boyd
an imprint of
Zeticula Ltd
Unit 13,
196 Rose Street,
Edinburgh,
EH2 4AT

http://www.kennedyandboyd.co.uk
admin@kennedyandboyd.co.uk

First published in 1917 by Herbert Jenkins.
This edition Copyright © Zeticula Ltd 2016
First published in this edition 2016

Note on the text
To produce this edition of *Helen of Four Gates* we
have used the first American edition, published by
E.P. Dutton & Co. in New York in 1917. The text
of the current edition, set in Bookman Old Style,
follows that of the original text as closely as possible,
retaining older forms of English usage and grammar.

Front cover image: Ethel Carnie Holdsworth.
Reproduced with kind permission from Helen Brown.

ISBN 978-1-84921-128-4
All rights reserved. No part of this publication may
be reproduced, stored in a retrieval system, or
transmitted in any form or by any means, electronic,
mechanical, photocopying, recording or otherwise,
without the prior permission of the publishers.

Acknowledgements

Pamela Fox: I would like to thank Nicola Wilson for the invitation to participate in the republishing of this novel and am grateful for her assistance with some hard-to-find sources. I also want to thank Nick Wilding and Christopher Lynch for their recovery of the film *Helen of Four Gates*—a significant contribution to silent film studies that will undoubtedly enrich future commentary on the novel as well as Carnie Holdsworth's work as a whole. Both have generously shared pertinent documents and information with me. Finally, I wish to thank three institutions: the Hebden Bridge Local History Society, particularly Diana Monahan, for providing me access to archival material; the George Eastman House, particularly Jared Case and Nancy Kauffman, for facilitating my viewing of the film; and Georgetown University's English Department for supporting my work on the Introduction with summer funding.

Nicola Wilson: I would like to thank all of those who continue to work to preserve Ethel Carnie Holdsworth's name and legacy. I would also like to acknowledge my 'Class Matters' students for the enthusiasm with which they have approached Ethel's writing, and to thank in particular Cariad Williams for her careful copy-editing on this new edition.

Stills from the film of *Helen of Four Gates*. Dir. Cecil Hepworth. Hepworth Picture Plays. 1920.
Kindly provided by Nancy Kauffman of George Eastman House in Rochester, NY.

Contents

Introduction
by Pamela Fox

In reviewing Ethel Carnie's 1913 novel *Miss Nobody*, recently brought back into print in this new Kennedy & Boyd series, *The Times Literary Supplement* enthuses that 'reissues like these are in everybody's interest'. But its reviewer also calls for further exploration: the former mill worker's surprisingly wide-ranging fiction, mixing popular literary styles with socialist-feminist polemics, raises 'questions not just about the canon' but also specifically 'about the functions of melodrama and romance within radical and feminist fictions.'[1] While much of Ethel Carnie Holdsworth's work incorporates those popular elements, *Helen of Four Gates*, published in 1917, positively embodies them. (Even the *TLS* reviewer in passing deems it pure 'unbuttoned melodrama'.) A bona fide best seller later brought to silent film by director Cecil Hepworth, *Helen* seems a particularly suitable novel (and film) for such consideration and, along the way, pushes twenty-first-century readers to reimagine what they think they know about the classed and gendered politics of literary study.

Although Carnie Holdsworth published ten novels, three poetry collections, a plethora of children's stories, popular serialised fiction, and journalistic commentary before her death in 1963, both her life story and literary reputation remained largely obscured until the 1980s. But thanks to more recent historical recovery efforts, we now have enough details to sketch out a basic biography as well as a more nuanced understanding of her contributions to what has been variously called British 'social problem', 'proletarian', or 'working-class' writing. Below, I briefly outline the years before she wrote *Helen of Four Gates* to provide a preliminary context for its ideas.

Born in 1886, Carnie Holdsworth spent her early childhood in the cotton mill towns of northeast Lancashire—Oswaldtwistle, Great Harwood—where she attended primary school until age thirteen, when she began working full-time as a winder in the St. Lawrence Mill. Two years earlier, she had begun her apprenticeship in textile labour by working part-time as a reacher. She sought to extend her schooling as well, however, by taking evening writing classes at the local technical institute. A confluence of educational and work experiences, along with her early exposure to socialist beliefs through her father's involvement with the Burnley branch of the Social Democratic Federation, fuelled her early poetry (*Rhymes from the Factory* and *Songs of a Factory Girl*), which gained recognition and spurred her recruitment in 1909 by prominent socialist Robert Blatchford to write for his newspaper the *Woman Worker*. But it was largely her working-class credentials that served as the badge of her literary success. During local filming of *Helen of Four Gates*, for instance, a 1920 profile on Carnie Holdsworth claims that her authentic portrayal of the mill community 'has been bred into her, through sharing their lives, their labours, their joys and sorrows, standing at the loom in a factory, living with them in tiny houses in poky streets.' The interviewer concludes that this 'premier novelist' of Lancashire 'is successful because she is certain of herself and her cast ... and as a consequence, her work possesses a richness and atmosphere, a boldness and truth ... extremely scarce in these days of problem stories.'[2]

However, soon after she moved to London at age twenty-two, Carnie Holdsworth had recorded her own sense of division from, as well as solidarity with, the Lancashire 'folk'. She confesses that she had 'hated the narrow, monotonous, long days' in the factory, but when hinting at her rebellious thoughts to her workmates, she was both 'shame[d]' and disturbed by their 'stolid patience', which 'never questioned but that the cage' is their 'birth-right'.[3] Brought in as a 'typical Lancashire factory girl'[4] to bolster the paper's working-class female readership, she made good on that promise through her weekly essays, poems, stories, and brief stint as editor—but not in the way Blatchford had intended.[5] Rather than extol the virtues of working-class life and a paternalistic version of cultural socialism, Carnie Holdsworth wielded her own brand of feminist critique addressing marital and family violence ('how are women to know these bullies from the rest?'[6]), women's 'dreary' daily existence as wives and mothers as well as paid workers, and their continuing marginalisation within socialist organisations. As she insists in 'Modern Womanhood', '[w]e shall help in the great fight—the only fight that is worth our strength ... For we are women, and refuse to stand on a hill, safe and afar, watching the struggle.'[7] Crucially, at this stage in her thinking she emphasised what 'half dead' working women *lack* as they exhaust themselves creating profit and sustenance for others: 'our right to play'.[8] She certainly urged her readers to value collective class fellowship and to organise for basic rights. Yet her insistence on pleasure, gained from reading literary classics, enjoying nature, or the potential thrill of romantic love, also called for individual space and consciousness within the mass. It would prove her calling card in the next decade as she largely turned to novel writing to propagate her political views.

After being fired from the *Woman Worker* (replaced by Blatchford's daughter under a retitled publication called *Women Folk*), Carnie Holdsworth returned to her home town and briefly to factory work while continuing to publish in women's periodicals, working in her mother's modest draper's shop, and resuming part-time study at a nearby college.[9] In 1913, she founded the Rebel Pen Club while working at Bebel House Women's College in London, which formed part of the Marxist-led Central Labour Colleges promotion of radical adult education. In attempting to clarify the Club's goals to a London-based suffrage paper, she archly noted that '[w]orking-class women ... must learn to cultivate powers of expression in writing and in speaking' so that they bring to light 'corners of life unseen by the many superior persons who have shown the necessity that the workers should speak for themselves.' Doing so, she argued, promoted 'women's forward movement in the widest sense of the term.'[10]

She proceeded to perform that work of literary exposure—lifting the veil on her own seemingly invisible class—in *Miss Nobody*, published that same year by Methuen Press. Like many debut novels, its uneven execution didn't quite match its aim, which perhaps explained its disappointing sales. But it provides a window onto Carnie Holdsworth's initial struggles to meet conflicting literary expectations for social fiction in the pre-war era, intermixing the urban and pastoral alongside variants of romance, proletarian, and folk narrative. She reveals a particular debt to the Victorian 'industrial novel' perfected by Elizabeth Gaskell, who incorporated more sensational elements—murder trials, cross-class romance and marriage, secretive family origins—into an otherwise realist story of class conflict featuring a spirited worker-heroine.[11]

Helen of Four Gates: Melodrama, Vision, and 'Colour'

The conditions under which Carnie Holdsworth began writing her second novel reflected a dramatically different type of upheaval on both personal and national fronts: marriage, children, and the First World War. In 1915, she married life insurance salesman, poet, and farmer Alfred Holdsworth; she gave birth to their first daughter a year later, the second in 1920. While trying to raise a young family and contend with her newfound status as wife and mother, Carnie Holdsworth also continued the anti-war work she had begun several years before as an extension of her internationalist brand of socialist politics by joining forces with Lancashire's British Citizen Party. She and Alfred both vehemently opposed conscription, yet he eventually went to the Western Front when called up in 1917 and was reported missing in action nearly a year later before being discovered alive as a prisoner of war at the war's end.[12]

In the midst of this tumult, Carnie Holdsworth managed to keep publishing creative writing alongside her more direct anti-war essays. Perhaps due to *Miss Nobody*'s largely poor reviews, she chose to make her next novel a more likely commercial success by adapting a narrative formula popularised by the Brontë sisters roughly seventy years earlier: Gothic melodrama set in the Yorkshire moors. Romance and other forms of 'escapist' fiction proved especially appealing to female readers and cinema-goers during World War I, and Roger Smalley makes the case that Carnie Holdsworth decided even earlier to adapt these modes for their 'propaganda potential.'[13] Certainly much of her *Woman Worker* material celebrated all kinds of literature, from so-called high to the low, for its power to make the working-class reader momentarily forget her plight—whether at the mill or at home—as well as raise her consciousness. In 'Living Pictures', she wants to know 'who invented the cinematograph, for assuredly he did more for the working classes than many who are knighted.' Recounting her experience at the picture show, she concludes '[a]ltogether it was a fine time; and the faces of the audience were as good to watch as the pictures, as tragedy or comedy swayed their minds, for there was sympathy with the wronged, a glad sense of the justice of things when the redress came, and even a forgiveness for the evil-doer.'[14] But beyond their simplistic morals, she suggests that popular fiction and film, directed at the masses and targeting emotion rather than intellect, potentially fostered a different type of vision—what she refers to as 'colour'.

In her 1909 essay 'How Colour is Introduced', Carnie Holdsworth distinguishes between two groups within the working class: those few who seek 'a splash of colour' by choosing to 'see and suffer'; and the 'colour-blind' majority who 'have not strayed from the straight and narrow way'. The former resist their parson's sermons and 'compress all the pleasure they can into the short weekend', while the 'respectable toilers' are likened to 'convicts' who 'drag the chains to their graves', mistakenly believing that 'they are happy'. In sum, those who 'welcome a thread of scarlet' represent 'the finest natures', as they 'have not forgotten how to feel'. The capacity to experience keen emotion thus spurs, rather than blocks, insight: 'a man of strong character and passions' is tantamount to '[t]he man who can see—who is alive to his position'.[15] It results in a kind of consciousness that she soon after equates with 'poetry'.[16]

Helen of Four Gates serves as the distillation of these theories. On the surface, it appears far removed from

Carnie Holdsworth's class preoccupations. Set on a remote farm in an especially 'wild', lawless portion of the Pennines renowned for its history of witch trials, the novel focuses on the pathological—indeed sadistic—father-daughter relationship of Abel and Helen Mason. Squatting on the borders of neighbouring villages, Four Gates farm is a perverse mockery of dominant social norms, a household that thrives not on domestic harmony but emotional and physical violence. Its patriarch, poisoned by a streak of family madness and an obsessive revenge plot over a broken engagement, dedicates his life to punishing the daughter of his now dead former fiancée, whom he passes off as his own flesh and blood. She in turn pursues an equally 'mad' love with farm hand Martin Scott while being literally sold to Abel's savage apprentice, Fielding Day. The novel's isolated country setting and hothouse focus on personal melodrama might appear curious choices for this avowed champion of the working class.

However, in drawing on both *Wuthering Heights* and *Jane Eyre* for Gothic mood and certain plot elements, Carnie Holdsworth is not simply capitalising on their dual sensationalist appeal and literary cachet.[17] She recognises both works' feminist recasting of the Gothic convention, creating in Helen Mason a strikingly transgressive female protagonist who battles all three men for various forms of freedom. Further, she arguably utilises the *class* tensions of her melodramatic framework to critique another kind of power structure. A highly adaptable genre, melodrama has its own complicated class roots in British culture, initially affiliated with the working-class music hall and other 'low' performance sites and styles, then gradually refashioned for middle-class audiences drawn to more realistic sentimental comedies and drama. By the early twentieth century, its starkly defined heroes and villains and cruder form of spectacle were frowned upon by critics and the intelligentsia, but as Carnie Holdsworth's essay on cinema demonstrates, melodrama remained popular with working-class audiences who perhaps found release in its outsized emotion and insistent moral schema often grounded in stories of class opposition.[18]

Helen of Four Gates's opening pages may invite the reader into a supernatural landscape of Druid worship and 'anarch[ic]'[19] darkness, but it swiftly incorporates modern class markers into its mythos: 'The valleys between were strewn with factory towns. Here and there was a furnace, whose glare and after-darkness would soon change the night sky like the eye of some fire-god opening and closing' (6). Additionally, both Scott and Day enter the narrative as outcast 'tramps' seeking food and shelter. Yet through his diabolical pact with Mason, Day assumes brutal authority over not only Helen but the everyday operations of Four Gates farm, so that the narrator simply labels him 'the boss'—he becomes a stand-in for capitalism's greed and selfishness, inciting fear in the villagers and, in the novel's climax, his own death by a resentful fellow tramp. Tellingly, he is dismissed as a 'tin-god' (212), invoking a key passage from 'How Colour is Introduced': 'We are not tin men and women: we have blood in our veins and eyes in our head, and want some sunshine and blue sky and bird-songs before we pass to the great majority.' The very exoticism of the story and its environs allows the novel to raise (as well as deflect) difficult questions concerning class solidarity and conflict.

Indeed, though this narrative's predominant palette may be black, its spectacular setting—alternately bleak and exhilarating—insists that nature offers the oppressed their greatest chance to seize redemptive 'colour'. In her earlier work, Carnie Holdsworth tends to romanticise the country and its 'folk' in keeping with pastoral tradition: 'The problems of life seem so simple here: in fact, there seems no problem at all when one gets close back to what Stevenson calls God's green caravanserai ... There is no past, no future, nothing but a glad present with sweet country lanes, wholesome country fare.'[20] *Helen of Four Gates* largely overturns such sentimentalism in its fevered portrait of the Mason farm and even the stinging gossip of Brungerley's women. But the surrounding moors prove to be Helen's genuine home precisely because they resist taming, domestication, 'sweetness'. Their wildness authorises her own fierce spirit, as she 'might have been some high priestess of Nature's—imbued with the holiness of life and its aspirations, and scorn of those who ran from its battles. ... from every inch of her tall form, issued a majestic pride, defiance, and dignity' (111-2). Declaring herself 'nothing but feeling' (39), Helen utilises this kinship with the natural world to withstand her bodily and psychic torture at the farm but also to pursue Martin, whose well-thumbed copy of the *Decline and Fall of the Roman Empire* signals his misguided faith in reason over mysticism, civilisation over primitivism.[21] Whether casting a spell in the woods to bind the two in a supernatural wedding or enticing him to frolic in the meadows, she poses her sheer life force against his 'thinking'. Not surprisingly, then, once Martin fully abandons Helen and she commits her sole mistake—succumbing to Day to avoid community shaming—her brief 'soullessness' (130) is registered in the snowy landscape's notable *absence* of colour, its 'blinding track of whiteness' (127).

As this last metaphor suggests, the novel overall casts her instinctive pantheism as an authentic mode of vision: 'she stared across a blaze of colour that was life ... beautiful, with all its struggle, that world of nature' (52). Martin's 'humanism' by contrast 'had made her see less in the woods, the moors, the hedgerows' (52). But this witch/wild cat/mad woman arrives at a new kind of liberating consciousness by honouring both her need for distinctly human companionship and her insistence on seeing clearly. As she declares to Martin in the closing pages, "'I allus want to look—what's comin'" (203). The novel essentially stages a contest of competing gazes, pitting Helen's instinctive stare against her antagonists' increasingly hidden mode of surveillance. Film historian Christine Gledhill has explained that cinematic melodrama typically stages a spectator on screen, such as the viewer of a theatrical performance within the storyline, in order to construct the film's own audience as a self-conscious 'witness' to its events.[22] Carnie Holdsworth exploits another version of that figure—the concealed adversary who spies on the action—as both Mason and Day turn to stalking and spying to monitor Helen's whereabouts. As will be particularly evident in the film version of *Helen* but is also the case here, the audience's own reading/viewing thus becomes uncomfortably aligned with the villains'; we not only serve as 'witness' to the plot's machinations but also threaten to become complicit in their regulatory gaze. For his part, Martin attempts to avoid looking at Helen at all in order to resist her allure. Yet after he has fled abroad and fallen deeply ill out of his suppressed desire, he returns to Brungerley to glimpse her face once more before he dies.

The novel's romance plot thus also plays a critical role in developing its alternate model of defiance. Martin's final 'recovery' is most recognisable in his transformed definition of both humanness and masculinity after the couple reunites against threat of both their deaths: 'He was a man. A woman cared about him' (180). As I've argued elsewhere, Carnie Holdsworth makes innovative use of romance not to divert from her socialist-feminist aims but to enhance them.[23] She bids her readers to join Martin in redefining their own core notions and beliefs—to reimagine freedom so that it privileges pleasure over duty, emotion over conventional reason, individual human bonds over property and profit. 'Love Triumphant', the title to *Helen of Four Gates'* final chapter, encompasses these possibilities as perhaps the ultimate example of 'colour'.

To be sure, in much of this author's writing about Lancashire daily life, romantic love is in short supply. She likens most working-class women's 'indifferent' marriages to 'prostitution' and exposes rampant spousal abuse, which she witnessed in her own parents' relationship.[24] At Carnie Holdsworth's request, her wedding to Alfred took place in a perfunctory registry office without a reception or honeymoon; she eventually left him in 1928.[25] Yet her long-held dream of 'comradeship'[26] between men and women attempts to retrieve and repurpose romance along feminist lines. In *Helen*, farming couple Lizzie and Teddy Trip's marriage potentially functions as one modest version of such a bond: their home is cheery and bright— the direct counter to Four Gates—and they express genuine affection for one another. At the same time, their relationship is hardly idealised, as Lizzie blames her husband for 'buryin' me alive' in the household with their children when he goes off on a drunken bender. They appear to embody Helen's professed desire late in the novel: 'I never wanted anything up i' th' air ... Just common things, an' a common life' (199).

But ultimately, Helen has no use for moderation in her relationship with Martin. She insists upon an all-or-nothing union that tilts comradeship onto another axis. Though Mason and Day display equally instinctive personalities ruled by extreme emotions, Helen represents a woman's model of visionary passion.

The men's ambitions are inherently immoral, intent on destroying another human being for twisted personal gain. She follows a single 'creed': the 'sacredness of first love, such as a tribal savage would have held, ere the complexities of modern life placed a barrier between body and soul' (110). Despite her fear of turning into either dying recluse Sue Marsh, who haunts the narrative with her tale of fanatical love gone awry, or Aunt Milly Mason locked away in another kind of asylum, Helen realises that her only hope of being truly 'alive' is to 'snatch' her 'mate—and die for it' (200). As a startlingly aggressive suitor who literally brings her man back to life, she mocks the role of the traditional romantic heroine.

But in exalting such love as the supreme goal and—no matter how contrived—engineering its successful fulfilment at the novel's conclusion, Carnie Holdsworth makes her boldest move as a working-class writer of this era. Challenging the Left's opposition to romance as so much bourgeois claptrap, she uses that plot formula both to critique gender relations within her own as well as other class communities and also to expand labour activists' sense of the mission itself: namely, to recognise the legitimacy of *individual* personal relationships and desires—or more broadly, the existence of 'selves' that shirk all forms of collective orthodoxy, be they Church of England or Marxist. Interestingly, earnings from *Helen of Four Gates*, along with income from three other novels Carnie Holdsworth published in 1920, were used to help fund a short-lived radical newspaper she produced with her husband in the early '20s, *The Clear Light,* which urged solidarity amongst Labour, Communist, and Anarchist movements in combatting the rise of European Fascism. A trailblazing internationalist into the next decade, she clearly saw no incompatibility between her 'popular' and 'political' writing projects.

Critical Reception and Film Version

If Carnie Holdsworth intended to reach a wider readership by adapting common genres, then she certainly succeeded with this novel. By the end of 1917 alone, *Helen of Four Gates* had gone through four editions, selling a total of 25,000 copies; by 1920, the number grew to 33,000. U.S. publishing house E. P. Dutton also brought out an edition in 1917. While these sales figures fall just shy of the 35,000 averaged by a highly popular British female writer during this same period, it seems fair to deem the novel a 'best seller'.[27] The savvy ad campaign launched by its publisher, Herbert Jenkins Ltd., surely contributed to its rise but also concealed its author's identity. Although her 1915 contract with Jenkins lists 'Ethel Carnie' as the book's provisional author, it was published anonymously two years later, with 'The Ex-Mill Girl' as pseudonym even through its later editions. [28] In promoting the novel, Jenkins ran ads under the provocative banner 'Who's the Lady?' accompanied by a small cameo of a masked female profile. Pairing *Helen of Four Gates* with a memoir by 'a Woman of No Importance', the ad exults '[t]wo of the great successes of the hour are anonymous books. They are being read and talked about everywhere. Who are the writers?' *Helen* is billed as '[t]he novel by an ex-Mill Girl that has created a sensation, and has been described as a great novel, an epic, the most sensational novel of recent years.'[29]

Though it would seem counter-intuitive to withhold an author's identity, in this case Jenkins tried to have it both ways by capitalising on the rarity of his writer's class background while distancing her from her prior novel's poor showing. A review of Carnie Holdsworth's subsequent book, *The Taming of Nan*, explains as much, stating that *Miss Nobody* 'sold so badly that when a very different book appeared—*Helen of Four Gates*—the authorship was concealed under the pseudonym of "an ex-mill girl."[30]   However, this state of affairs also confused reviewers, who almost uniformly hail *Helen* as a first novel (which allowed for both praise and criticism) and occasionally find the pen name itself misleading. Such is the case for the American commentator of *The Living Age*: "'By an Ex-Mill-Girl' on the title-page suggests that "Helen of Four Gates" is a story of factory life, but the reader who takes it up with that expectation will be disappointed, and perhaps annoyed. It is a study of individual rather than social problems, and its scene is a farming district in the north of England.' Unable to fathom a connection between these two modes of the 'problem' novel, the reviewer concedes 'the story makes a strong impression' but warns 'it is needlessly repulsive, and only those who enjoy supping on horrors will recommend it to their friends.'[31] Herbert Jenkins clearly hoped to attract new readers for Carnie Holdsworth by either appealing to those who could identify with a female textile worker's outlook or provoking others' curiosity.

For the most part, contemporary critics were drawn to the novel's power. Two lengthier reviews by women attempt to pinpoint its accomplishments. Ruth McIntire, writing for modernist journal the *Dial*, compares the unknown author to Thomas Hardy for her authentic rendering of 'the eternal struggle of all elemental, living things to maintain their birthright to freedom of expression in living terms.' She appreciates the 'truth that the "Ex-Mill-Girl" makes you feel' and acknowledges that '[s]he has run a certain amount of danger in making you feel it.' McIntire credits this realism to the author's own life, writing '[s]he herself must have experienced to an unusual degree the sense of a common heritage with all sentient and growing things.'[32] Lola Ridge of the *New*

Republic likens the novel to *Wuthering Heights* and its author to Emily Brontë for their 'intensity', particularly in the nuanced exchanges between Helen and Martin. Ridge similarly calls *Helen* 'a remarkable book—a first offering of genius ... It is an essence, however crudely distilled, out of our common life, with an authentic if ill-dressed beauty.'[33] Yet she objects to the author's intrusive, almost hectoring voice channelled through the narrator. And perhaps predictably, both critics find the novel's improbable closing—replete with the timely deaths of Day, Mason, and Helen's stillborn child, freeing her to marry Martin—a distasteful 'concession to the gods of credulity that rule our modern marketplace.'[34] Or as Ridge more pointedly charges, its 'miraculous intervention on the hill-side is a subterfuge of the cheapest movie drama.' They applaud the story's universality, its 'sense of a common heritage', as long as its ploys aren't *too* common.

But like it or not, Carnie Holdsworth was keen on getting *Helen of Four Gates* made into just such a 'movie drama', as she found cinema a captivating new device capable of reaching untold numbers of viewers. Its literal 'cheapness' was its virtue: the early film industry primarily targeted working-class audiences in both its content and pricing. In England, cinema houses began popping up in major metropolitan areas in the 1890s; by 1912, 500 could be found in London, 111 in Manchester. On the eve of World War I, 'going to the picture palaces had become a normal activity' for the likes of many in Carnie Holdsworth's position.[35] By 1917, the same year as *Helen*'s publication, approximately half of Britain's populace routinely went to the cinema. As mentioned previously, women were especially drawn to movies for the stories and star spectacles but also for the opportunity to enjoy themselves *independently* in a public setting.[36] Cinema houses offered excitement and escape. One harried mother tells a 1919 movie magazine that she would 'go mad without the pictures; her days are terribly monotonous except for Mondays and Thursdays—the days I come here.' And as letters to such fan publications attest, single young women also flocked to films to learn about distinctly modern femininity.[37]

Armed with her best-selling novel, Carnie Holdsworth apparently sought out filmmakers' ads, placed in a handful of cinema journals, seeking new material.[38] This was a common practice during World War I and beyond as British film offerings became increasingly threatened by the new Hollywood imports from abroad. Producers struggled to keep up and began to rely on popular plays or novels to attract audiences. One such filmmaker was Cecil Hepworth, a lauded 'pioneer' of silent cinema.[39] Born of modest means in South London, Hepworth followed in his father's footsteps to break into the cinematograph business; his first company was formed in 1904. He specialised in literary and stage adaptations and soon became known for 'pictorialist' films prizing the English landscape (a precursor of the later national heritage cinema phenomenon).[40] During the war, he realised he needed to make more commercial films and turned to both past and recent best-selling stories, such as in his most highly regarded film, *Comin' Thro' the Rye*, to 'cash in on the popularity already secured.'[41] In 1920, he must have placed the notice that attracted Carnie Holdsworth's eye, as they began working together to bring *Helen of Four Gates* to the screen.

Hepworth filmed in Yorkshire's Hebden Bridge area, where his author and her daughters had moved during the war (Alfred joined them upon his release). The experience merits a brief passage in his autobiography, where he recounts wanting 'to capture the wonderful atmosphere' of her novel and of that found in nearby Haworth, famed for its connection to the Brontës. The moors offered 'the dour, cruel environment' he had in mind.[42] The film's principal star, Alma Taylor, had become one of the few British silent film actresses to gain a national profile through her long association with Hepworth and was particularly admired for her 'natural' look—'the embodiment of charming, unspoilt British girlhood'.[43] According to one local woman's account, the Hepworth Company's presence in Hebden Bridge caused quite a sensation when she was a girl, providing 'a new adventure' to its residents (including at least one who was an extra on the set). Once the film was released in 1921 and screened in their local cinema, they all found it 'immensely exciting'. Pondering the novel's popularity, she affirms one main reason for its appeal: 'Helen of Four Gates produced a modicum of romance into what by modern life was a fairly bleak Childhood.'[44] It remains unclear, however, whether the film version achieved the same level of success. Hepworth notes that he was 'pleased with the whole job' but claims 'it was not a popular film',[45] despite a positive review from one of the leading cinema magazines, *Kinematograph Weekly*. It may be that its more visceral images of violence, especially directed at a woman, deterred some cinema-goers from recommending it to others.[46] Or perhaps Carnie Holdsworth's class narrative as a whole took Hepworth's 'heritage film' model in an unanticipated, more unsettling direction?

Until several years ago, we could only speculate about the film's treatment of *Helen*'s storyline because it was presumed to be damaged beyond repair or lost entirely. Amidst a national shutdown in film production during 1924 that compounded Hepworth Studios' increasing financial difficulties, the company shortly thereafter declared bankruptcy, and most of

Hepworth's film stock was destroyed to recover its silver nitrate.[47] But due to the recent unflagging efforts of Lancashire historian Christopher Lynch and Hebden Bridge-based filmmaker Nick Wilding, who conducted a five-year search for the last remaining film negative of *Helen of Four Gates*, a new 16 mm print was made available in 2010.[48] Though most cinema scholars fail to mention this film when discussing Hepworth's main body of work, it clearly showcases his signature style, particularly its nearly reverential depiction of the Yorkshire landscape. As Wilding notes, 'it is dreamy and luscious in Hepworth's hands'.[49] In keeping with Carnie Holdsworth's own philosophy, nature has the true starring role, the moors and sky filling nearly every inch of screen and almost always serving as both literal and conceptual frame for the human drama unfolding within its space.

Adapted for the screen by Hepworth's long-time 'scenario writer' Blanche MacIntosh, the approximately one-hour silent film remains faithful to the novel overall, frequently incorporating direct quotes—often in local dialect—into its intertitle captions. Yet it does streamline the narrative to concentrate squarely on the dramatic set of conflicts at Four Gates farm.[50] Lizzie and Teddy Trip make more of a cameo appearance, for instance, and Sue Marsh is excised entirely. More significantly, the novel's opening 'tramping' scenario, featuring Day and Scott's initial meeting alongside other village folk, has been replaced by a flash back scene contextualising Mason's revenge plot (which in the novel is hastily relayed to Day by Abel himself). Doing so helps establish his youthful identity as a man in love, disappointed and ultimately betrayed by his friend/rival who marries his fiancée (Helen's mother). But this altered plot introduction also has the effect of diminishing the narrative's more overt class dimensions—its 'social problem' framing—even as it briefly humanises the man who emerges as the film's most repellent figure. Additionally, the opening betrothal scene echoes later ones introducing Helen and Martin as young lovers: both take place on the moors and involve a concealed male spectator watching the action. Their costuming may have different class coding—Abel and Helen Sr. appear respectable townsfolk while Helen and Martin are in country dress—yet the doubling of the two scenes suggests an almost fated replication of family history. With such telescoping and scene mirroring, the opening's departure from the original text intimates that this story is an entirely private matter.[51]

The film's most significant modification, however, comes in its arguable centrepiece: a fantastical 'witchery' scene of Helen conjuring spirits in the woods. Whereas the novel never actually depicts this incident—we only hear about it early on when Teddy Trip tells of overhearing Helen's wedding incantation—here the cinematography casts Helen as a 'high priestess of Nature'. Chanting 'by the magic of fire, air, and water, I draw thee to me', she contorts her body in a riveting mystical rite. Hepworth clearly exploits the setting's history of witchcraft and magic, made all the more compelling by the public's recent interest in 'fairy lore' prompted by the Cottingley fairies ostensibly photographed by two children in 1917 in West Yorkshire. Although Arthur Conan Doyle didn't publish his book about the incident, *The Coming of the Fairies*, until 1922, he did include two prints of the fairy photographs in an explosive 1920 article for the *Strand*—the year in which Hepworth was filming *Helen*.[52] Beyond its potential commercial value, however, the scene also endorses Helen's bond with the natural world: she doesn't appear frightening, just a unique blend of strength, vulnerability, and sensuality.

Earlier, when she first appears on screen, the camera deviates from its previously distanced, wide-angled shots to an intense close-up of her light-hearted play with several baby farm animals. She takes a duckling to her breast, laughing and caressing as it walks around her neck; a calf licks her fingers. The scene commingles traditional qualities of femininity—innocence, the maternal—with intimations of budding sexuality. The later incantation scene presents a more dramatic spectacle. But for the viewer, both depictions of Helen create an almost privileged sense of intimacy as we watch public moments that feel intensely private. Close-up shots themselves can help foster our identification with specific characters, and she no doubt serves as a distinctly gendered display within them, but these moments of vulnerability also establish Helen as a particularly sympathetic *individual* who exceeds melodramatic typecasting.

The film soon disrupts that audience connection, however, by intercutting shots of a hidden spectator. In the duckling scene (this one entirely invented for the screen) we discover that Mason is secretly watching Helen, so angered by her momentary pleasure that he throws a rock to thwart her. In the lengthier woodland scene, it is Day who privately watches, entering the story by accidentally stumbling upon Helen in the midst of her 'sorcery'. As hinted earlier, the continual fades between his gaze and the scene itself suggestively line up our viewing with his, so that our enjoyment of watching Helen becomes refracted through Day's malevolent voyeurism, underscored by the caption, 'But cruel Fate steps in ... Fielding Day—Now a Tramp but Once an Evil Companion of Mason's Youth.' As the film moves forward, our 'corrupted' sight line—repeatedly framed by both men's and perhaps culminating in Mason's grotesquely gleeful viewing of Helen's whipping—contrasts with Helen's clear vision (as well as Martin's once he rejects the 'modern' lens of social propriety).

In the closing scene the lovers mimic their tormentors' practice of spying when Day, hotly pursuing them with weapon in hand, is tackled from behind and thrown down the hill. They silently watch, their eyes following the figure to his death below. However, they get no visible pleasure from his demise, despite the fact that it spares their own lives. Ending abruptly on that shot, the film completes its lesson in teaching the viewer how to 'look' differently.

The film version of *Helen of Four Gates* may on surface appear a standard melodrama of the silent era, complete with villainous hand-wringing, lecherous leers, and a tidy moral outcome. But Carnie Holdsworth's subversive take on that genre's formula, combined with Hepworth's aesthetic sensibility, set it apart—even from amongst the filmmaker's most acclaimed works. While Hepworth is thought to subscribe to the most conservative tendencies of English pastoralism in his own examples of British heritage cinema—'nostalgic, ruralist, escapist'[53]—those films tend to feature upper class country 'manses' or more romanticised rural hamlets where classes and sexes remain in their fixed positions and the landscape represents an ostensibly harmonious nation. *Helen* creates a much darker post-war portrait, even as the moors offer breath-taking views. Both the class and gender politics of such films are complicated, if not overturned entirely, in Helen Mason's triumph of *self*. That, in turn, proved a victory for Carnie Holdsworth and for working-class literature as a whole.

Notes

1   David Malcolm, 'Bedazzled', *Times Literary Supplement*, 7 March 2014, p. 28.
2   'Ethel Carnie Holdsworth: A Notable Lancashire Woman Novelist', *Woman's Outlook* 23, September 1920, p.294-5.
3   Ethel Carnie, 'We Who Work', *Woman Worker* 33, 16 September 1910, p. 716.
4   Robert Blatchford, 'A Lancashire Fairy: An Interview with Miss Ethel Carnie', *Woman Worker*, 10 July 1908, p. 155.
5   Roger Smalley, *Breaking the Bonds of Capitalism: The political vision of a Lancashire mill girl* (Lancaster: Lancaster University, 2014), pp. 24-31.
6   Ethel Carnie, 'The Cry in the Night', *Woman Worker* 19, 10 November 1909, p. 430.
7   *Woman Worker*, 4 August 1909, p. 100.
8   'Our Right to Play', *Woman Worker*, 14 April 1909, p. 342.
9   Smalley, pp. 30-1; 49.
10 Ethel Carnie, 'Letter to the Editor', *Votes For Women* 228, 12 September 1913, 718. She was not a member of the infamous Women's Social and Political Union (WSPU) or smaller Lancashire-based suffrage organizations in large part because she objected to any mode of political violence, regardless of the cause. But as Nicola Wilson points out, she did at this time dedicate two poems to Emmeline and Christabel Pankhurst that composer Ethel Smyth set to music. See Wilson's Introduction to *This Slavery* (Nottingham: Trent Editions, 2011), p. xi.
11 Carnie Holdsworth was also undoubtedly influenced by late 19th-century socialist women writers such as Margaret Harkness and Isabella Ford. For more commentary on the novel itself, see Belinda Webb's Introduction to *Miss Nobody* (Scotland: Kennedy & Boyd, 2013), viii-xxxii.
12 Smalley, pp. 66-7.
13 Smalley, p. 50. For more on women's complex attraction to popular romance narratives in the Edwardian era, particularly in film, see Lisa Rose Stead, '"So Oft to the Movies They've Been": British Fan Writing and Female Audiences in the Silent Cinema', *Transformative Works and Cultures* 6 (2011) http://journal.transformativeworks.

com/index.php/twc/article/view/224/210. Accessed 7/16/14.

14 Ethel Carnie, 'Living Pictures', *Woman Worker* 18, 3 November 1909, p. 416.

15 Ethel Carnie, 'How Colour is Introduced', *Woman Worker* 14, 7 April 1909, p. 323.

16 Ethel Carnie, 'The Poetry of the Streets', *Woman Worker* 19, 5 May 1909, p. 442.

17 Cf. haunting moor locales, revenge, forbidden love, family histories of insanity—even the name Mason resonant of *Jane Eyre*'s 'mad' Bertha Mason—and domineering men brought low by illness or calamity. Numerous contemporary reviews of *Helen of Four Gates* referenced *Wuthering Heights* and/or Emily Brontë as comparisons.

18 On the history of melodrama, see Christine Gledhill, *Reframing British Cinema, 1918-28: Between Restraint and Passion* (London: BFI Publishing, 2003), pp. 11-18; Raymond Williams, 'British Film History: New Perspectives', in *British Cinema History*, eds. James Curran and Vincent Porter (New Jersey, USA: Barnes & Noble Books, 1983), pp. 9-23.

19 All further text citations to this edition will appear as parenthetical references.

20 Ethel Carnie, 'A Country Village', *Woman Worker* 20, 17 November 1909, p. 450.

21 Martin is also likened to Hamlet. The film introduces him as a 'Queer Mixture of Labourer and Student.'

22 Gledhill, pp. 28-9.

23 See Pamela Fox, *Class Fictions: Shame and Resistance in the British Working-Class Novel, 1890-1945* (Durham, N.C.: Duke U P, 1994), pp. 145-69.

24 Quotes from Carnie, 'How Colour is Introduced'.

25 Smalley, p. 63; 118.

26 Ethel Carnie, 'Why I Have Never Married', *The Woman Worker* 22, 1 December 1909, p. 495.

27 Sales figures in Smalley, p. 70.

28 It's unclear why the contract specifies her maiden name for publication, when she had married a month before and, as the contractual party, is listed as 'Ethel Holdsworth.' See Smalley, p. 71.

29 *The Times,* 26 June 1917, p. 10.

30 *The Wheatsheaf* 282 (December 1919).

31 *The Living Age,* 15 September, 1917: 703. The reviewer's objection to the novel's depicted 'horrors' strikingly recalls commentary on Charlotte Perkins Gilman's Gothic feminist classic, *The Yellow Wallpaper.*

32 Ruth McIntire, 'Primitive Emotion', *The Dial: A Semi-Monthly Journal of Literary Criticism, Discussion, and Information* (13 September 1917): 211.

33 Lola Ridge, 'Essence of Life', *New Republic* (4 May 1918): 27-8.

34 McIntire, 'Primitive Emotion.'

35 Philip Corrigan, 'Film Entertainment as Ideology and Pleasure: Towards a History of Audiences', in *British Cinema History,* eds. James Curran and Vincent Porter (New Jersey, USA: Barnes & Noble Books, 1983), p. 27.

36 Stead, "So Oft to the Movies They've Been."'

37 As quoted in Lisa Rose Stead, 'Audiences From the Film Archive: Women's Writing and Silent Cinema', in *Using Moving Image Archives,* eds. Nandana Bose and Lee Grieveson, *Scope: An Online Journal of Film and Television Studies,* 2010, 35. http://www.archivalplatform.org/images/resources/Archives_eBook.pdf#page=42. Accessed 7/16/14.

38 Smalley, p. 72. He cites a local source, F. Lake, for this information.

39 He is typically described as such by film historians. Hepworth also uses the term in his own memoir, *Came the Dawn: Memories of a Film Pioneer* (London: Phoenix House Ltd., 1951).

40 See Hepworth; Gledhill, Chapter 4. On Hepworth's relationship to heritage film, see Andrew Higson, *Waving the Flag: Constructing a National Cinema in Britain* (Oxford: Clarendon Press, 1995), Chapter 3.

41 Hepworth, p. 148.

42 Hepworth, p. 150.

43 *Picturegoer* female fan letter, 1918, as cited in Stead, ' "So Oft to the Movies."'

44 Reminiscences of Dilys Thomas, MISC 91/16, 'Helen of Four Gates: Filming in West Yorkshire Generations Ago', Hebden Bridge Local Historical Society Archive.

45 Hepworth, p. 150.

46 See Smalley, p. 72.

47 Gledhill, p. 5. Also see Michael Chanan, 'The Emergence of an Industry', *British Cinema History*, 52.

48 For more on the film's remarkable recovery and two 2010 screenings, see 'Helen of Four Gates to get screening after 80-year hiatus', *Guardian*, 31 May 2010: http://www.theguardian.com/film/2010/may/31/helen-of-four-gates-film. Accessed 6/17/2014. The new print is housed in the BFI Archive, made from a negative found in the archive of Montreal's Cinematheque Quebecoise. Another print is housed in the George Eastman House archives, Rochester, NY.

49 See *Guardian* article, above.

50 My thanks to Jared Case and Nancy Kauffman at the George Eastman House for facilitating my viewing of the film.

51 One other noteworthy deviation from the original text: Fielding Day's murder at the novel's end is accomplished by Jim Brett, a tramp who hopes to befriend Day but is later mocked by him. In the film, it is a recently hired farm hand poorly treated by Day. However, he primarily commits the act due to the overseer's cruelty to Helen, overhearing her vicious beating (and thus serving as another kind of witness/'stand-in' for the film's viewing audience).

52 See Gledhill, pp. 98-100, for more on the Cottingley fairies and their use by filmmakers in the post-war period. In 1923, Hepworth produced *The Pipes of Pan* which included an inventive woodland fairy scene. (Gledhill does not mention *Helen of Four Gates*.)

53 Higson, *Waving the Flag*, p. 44. Here Higson is referring to the novel version of *Comin' Thro' the Rye*, arguing that the 1916 film served a nationalist purpose by showcasing England as a pastoral 'nation' during a time of 'Martial horrors', p. 44.

Suggestions for Further Reading

Alves, Susan, "'Whilst Working at My Frame'": The Poetic Production of Ethel Carnie Holdsworth', *Victorian Poetry*, 38:1 (2000): 77-93.

Ashraf, Phyllis Mary, *Introduction to Working-Class Literature in Great Britain: Part II: Prose* (Berlin: Ministerium fur Volksbildung, 1979).

Barr, Charles, 'Before *Blackmail*: Silent British Cinema', in *The British Cinema Book*, ed. by Robert Murphy (London: BFI Publishing, 1997), pp. 5-16.

Batsleer, Janet, et al., *Rewriting English: Cultural Politics of Gender and Class* (London: Methuen, 1985).

Bourke, Joanna, *Working-Class Cultures in Britain, 1880-1960: Gender, Class, Ethnicity* (London: Routledge, 1994).

Enstad, Nan, *Ladies of Labour, Girls of Adventure: Working Women, Popular Culture, and Labor Politics at the Turn of the Century* (New York: Columbia UP, 1999).

Fox, Pamela, *Class Fictions: Shame and Resistance in the British Working-Class Novel, 1890-1945* (Durham, N.C.: Duke UP, 1994).

Frow, Edmund, and Ruth Frow, 'Ethel Carnie: Writer, Feminist, and Socialist', in *The Rise of Socialist Fiction, 1880-1914*, ed. by H. Gustav Klaus (Brighton: Harvester, 1987), pp. 251-56.

Gledhill, Christine, 'An Ephemeral History: Women and British Cinema Culture in the Silent Era', in *Researching Women in Silent Cinema: New Findings and Perspectives*, eds. Monica Dall'Asta, Victoria Duckett, Lucia Tralli (University of Bologna, 2013), pp. 131-48.

---'Reframing Women in 1920s British Cinema: The Case of Violet Hopson and Dinah Shurey', *Journal of British Cinema and Television*, 4 (May 2007): 1-17.

Hawkridge, John, 'British Cinema From Hepworth to Hitchcock', in *The Oxford History of World Cinema* (Oxford: Oxford UP, 1996), pp. 130-36.

Higson, Andrew, 'Figures in a Landscape: The Performance of Englishness in Cecil Hepworth's *Tansy* (1921)', in *The Showman, the Spectacle and the Two-Minute Silence: Performing British Cinema Before 1930*, eds. A. Burton and L. Porter (Trowbridge, Wiltshire: Flicks Books, 2001).

Hunt, Karen, *Equivocal Feminists: The Social Democratic Federation and the Woman Question, 1884-1911* (Cambridge: Cambridge UP, 1996).

Joannou, Maroula, 'Reclaiming the Romance: Ellen Wilkinson's *Clash* and the Cultural Legacy of Socialist-Feminism', in *Heart of the Heartless World: Essays in Cultural Resistance in Memory of Margot Heinemann*, eds. David Margolies and Maroula Joannou (London: Pluto Press, 1995), pp. 148-60.

Johnson, Patricia E., 'Finding Her Voice(s): The Development of a Working-Class Feminist Vision in Ethel Carnie's Poetry', *Victorian Poetry* 43:3 (Fall 2005): 297-315.

Kirk, John, *The British Working Class in the Twentieth Century: Film, Literature and Television* (Cardiff: University of Wales Press, 2009).

Klaus, H. Gustav, ed. *The Rise of Socialist Fiction, 1880-1914* (Brighton: Harvester, 1987).

Martin, Anna, *The Married Working Woman: A Study* (New York and London: Garland, 1911, 1980).

Mitchell, Jack, 'Early Harvest: Three Anti-Capitalist Novels Published in 1914', in *The Socialist Novel in Britain*, ed. by H. Gustav Klaus (Brighton: Harvester, 1982), pp. 67-88.

Ross, Steven J., *Working-Class Hollywood: Silent Film and the Shaping of Class in America* (Princeton, NJ: Princeton University Press, 1998).

Smalley, Roger, *Breaking the Bonds of Capitalism: The political vision of a Lancashire mill girl* (Lancaster: Lancaster University, 2014).

Stead, Peter, *Film and the Working Class: The Feature Film in British and American Society* (London: Routledge, 1989).

Steedman, Carolyn Kay, *Landscape For a Good Woman: A Story of Two Lives* (New Brunswick, NJ: Rutgers University Press, 1987).

Taylor, Elinor, 'Ethel Carnie Holdsworth: A Centenary Celebration', Radical Studies Network, https://radicalstudiesnetwork.wordpress.com/2013/09/08/ethel-carnie-holdsworth-a-centenary-celebration/ Accessed 6/3/14.

Waters, Chris, 'New Women and Socialist-Feminist Fiction: The Novels of Isabella Ford and Katherine Bruce Glasier', in *Rediscovering Forgotten Radicals: British Women Writers, 1889-1939*, eds. Angela Ingram and Daphne Patel (Chapel Hill: University of North Carolina Press, 1993), pp. 25-42.

Wilson, Nicola, *Home in British Working-Class Writing* (Farnham: Ashgate, 2015).

----'Politicizing the Home in Ethel Carnie Holdsworth's *This Slavery* (1925) and Ellen Wilkinson's *Clash* (1929)', *Key Words: A Journal of Cultural Materialism* 5 (2007-8): 26-42.

HELEN OF FOUR GATES BY AN EX-MILL-GIRL

TO
MY DEAR FRIEND
ERNEST WHARRIER SOULSBY
IN TOKEN OF HELPFUL COMRADESHIP

Helen of Four Gates

Chapters

CHAPTER I

A RISE IN THE WORLD

A DAY in May was drawing to its close. The country between Brungerly and Little Moreton took on a wilder look as shadow after shadow obliterated signpost, trespass-board, gate, stile, and the little fences put up by small farmers. This North England changed subtly from a domesticated, intersected land into one huge dark county. Night with a laugh of anarchy blotted out the symbols of law and order, gave infinity for acres, reclaimed for a short time the wild that was half tame, and lent a sense that here fierce dark deeds had been done, and might be done again. For why should not fierce dark deeds happen here again?

The glimmering before the final closing down of darkness showed woods blackening against the sunset, woods bearing names that told of the worship of Odin and Thor. Rocks going up blackly into the gloaming were said to be the altars of the Druids; rain from the northern clouds had fallen into those rock-basins unprofaned by the human hand. Those bridges, becoming dense and iron-thick in their blue-blackness as they spanned river and broad stream, were many of them the work of Roman soldiery. A few watercourses still held the red rays of sunset. They glittered like fire-snakes, twining through the dark opaqueness of the landscape, murmuring through funereal waving plumes of blackening grass and rushes. They had witnessed the chasing of witches to their deaths. Here, where all was now still, save for the wailing cry of the peewit, those beings had shrieked aloud their innocence, or, borne aloft on the maddened wings of ambitious ecstasy, had proclaimed their power to raise the quick and the dead, to curse if they could not bless, hate if they could not love—clothing themselves with sombre majesty, playing with elemental fires, rather than eat porridge humbly, bow to the squire, and tremble before the priest.

A shuttle of darkness ran across the sky, weaving a web over earth, water, and the air, making a scene fit for such power-loving mortals to move in, as seen from the old road running between stone walls.

High on the darkening hills those stone walls encroached. Storm-driven sheep might cower behind them, their impotent bleatings drowned in the crash of thunder and clap of cloud-burst. The hills looked broader, higher, as they blackened. The sky, still red between the gaps in the highest of the hill-walls, gave an uncanny, dizzying look to those rifts in the ebon gloom, as if they led down and under the edge of the earth. But over there were other hill-ridges, their peaks hidden in mist and cloud. The valleys between were strewn with factory towns. Here and there was a furnace, whose glare and after-darkness would soon change the night sky like the eye of some fire-god opening and closing.

Over there, too, lay Little Moreton, the Tramp Hole. Overshadowed by the Pennines, damp with the rolling vapours of their heads, it received into its arms of crooked streets the weak, the broken, the incapable, the unwanted, and, anon, the rebellious. It was a bowl in the hills. The towns round about spat away from themselves those who were broken, or those who would not bend. They became Tramps. They fell into this giant spittoon of sober sorrow, drunken mirth, where the man who was not wanted took the woman who was not wanted, where they toiled together, drank together, fought together, recognising no law but necessity.

The old road knew the feet of the weary race who floated in and out of Little Moreton, each time disgusted and desperate. It ran away from it, towards the grand sweep of moors. But it ran back to it hopelessly, helplessly.

Curlew, peewit, and grouse called apart and together. It was like the cries of three separate hearts. Yet the moor had homed them all. A few scranny bushes bending over the stone wall were caught by a wind which started up in the darkness. The unseen hand of it swept the branches. A little croon of shuddering joy ran through bush, furze-clump, the million field rushes, the rusty heather. Soon everything was shouting with wild, restless music, like the fierce cry of a fierce heart for Love, or Hate, or Power—all sweet things.

It grew ever darker.

Wind! Blackness! Solitude!

It was Witches' Country, at the hour when their spells were worked; when Will-o'-the-Wisp carried his wavering lamp over black moss, blacker pool, and shaking bog; when Barguest, the moorland spirit-dog, followed the lonely traveller caught in the net of darkness, the weird paws sounding splosh-splosh behind him on the soppy ground. It was the hour when children spawned by the bog were found—to be claimed at length by the bog, after they had tasted human joy, human sorrow. In the sky one lingering beam of light trembled like a sword dipped in red, against a pall of death.

Wh-oo! wh-oo-o! shouted the wind deliriously.

Two pairs of heavy footsteps sounded through the darkness. By and by they paused. The light of a match spluttered upon the gloom.

On they came again.

Beside a milestone they paused. Two dark figures were almost indistinguishable from the surroundings. But their voices flowed into the night. The tone of them was like a tired curse.

"The nigher I get th' more I feel like turnin' back," confessed one voice.

In answer there was the sound of a laugh that had in it callous scorn.

"Fleyed of a woman," gibed the one that had laughed.

"Tha doesn't know Sally," said the first man weakly. "When I think of her face—it a' seems madness, what I dreamt by th' doss-house fire. It's a sort o' madness comes ower a tramp now an' then, to go back to th' respectable folk."

The footsteps came to a pause.

The second man laughed again.

"Tha really means it—to ha' walked a' this way for nowt!" he exclaimed, a comical wonderment in his voice.

"Nay, not for nowt," said his companion; "for I'll sort o' be satisfied—for another year."

"A man 'at can't manage a woman—" gibed the other.

"Give us a leet," said his companion. "Then I'll be off—back. An' mind tha never meets thy match."

There was the sound of his pal fumbling in his pocket.

"I'd smash her jaw—or her heart," he said determinedly. "Here tha art. But buck up, owd lad. There's a pub i' th' village only half a mile away. A pub wi' a soft-hearted landlord, an' a dowter as hard as nails. Come an' take lessons off me how to deal wi' th' creatures. I'll promise to get snap an' rattle[1] for thee and me, without wearin' a penny piece."

There was a pause.

This last appeal seemed to be effective. His mate was thinking of that lonely stretch of darkness behind him—then of the picture he had just had conjured up before him.

---

1   Oatcake.

"Comin'?"

There was silence again. Then Jim Brett spoke.

"I'll get back," he said briefly. In his voice there was something of rude dignity.

"A' reight," answered the other. "That'll be walkin' a' neet. Mind tha doesn't meet th' ghost o' that pack-horse man. He carries his own head under his arm."

Jim Brett chuckled now.

"I'm noan fleyed o' ghosts," he said; "but, by goff, I were fleyed when I thowt o' Sally's eyes lookin' me through. Well, good luck, owd lad. I hope tha'll get on at Brungerly. Tha'll be back again, soon. Little Moreton is th' last place God made—but they a' come back!"

"I'm never comin' back any more," was the answer he got, given with quiet determination.

Jim Brett laughed.

"Never any more," repeated the other quietly, firmly.

"I' that case, we shan't meet again," said Brett. "So-long. I've got a long way to go." He swung round, and disappeared in the darkness.

Fielding Day struck on towards the village inn. He soon reached it, a low-built, homely place, with red window curtains.

His eyes glinted with hungry longing.

He entered, standing in the full light of the bar. Dainty Polly Cherry looked up—paused, and stared at that which stood before her.

If a scarecrow could look handsome, it might be said that Fielding Day was such a handsome scarecrow. His rags appeared to have been gathered with a harlequin-like disregard for harmony. But it was the boots upon him, peering below the frayed edges of his trousers, that told his class and clan. They clung to his feet by some miracle, revealing at intervals pallid, dirty toes. He was a Tramp Weaver—"on the rocks," as his clan would put it, rude poetry in the symbolism they use so callously.

He had the face of a man who has left dreams behind.

9

"Grand neet," he remarked to Polly Cherry, with a nod almost of patronage. She looked at his clothes, baffled by his own unconsciousness of his position. He was a Tramp. Yet he spoke as if he had honoured the place by straying in. She decided not to notice him, but even as she did so, his eyes caught and held hers.

"It might be a worse night," she said, astounded to hear herself say it. "The kitchen's to the left."

The tramp nodded, passing along till he came to the open door of the kitchen. Entering, he sat down on a form, then took out a broken-stemmed pipe, and lit it.

He looked through the smoke that curled from the pipe upon the scene before him. Low-roofed, black-beamed, hunting pictures on the buff-painted walls, the room was occupied by a company of rough, homely men. They also sat on forms ranged round by the walls, white-boarded tables before them holding their blue-banded pint pots. From the rafters hung oaten cakes, sweet herbs a-drying, and flitches of home-cured. A big fire spluttered in the wide grate. Over it hung a stew-pot, occasionally spitting into the fire. The scent from that pot penetrated every corner of the long room. Firelight and lamplight brought gleams from silver and pewter in a corner cupboard. In a large, brass-wired cage a parrot strutted upon its perch.

There was a lull in the conversation, a waiting expression on the various faces. Some rivalry appeared to exist between a ruddy, pumpkin-bellied man and a pale little chap whose coat, covered with threads of cotton weft, stamped him as a weaver, whilst the tin food-box and tea-can standing on the floor between his feet intimated that he had not yet een home to his tea.

The ruddy man looked scorn at his opponent, then, leaning across the table towards him, he apparently went on where he had left off.

"She's th' finest pair of e'en in her head fro' here to John o' Groats," he said warmly. "I'm noan defendin' her hats bein' queer, but she never handles a penny piece in yon house, an' th' old cracked-pot buys everything for her. Andry there says no woman as 'd wear such hats can be reight i' her head. She doesn't buy them hats hersel'. Then he says she goes maunderin' round in th' dark an' weet as if she were a Pendle Forest witch. Why shouldn't a lass go out in th' weet an' dark, if she wants? It's hardly darker anywheer nor in yon farm kitchen, wi' th' hill comin' down nigh to th' window-stone, an' th' river cryin' away below like it can't help it, an' all them dark, mutterin' trees about. An' then, look at th' old chap—allus quiet an' broody, or chunnerin' to hissel, or else daft an' in all maks o' mischief when th' moon's at full. An' she's got no friends, save my wife, Lizzie. If that lass had had a grain o' madness in her she'd have gone by this. She's all reight. I'd lay my neck to a hay-seed on it! An' any chap 'at says otherwise has got to prove his words, or I'll make him eat 'em. So look snarp, Andry, for I want to be toddlin' home."

"Ay, prove thy point, Andry," said an old man with a white pow, his nostrils dark with snuff-taking, his eyes cute as a weasel's. "She's a lass I shouldn't fancy, as sure as my name's Ben Ling, for she looks like she wouldn't wait to be axed. But it's a serious thing to say anybody is only ninepence to th' shillin'. An' th' least tha can do is to prove she's dotty."

"I could prove it, reight enough," said Andry knowingly, "but I don't want to do th' lass any harm."

His opponent pricked his ears up at this.

"There," said Teddy Trip triumphantly, "he can only cast innuendoes—"

"None o' them long words, Teddy," drawled somebody. "It isn't fair in an argyment. Plain English'll do for us."

Andry sniggered.

"What I say is," said he, "to use short words as everybody knows, an' not try an' knock folk down with a foreign language." There was a murmur of applause. Teddy got restive.

"Arta goin' to prove what tha said about Helen Mason—or come round th' back?" he exploded, after a moment in which the blood of a race of fighting men had risen in him. Somebody pulled him down in his seat.

"I've told thee," said Andry solemnly, "I don't want to harm th' lass. It were only by accident th' subject came up. But—I could prove it, reight enough."

"Tha can't," sneered Teddy. "Tha'rt wrigglin' now."
"Can't I, by goff!" said the little man.

He squared his narrow shoulders at the challenge.

"An old beer for Andry," called someone, and Polly Cherry entered, bringing it. She cast a look at the tramp as she set it down. He did not order. She saw the game. He was waiting until snap and rattle was served out—to get it for nothing. She determined he should not have it.

The tramp smiled, meeting her eye—and again she did not say what she wanted to say.

"Well," said Andry, "it's five years sin', this fall. I were out o' work, an' th' wife had been cryin' all mornin'. We'd little i' th' cupboard. I couldn't stand it no longer, so I set out I didn't know where. We lived at Green Booth then. Somehow my feet turned this way, an I'd got about a mile fro' Four Gates yonder, when down came th' rain like th' sky were opened. Well, I traunched on through it, till I came to a lane. I can see it now, full o' red leaves, an' th' water gugglin' in th' ditches cowd-like, an' th' wind blowin' hell for leather, an a' th' leaves flutterin' about like they were birds. Old Mother Chattox might ha' been after 'em wi' her broom. An', by goff, if I didn't pass under a tree with one o' them dark clots i' th' branches, they ca' 'em witches' brooms. Seemed like an ill sign. Then I came to a brig, wi' water as black as th' ace o' spades. I stood there, an' tried to leet mi pipe. But it wouldn't leet, for mi matches had got soddened. Then I see there were a little stile at one side o' th' brig, leading down into a wood, an' I thowt I'd find a bit o' shelter there, so I hopped through. Th' sky were dark where there weren't no trees, but it were that thick yo' could ha' cut th' blackness wi' a knife an' fork i' th' wood. Bits o' leet glimmered through on red leaves. I found a place under a holly, wi' th' ground under as dry as snuff, an' I felt tired an' threw mysel' down to rest. It were welly pitch dark where I lay. I could hear th' rain tipplin' down like it were bein' poured out of a bucket 'at would never be empty. An' I lies there, wishin' I were at hoam—when just then th' wind stopped, an' I hears a voice that made my blood run cowd. It were rayther a nice voice—but there were summat i' th' way it spoke made my heart go pit-a-pat. It were like it were chantin'—an' fiercer nor aught I've ever heard, though it weren't loud, but it said every word like it were bein' burnt into Eternity. It were callin' a name, a man's christian name—but aught more unchristian I ne'er heard. Then it goes on to address him, as if he stood there—an' all were dark. I could see nowt. An' suddenly, it dawns on me, as I lies wi' my breath held for fear, that I'm hearkenin' some sort of a weddin', between two folk, though I can see neither—"

Andry stopped, and shivered. His pale eyes appeared to look beyond the room he sat in. What he was feeling conveyed itself eloquently to the company.

"Don't give us th' creeps, Andry," said Ben Ling.

"Creeps isn't the word for what I felt," he said, lifting up his empty glass.

He set it down, and moistened his lips, whilst someone gave the order he had forgotten. "Well, th' voice goes on, repeatin' a ceremony more or less like they have i' Four Gates Church yon—save for queer little bits pushed in, an' save that this same voice answered for both parties, th' chap never havin' a word to say for hissel'. An' nowt to be seen o' either. Th' words o' th' wind-up were th' wildest o' a'. I'd a good memory at that time, an' when I got home I wrote 'em down, an' they sort o' fascinated me. I got 'em off by heart. I used to say 'em ower to mysel' before goin' to sleep o' neets just to be thankful I'd a daycent lass by my side. I'll just see if I can bethink me—."

There was silence whilst Andry pondered. Finally his face lit up with satisfaction.

"I've getten th' beginning" he said, "an' it'll a' come back, for I went ower 'em that often." Then closing his eyes, he began to murmur the words he had heard in the dark wood, five years back.

"'Thus, thus, and thus,'" he incanted, "'by the magic of fire, air, and water, I draw thee to me. By the seven colours that make earth an' heaven, by moon, sun, and stars, I draw thee to me. By the four Seasons, I draw thee to me. From the four corners of the globe I will draw thee to me. By my strength and weakness, my hardness, my softness, my tears and my laughter, I draw thee to me. By every strand of my black hair, and the dew o' my mouth, I draw thee to me. Mine, mine, all mine! I draw thee into my blood, my heart, my bone, my mind—all mine, mine, mine! For richer, for poorer, for better, for worse, in health and in sickness, till Death us do part. The same grave shall hold us. Dust to dust, earth to earth, ashes to ashes, as in the beginning, yesterday, to-day, and to-morrow. I scatter these red leaves. Thus I claim thee, who wast mine from the beginning of the world. Those whom Love hath joined together—let no man put asunder.'"

Andry finished, looked pleased with himself, coughed as he looked at Teddy, and waited.

The latter did not speak.

"An' then what?" asked Ben Ling.

"Then I hears summat stir, an' a ray o' leet filters in somehow, an' I sees a lot o' red leaves fa'in', an' sittin' among 'em, on a high branch, a young woman, wi' a face as white as a warmed-up corpse, an' black hair round it, an' a look in her e'en—oh, Lord, I don't like to think on't! It were Helen Mason. I foun' it out afterwards. But I thowt then for sure she were a witch, an' I took to my heels as if Owd Nick were after me. An' I foun' out afterwards she were Helen Mason, an' how they'd all gone i' th' top storey—an'—I puts it to th' company o' sound English chaps, to say if any young woman would sit up in a tree-top, in a storm, wi' her hair down her back, weddin' herself to a chap 'at weren't there? Mad. If that's sane, what's mad? An' look at her pedigree!"

Teddy Trip stood upon his pins, drank up his beer, and went out looking glum.

"What were th' name of him she wor weddin' hersel' to?" asked the old man with the white hair, softly.

Andry looked at him, tapped his nose, as much as to ask him if he saw any green in the corner of his eye. Then the talk turned on ferrets and had barely got going when a step sounded in the doorway. The others started, smiling in extra efforts to look at ease.

"Hello, Martin!" they greeted him. "Come an' sit here."

The new-comer, a man of some twenty-five years, took a seat next the tramp, saying the fire was too warm. His voice was monotonous to dullness, as if he were dog-tired, or without feelings. No one would have expected geniality from that sallow-tinctured, immobile countenance. A broad brow shadowed a pair of brown eyes that were the antithesis of the rest of the reserved, monotonous man. He was clad in coarse clothes, stained with, and smelling of, the earth.

His eyes turned upon the tramp now. Fielding Day was conscious of a curious antagonism, a losing of half of his own animal magnetism. He was vaguely angry, as one who is challenged. And yet the eyes did not rest on him more than two seconds.

"Beer?" queried the dull voice. The tramp nodded.

Martin tapped the bell on the table. Polly Cherry brought in the drinks. Then she served out the stew and oaten cakes. Soon there was no sound but the clatter of spoon and plate, the smacking of lips, and remarks appropriate, with a desultory, broken thread of conversations that generally ended among the stew.

The tramp ate ravenously. "Hungry?" asked Martin. Fielding Day nodded.

"Twenty-four hours sin' I'd owt," he answered unsentimentally. Martin nodded understandingly.

"Ever bin hungry?" asked the tramp.

The eyes that lit up the whole face glowed for a moment. Looking into them it was as if he saw into a pit of flame.

"Ay!"

The tone was more monotonous than ever.

"Nice comfortable feelin'," joked the tramp. "Nice to see other men's fires shinin', an' ha' to sleep under th' stars. Tha knows a' about it, I see. What part o' th' country did tha tramp?"

"I've never been a tramp," said Martin.

"Tha said tha'd been hungry," said Fielding.

"Ay," said Martin laconically, "so I have. But it weren't bread-hunger I were thinkin' on. What's that like? Does it pass off after a bit? Does it bite less an' less?"

"When tha's eaten," said the tramp. "Till it's comin' round to next meal-time. Or if tha goes on long enough, fastin', girnin', tightenin' thy belt, tha gets used to it, an'—just as tha'rt gettin' used to it, tha dees."

"So hunger never dies," said Martin wearily, as one who sees some hope vanish. They sat in silence for some moments. Then Martin found out how far the tramp had come, his being without a penny, without work, without aim.

"It's a cold night," he remarked, as one who has experienced the deepest horrors of starvation, though he had confessed that he had never been without a roof over his head or without bread to eat.

"Ay," said the tramp, "it's gettin' cowder, an' there's not much poetry sleepin' under th' stars—particularly about two i' th' mornin'. Everythin' sort o' shivers."

"Old Mason might give thee a doss in th' barn," said Martin, "but tha'd have to double earn it to-morrow."

The tramp signified his willingness to accompany Martin to the farm, and try. If it failed, it only meant sleeping out, just the same.

In five minutes they were making their way through the night towards Four Gates Farm. They were walking into a boundless blackness save for the gleam of a few stars. The turf under their feet was soft after the limestone road. Then a deeper blackness rose before them. They were ascending a small hill. It was this that deepened the darkness. Somewhere in the distance a dog barked. The echoes shouted it back.

"Is it far?" began the tramp.

His companion did not answer. He had stopped. Fielding felt that he was peering into the gloom. A tiny speck of light penetrated the darkness. It came nearer. Martin took a step or two forwards, then paused again irresolute. From the depths of his throat stole a muffled oath—the tone of which conveyed a weary impotence, irritation, despair, anger, and yet something that had in it admiring wonder.

"Is't a will-o'-the-wisp?" asked the tramp.

Martin Scott mumbled something in confusion.

"I think it's Miss Helen," he said in his monotone, after another silence.

"She'll be comin' for a walk to the yew-tree. She generally gets so far of a night."

The wavering light came nearer to them.

A dark figure was silhouetted on the light made by the lantern. Fielding was walking behind Martin, as the path was narrow. The woman did not see him.

"Martin!" she called. In her voice was the abandon of a wild thing that has been caged, and has slipped out by chance into freedom. "Martin!"

It was a voice with passionate cadence. She might have repeated that name over to herself in a hundred moods. It made the tramp feel one too many, to wonder what she would say next. Even as he wondered she lifted up her lantern, stared into Martin's mask-like face, and said with a sudden restraint: "I was just setting off to the yew-tree, that's all, Martin Scott. An' the wind got in my blood coming down the hill."

Fielding Day did not know whether she had seen him or not, but the next moment her glance included him. He stared back at her as boldly. Then she turned from him to Martin, ignoring his presence.

CHAPTER II

AN OFFER OF MARRIAGE

MARTIN pulled his cap down closer upon his eyes. The movement, natural as it seemed, made the tramp suspect that he wished to hide anything they revealed of his feelings. The eyes of the cloaked woman went immediately to those eyes. She raised her lantern higher, to flood the shadow, woven over the upper portion of the face, with light. As she moved Martin moved. The deep-nebbed cap served its purpose well. Some of the lantern-rays caught her own countenance.

It was a face too thin, too sullen, too strongly charactered for beauty. Perhaps it was the blackness of the nun-like garments made her face seem so alabaster pale, or the cloud of blown dusky hair that had escaped the hood. The only colour in the face was the line of red made by fullish lips, and the greenish glow of a pair of eyes set widely apart under brows so straightly black that they lent to the whole an austerity bordering on the disagreeable. The expression of those eyes was of an unflinching courage, mingled with something stoical. She might have been fighting things all her life from their look. The nose was ordinary, but the chin might have belonged to a statesman. A string of coral beads gleamed on her throat where the cloak opened, giving a hint of something essentially primitive and elemental.

"Going as far as the yew-tree, Martin?" was her greeting.

19

The voice was slow, clear, incisive. She spoke as one whose passionate utterance of swift speech has been long checked by some habit developed by necessity. After that voice the labourer's speech sounded faltering and mumbling.

"I'm tir't," he said.

"The stars'll be shining through the black boughs, Martin," said the young woman.

She smiled. The sullen lines faded from her face. It was a sudden revelation of beauty.

"I'm tir't," reiterated Martin.

The smile died away. The old stoicism, the old fight, came back to The woman's eyes. The lips tightened.

"We shall be a long time dead, Martin," she said. "There's some in the old churchyard would be glad to shake the mould off themselves, and be amongst the wind and stars to-night."

Martin hitched his cap lower down.

"I've got to take this chap up to the farm to ask the old man if he'll let him sleep in the hay-mow. He's nowhere to sleep. An' he wants to know now. If he can't sleep there he'll want to be journeying on."

Helen looked at the tramp.

There was a slight resentment in her voice as she said, "The farm's right on. You can't miss it. You'll see the light twinkle through the trees. I've never heard there's boggarts about,—but, of course, you might get lost."

She was hinting that the tramp might be afraid to go alone.

"I'm feared o' neither man, God, nor devil," was his answer. Even as he gave it he was made aware by the gleam in her eyes that he had fallen into a trap. She had used him to overcome Martin's refusal. The latter stood dumb for a moment.

"I'll go on with thee," he said to the tramp, and the latter had perforce to follow with the conventional refusal to be accompanied.

"All right, I'll be on soon," said Martin, "Go right on. Tha'll find it, all right. The first farm." He passed down the slope with Helen. The tramp stood gazing after the two figures, a track of light behind them. He saw in Martin's attitude that of a rebellious but conquered slave.

The thought of how he would have dealt with her brought a laugh to his lips—the laugh of one who has been under the chariot wheels of power and learnt to reverence them, to envy them, to desire to be as they, grinding, breaking, rolling along over the crushed hearts of others.

Walking on, dead tired, the darkness got into his head, giving him a drunken feeling. Soon he confessed himself lost. But a twinkle of light amongst trees lured him on. He headed for it, to find himself on a path through a copse. As he paused bewildered, he caught again the gleam of the light he had fancied was the farm window. There were voices, too. He listened intently, then held his breath. They were the voices of the couple he had left not long ago. It was Martin's mumble and Helen's clear tones. The light that he had seen came from the lantern, hung up in the boughs of a tree. They were speaking in the dialect, as half- cultured people do under stress of excitement.

He drew back and paused, not daring to move away lest they should hear him.

"Somebody's comin'," said Martin.

There was tired thankfulness in his voice.

"'Twere th' wind, that's a', Martin," said the woman.

"There's th' church clock," answered Martin. "We've bin here a quarter. There's th' proven' to make ready against mornin'."

"Promise me, then, Martin," she asked earnestly, "tha'll never go away, like I dreamt last neet. 'Twere horrible, Martin. I'd never leave thee, Martin, never.

Tha doesn't know what 't were like. 'T were that awful I had to creep downstairs, and see that thy shoon were under th' table. An' a' the way up th' stairs I looked at my own shadow, an' it looked that lonesome. Promise, Martin."

There was silence. Helen herself broke it.

"Tha wants to get away—to leave me," she accused hotly.

"Listen, Helen," said Martin Scott. "Last neet I ne'er slept, nor th' neet afore, an' I've got tir't out. What's th' good of startin' it all ower again? All I know is—I want to sleep, sound, sound as somebody dead."

"Poor Martin!" crooned the voice. "Creep close to me. Rest near me." Martin laughed.

"Rest!" he ejaculated, in mockery. "Rest—when my days an' neets are a hunger an' a thirst. I go in th' wood. Tha's bin there. Tha seems to laugh at me, peeping fro' th' leaves o' the trees. Th' house is full o' thee when tha'rt out. Every walk around for miles knows thee. I try to find places where tha hasn't bin—to rest, to get away, where I could sleep sound for a month. It's like livin' in a cross between a madhouse an' a tomb yonder—an' added to that, to hunger in the sight o' what I hunger for. It's cruel—and tha's no mercy. Tha can sleep."

"I learnt to sleep wi' heart-break when I were a child, Martin," said Helen. "I make myself sleep. It's how I keep up. What days! He got me by th' throat to-day, Martin. Sometimes he looks at me like he hates me more'n any thin' on earth. An' yet—he loved my mother."

"Did he hurt thee, Helen?" murmured Martin.

There was silence for a moment. Then against that softness in Martin she made her attack.

"Kiss!" she breathed, with the abandon of a child.

There was silence. When she broke it, it was as if some vial of pride spilt itself in her voice.

"To whine—to grovel—like a beggar—for a kiss," she said jerkily. "Some day, Martin, I think I shall punish thee for this. Some day tha'll beg a kiss o' me like 't were th' breath o' life, an'—I'll let thee dee."

Martin Scott still made no reply. He was reaching the lantern down from the tree. As he got it safely he drew near to the woman. Whilst she looked at him with that threat upon her lips—with almost antagonism in her eyes—he kissed her swiftly, then, as a man who dares not stay, strode on in front with bent head.

"Martin, Martin," called Helen gaspingly. "There's no need to run." The pride was gone out of her voice. Her limbs were unsteady with joy. She was building wild dreams—and in front walked the labourer with bent head. Behind them both, in the shadows, followed the tramp. He could see that Helen would only overtake Martin at the gate of the farm. Its lights could be seen now through the darkness. He hung back until he heard Martin and Helen pass through a gate that clicked after them. Then he advanced towards the farm.

The dog barked furiously as he neared the gate. The house-door opened—light flowed into a cobbled yard, showing a giant of a man standing in the doorway.

"Who's mellin', Nero?" asked a harsh voice.

The dog snarled and barked.

Martin now came into the doorway, peering out.

"It'll be a man asked to sleep in the haymow," he explained.

"Oh, will it?" snarled the old man. "Well, come into th' leet, mon, an' let's see what manner o' beast tha art."

"Keep this dog off," said the tramp, as he entered the yard. The old man cackled in answer. Fielding could see more of him now. His hair looked like white moss in the semi-light—white moss, long and unkempt, on a large head.

"Keep it off thisel'," he answered jeeringly. "Come on, mon. It'll noan hurt thee. It's only its playful little ways." His whole figure grinned.

The tramp whitened with rage. He let out a string of oaths. Again the old man laughed.

"Think I daren't pass it?" asked the tramp.

"It's dam would worry a man," said the old man. "Helen, bring th' lantern here, an' let him see th' beast." He yelled out the command as to a dog. Helen sullenly brought the lantern. He cursed at her to hold it higher.

The light shone on a great Airedale, its tawny eyes infuriated, low growls of intense hatred sounding as if they tore at his throat. That throat was a red cavern, jabbed with long, white fangs. Rough hair bristled from its back. The tramp was within two feet of it, with no protection but his broken boots, hopeless to kick with. In his eyes surged up a hatred like that in the beast's.

"Pass *that*—an' tha can sleep in th' haymow," laughed Abel Mason.

Martin had come out. He stood beside Helen. The beast was straining at its chain. The tramp was now within a foot of it. Quite suddenly he went down on all-fours, making a low, savage cry. Low, answering rumbles came from the dog. The fangs bared themselves to plunge into the man's throat—and all the time the moss-headed old man was laughing as at some pleasing sight.

"At him, Nero, at him!" he urged the dog.

The dog growled. But the growl was not so certain as his last. There was something weirdly strange, not understandable, in the man on all-fours, growling like a beast, menacing, with his eyes, narrowed like slits, glistening and watchful, defying the thousand years' savage ancestry in the dog. Nearer and nearer he crept now. Man and dog looked into each other's eyes—deep into each other's souls—challenging. Nero growled—thunder as from the depths of the earth. His chain rattled as he hurled himself back to spring. But in the undercurrents of that growl was a whimper, a whimper of fear as against the strange thing not understood, and the something in the eyes of the man. Fiercely burning, steady, fearless, those eyes looked into the wild soul of the dog—and then—with one swift leap he cleared the length of the chain. The dog gave a howl of impotent fury. The man had passed. He was on his feet. Abel Mason approached the tramp, and looked into his face.

"Come in, lad," he said, with a rude geniality. Then, with a swift change as he turned to his daughter, "Helen, supper, sharp. An' shake him up something to lie on i' th' spare room."

Helen Mason regarded her father with sullen rebellion.

"Can't he sleep in th' hay-mow?" she queried.

The old man laughed, with a cruelty in his tone such as the tramp had not yet heard in all his experience.

"He'll sleep i' th' sacred chamber," said her father. "Not another word, or tha'll rue it. Bring out the best for this lad."

Helen seemed as surprised as the tramp felt. She flashed a vindictive look at him. He lifted his greasy cap in response to it. The moss-headed old man broke into hoarse laughter. Helen passed on into the house. The farmer and the tramp followed.

It was a chaotic kitchen in which the tramp sat down. Books, cattle-trappings, farm utensils littered the place. Milk-kits scoured to the brightness of silver blockaded one side of the kitchen. Dark furniture stood against walls stained with the beating of winter rains. The sanded floor was naked, save for a rug literally dropping to pieces. The pictures were the weirdest that could be collected. Even at a distance they gave an impression of ferocity. A huge fire roared half-way up the chimney, despite the time of the year, the red light reflecting itself in a broad, steel-topped fender. In an old cap under it, newly hatched chickens were drying.

In every corner hung men's garments. Martin Scott had seated himself in one of these ingle-nooks, in an arm-chair, and was apparently reading.

"Martin, lad," said the old man, "just shift into that other chair, an' let this mon sit there." Helen looked up swiftly from where she stood, over the sink, scraping potatoes. Martin moved without a word, taking the book with him. He had the mask-like expression he had worn in the inn. Only, at times, one hand restlessly tapped on the arm of the chair he had taken.

Abel Mason seated himself in an arm-chair, on the opposite side of the hearth to the tramp. In the light of a couple of swing-lamps his face was clearly revealed. It was a curious face. Eyes of child-like blue shone under brows of bushy white, the mouth had a cunning weakness, every line of the face told of cynicism, of hatred. There was stealthy observation in his looks. He missed nothing of what passed around him. If was hard to think that hospitality was a characteristic of that disagreeable nature. Yet the fact remained that he had commanded Helen to lay out the best in the house.

She had sometimes to pass round the back of Martin's chair, in order to open the cupboard door. Fielding Day felt that the old man did not miss the fact that she lingered near that chair with the undemonstrative man—as if it held some joy that made her crushed life endurable.

The best that Helen laid out was very good. Steaming potatoes, slices of beef in which the blood lingered redly, crusty bread, and a slab of Cheddar cheese, with apple pie to finish off. She set their chairs, her own next to Martin's. They sat down. The meal passed in gloomy silence. Helen turned once, with a restrained sort of smile, towards Martin. Immediately the knife-haft of her father came down upon the table-top.

"Let your meat stop your mouths!" he snarled.

After the meal Martin prepared the provender, then pulled off his shoes and went to bed. Helen was drawing a half-broken-down chair before the fire, when her parent commanded her to get the shake-down ready for the guest, and that she needn't come back. Sullenly she obeyed, and left the room.

Fielding Day picked up and glanced at the title-page of the book Martin had been reading. It was *The Decline and Fall of the Roman Empire.*

In the other room they could hear Helen bustling about. They sat in silence. Abel Mason occasionally looked from the fire towards his guest. It seemed to Fielding Day whenever he met those blue eyes that they were engaged in looking him through. It was not until Helen's steps sounded along a stone corridor, leading upstairs, that Abel Mason addressed him.

"Shut that door," he said, jerking a huge thumb in the direction Helen had gone. Fielding did so, and sat down again.

"Now," said the old man, "we can talk." There was silence again.

"Who arta?" leered the old man, leaning forwards. "Hell-spawn o' somebody's."

Fielding Day smiled.

Briefly he gave his autobiography, finishing with bitter reference to his position down under.

"How would ta like to be top dog?" asked the old man.

He laughed, showing a row of broken yellow stumps.

"I'd never look back if I got on th' first rung," said Fielding Day, his eyes gleaming. "God! How I'd crush!" He laughed, and old Mason joined him.

"I knew tha were hell-spawn soon as I clapped e'en on thee," he said.

"Lad—I've an offer to make thee." He paused to knock the ashes from his blackened clay. Then he rose from his chair, opened the door Fielding had closed, and peered into the corridor.

"She's terrible cunnin'," he said. "They all are, women; but she can't beat me. It's all reight."

Fielding Day waited. There was a wild gleam in the old man's eyes, a delirium in his voice, as if he was not quite master of himself.

"Tha'rt wonderin' an' wonderin'," laughed the old man. "Mon—I've been waitin' for a mon like thee these years back. An' tha's come. Th' moor-winds has blown thee here, reight to my hand. Lad—tha can be a rich mon i' three years' time. Three short years, think on it! All tha's to do is to do as I want thee. Look at me! I don't look it, but I'm rich. An' I want to use my brass to carry out my dreams, same as tha'd use it to carry thine out. Lad—marry yon lass 'at's gone out just now, wed her, mak her as miserable as only a mon like thee can mak a woman, an' I'll see tha goes on an' up wi' Abel Mason's brass an' thy own brains. A mon 'at can lick yon dog can get to th' top. What says ta?"

The tramp looked bewildered.

"What's th' game?" he queried. "Why should yo' want me to wed?"

The old man looked into the tramp's face, looked as if he were reading its every line with pleasure.

"Because there's not another mon within a three-days' march would mak that lass so miserable as thee— if tha just got started on th' gettin'-on business. That's why. Tha'rt hell-spawn."

He laughed.

"But why should yo' wish her to be miserable?" asked Fielding. He could scarcely believe this that was happening to him. A short time ago there had been nothing before him but Tramp weaving shops, casual wards, being ground down. Now—he was offered a chance to get on in life, be in clover, get his own back, and the thing he had to do was to marry a woman.

"Will ta have her?" said the old man tensely. "Ay, or No?"

"Have yo' heard I'm a millionaire i' disguise?" asked the tramp, looking at his broken boots. "Look here! I've nowt, not a red, but I'm not goin' to buy a pig in a poke." He leaned back in his chair, pushed his hands in his pockets, and regarded Mason closely.

Again the old man laughed.

"What the hell has ta to lose?" he asked, regarding Fielding from top to toe.

"It's not that," acknowledged the other. "I want to know exactly what I stand to gain. I've no use for a woman. They're cheap enough, anyhow. But I'd put up wi' one—that is, I shouldn't let her get i' th' way. But I want to know what's in it. An' I want to know all th' ins an' outs, so I'll be able to judge I'm not bein' done." And all the time he and Mason were looking at each other like two driving a bargain.

"I'll tell thee everything, lad," said the old man. "That lass is all reight. When tha gets her tha'll get a woman—barrin' she's had th' heart ripped out o' her an' th' place where it were filled up wi' hell-fire. But that's nowt to do wi' thee."

"What she feels is nowt to do wi' me," said Fielding. "All I want to be sure on is what I get out o' th' bargain, an' that she doesn't get i' th' way."

Old Mason was staring into the fire-depths. He did not appear to have heard Fielding's last words. His brow was knit, his bushy eyebrows bristling, his hair had fallen about him in a way that gave him a look of savage ferocity.

"Listen!" he said, starting up, and speaking with a suddenness that startled his hearer. "I'd spend every farthin', give up every acre o' my lands, just to know she were as miserable as she would be with thee. Tha wants to know why I make this offer. It's answered i' four letters—four little letters that has toppled lives, an' homes, an' kingdoms down. H-A-T-E! That's why."

"It's not common for a man to hate his own flesh an' blood," said Fielding, as if speaking to himself. He was staring into eyes so malignant that they blazed like blue lightning.

A terrible gust of silent laughter shook the giant form, distorted the massive face of the man opposite. There was something almost unearthly in this soundless mirth. It died away. He leaned forward, gripping the arms of his chair so tensely that it groaned.

"My flesh an' blood! Mine!" he said, at length, mockingly.

"Isn't she?" asked Fielding.

"No," growled the other, "she's none mine. She's his. Hinson's!"

There was an essence of venom in the last syllable. The wind groaned hollowly outside, shaking the crazy window-sashes. The dark gloom of the house seemed to grow more sombre. The old man leaning forwards, with livid face, blazing eyes, and the look of one burnt up with one idea, might indeed have been the incarnation of Hatred—Hatred that rides across the world with fiery sword, smiting the hearts and blasting the lives of men.

"Who were he?" asked Fielding, after a moment's silence.

"My mate," replied the old man, growing more like the personification of Hate, the purger as well as the destroyer of kingdoms. "My mate. Th' lad I went to school wi', the David to my Jonathan. He-he! What fools young folk are. I showed him her photo—an' he looked at it curious like, an' then says she isn't as nice as some to look at, an' axes where she lives. An' I tells him th' village, thirty miles away, an' her name. An' off he goes to see her. My mate! An' he tells her what none but he knew, then—though it soon spread after. He tells her the Masons is a' fairy-kissed, mad, dottled, moonstruck, an accursed race, an' how there were one shut away had tried to murder one he loved best. An' th' week after, I meets her by th' Corple Stones, on th' Heights, an' she looks at me fearsome, but courageous like, too, an' she puts strange questions. I'd planned it for a holiday. An' she blurts out, sudden, just as we sat down to eat, an' I tried to get a kiss—'Abel, I dursen't. It's a' finished, Abel. Think o' the childer!' An' I looks into her face, an' knows what she knows, and it's a' finished, an' Hinson has done it—an' then, th' blood rushes before my e'en, an' th' moor fades away, an' th' big valley, an' th' rocks, an' Helen's face—an' I hears her scream, an' then I knows no more till I wakens up an' finds th' moon has risen, an' I'm lyin' in one o' th' hollows i' the rocks they say the Druids had for their altars. An' down i' th' valley there's a lamb cryin' after its mother, an' th' sound sort o' shivers through me, like it's tryin' to tell me something. An' I creeps down, fro' th' black rock, an' sits on th' slope to rest. An'—then I sees something on my hand—an' it's blood where I've struck my head, an' there's froth on my chin. An' I knows *It's* come, an' ta'en everything, everything. An' I sees the Corple Stones stickin' up into th' sky, black figures like wild beasts, an' below th' valley, an' about th' rocks it might be Druids' spirits, whisperin', mutterin', an' everywhere loneliness, dead loneliness, an' Helen fled from me. An' I goes up th' slope again, reight up to th' highest of the Corple Stones, that one that's shapen like a black swine—though it's only wind an' rain has carved it—an' I says if I've to wait thirty, forty, fifty years, I'll be even wi' Hinson, an' his childer, an' his childer's childer. An' then I goes down into th' valley, an' I meets a couple o' young lovers, an' th' lad says it's a beautiful neet. He-he! A beautiful neet! An' it's just three hours sin', thirty years back, by that clock, that I came down fro' th' Corple Stones—to look down on an accursed world. An' three hours sin', as th' clock struck, an' I thought of it, tha blew in through that door-hoyle."

His voice died away. His tones had made the rude words an epic of hatred, chanted on a black altar, spattered with a madman's blood.

"An' then—?" prompted Fielding.

The old man started out of a dark brooding fit.

"Eh—wert speakin'?" he asked.

"How did yo' come by Helen?" asked the tramp.

"Hinson an' her got wed, then he were killed by a fall o' coal, an' she took it to heart, an' she seemed to ha' forgotten 'at I might go mad—or else she were hard up what to do wi' th' child, an' she sent for me, an' asks me wi' her deein' breath will I take her little lamb, an' I promises, an' brings the child back wi' me here, where nobody knows her, or me, or aught—to Four Gates, off th' map. An' I says my wife is dead, an' has left me wi' this child. An' then I teaches th' child to call me father. An' she shows some soft little ways—but I checks 'em, an' speaks harsh to her, an' she shows a hardness strange in a child, an' when I swears at her she swears back at me, an' when I threaten her she defies me, wi' her mother's e'en starin' full at me, an' her hair the colour o' his streamin' round her face, an' they calls her a wild cat down i' th' village, an' she leads such a life as no child ever lived before, I think, for loneliness, an' hardness, an' she's as proud an' cowd as a wintry day. An' then—just as she's reached the point o' not carin' for death, if I killed her, Martin comes, to be a farmer's boy. An' she turns to him like a plant to th' leet. They read together, an' play together, an' work the fields together. An' they keep's growin'. An' one neet they ax me can they go to the fair—an' Helen has her hair up, an' a longer frock, an' won't tell Martin what she's altered herself to—an' they go. An' they come back, changed out o' girlhood an' boyhood, an' stand there, hand i' hand, axin' me to say it's all reight. Ay. They looked at me for my blessing. Mine," and he laughed again, as if the vision of those trembling lovers, standing before him in the firelight, brought gladness to his soul.

Fielding puffed at his pipe. Even his callousness faltered a little before that vision and the man's relentless cruelty.

"An' what did yo' say?" he asked.

"I told 'em Helen come of a mad race, a race wi' a murderer in it—an' her aunt shut away, thinkin' she were the Queen o' England bein' in danger o' bein' poisoned for her crown, an' Martin he turns fierce-like an' says 'It's a lie!' an' I says 'Go an' see her Aunt Milly Mason', an' he looks at me like somebody drownin', an' th' water closin' round his head, an' his hand drops fro' Helen's, an' her eyes grows wild, an' she sort o' screams at him, 'Martin, don't leave me. I'm not fleyed, Martin. Don't leave me, I'm not fleyed', an' I knows she's got a spirit 'at doesn't trembled before madness, only at bein' left lonely, like I were left by th' Corple Stones. An' Martin turns to her, an' all th' boyhood has gone out o' his e'en, an' th' leet, an' he shivers, an' says, 'I once saw a mad woman—when I were a little lad'—an' he covers his face wi' his hand, an' staggers upstairs. An' next mornin' when he comes down he looks ten years owder, an' talks o' goin' away, an' then Helen fastens hersel' to him, an'—he promises to stay, but not to be married, or lovers, an' she promises, an' they struggle, an' every day the struggle gettin' harder, an' yet more sweet nor absence to either—hell together—that sort o' thing, an' every time when Martin's forgettin', I sends him to see her Aunt Milly. He-he! Five o' the best years o' their two lives I've had 'em on my rack—an' Tom Hinson said I was mad. An' I acts mad betimes, just to be cruel, to drag her by the hair that's like Hinson's, an' my only fear has lest I kill her outright, an' miss my revenge.

That's a'. An' now, tha's come. Lad—will ta have her? Two thousand pounds handed over to thee before tha weds her—on conditions tha weds her."

"I'll wed her," said the tramp, "if it can be done."

"She'll be glad an' fain," said Mason, with certainty in his voice. "She'll be glad an' fain." Fielding did not look so sure. He detailed to Mason what he had overheard in the wood.

"Martin wouldn't promise?" asked the old man, laughing once more, and rubbing his hands.

"No," said the other. "He's worn out. He'll give in to Helen or run away from her soon. He's got to go away. She's got to sup the cup I supped by the Corple Stones, soon," and he gloated over the misery to fall.

Then, with the lamplight extinguished, and only the light from the red fire, the shadows plotting in the corners, they pledged themselves to the bargain. Nothing would please old Mason but that the paper be signed with their blood. So the blood of the penniless and brutalised tramp and that of the man who was either a maniac or a builder of revenge, met on the paper. It might have made one other than Fielding Day shrink—that scene in the gloomy farm kitchen, with the moss-headed old man, shaken with silent laughter that ended up in a harsh note like a raven's. But to the tramp that paper spelt an entry into a world where he would taste the sweetness of power. And if the old fool wanted a blood-oath, well, why not chuck in the blood-oath and please him, since he had a love for melodrama. Then he departed, departed to the room where Martin Scott had come twelve years ago, as an awkward, lonely, love-starved lad, to be a farmer's boy. He was soon stretched on the bed that was made up on the floor, but as he blew out the candle that guttered in a winding-sheet, he could hear Abel Mason building up the kitchen fire, as though he would sit gloating by it all night, and at times in his broken slumbers he half fancied that he heard the cackling wind-up of that horrible, silent laughter—and anon the wind beating against the windows or groaning in the chimney.

CHAPTER III

ALL ON A SWEET MAY MORNING!

ALL on a sweet May morning!

The wood below Four Gates Farm.

Everything a-hush, a-glimmer, a-silence in the heart of leafy green.

Sw-i-i-sh!

The wind stole along, creeping low amongst the fragrant flesh-like stems of the bluebells on river bank. The flowers trembled, swayed. In the movement their colour seemed to darken, the dancing joy of each hidden heart of burning gold making them change to richer pomp. The bluebells reflected in the clear river swayed to and fro. It was a dream within a dream, beauty, within beauty. S-sh! The wind came softly a breath, a sigh. Some exquisite nymph of Silence stood, her finger laid across her lips, whispered "Hush!" And then—the wind came again, jocular, merry, and the million leaves clapped their hands for glee, as if they heard in the distance the pipes of Pan, Pan the wild, the fierce, with his half-animal body and singing soul, Pan, the god who shall not die whilst one tiny wood is left to murmur through the opal and gold of a May morn.

The gladness of a morning wood! Who shall tell it? Only Pan, Pan with his wild, sweet notes, and the throstle with her swelling rapture, the blackbird with his mellow contralto, the kingfisher with his brilliance, as he darts from under an old mossy bridge, the dark blue of his plumage not seen at all, so swiftly he flies—nothing but a flash of red and gold.

Another day has dawned in a world that knows nothing but the present.

A flower opens, a flower fades, a bird-song ends, but the rest flow on. There is perfect Immortality here, and the birds on the boughs sing denial of the doctrine of Pain, each note a chant for joy of life, of love, of the fulfilment of Nature's ends. Whilst all the time the wood glows a brighter emerald, the grass stirs to a livelier tint, and the bluebells blaze into sapphire.

Helen was coming along the twisting path that led from the garden gate down through the trees to the water-edge. She was singing. In the light of day her haggard, passionate-eyed beauty was more striking. She looked like a Joan of Arc rather than a village belle, a fighter, a listener to voices—yet all she was fighting for was human love.

Behind her stepped the dog, nosing her footsteps.

At the edge of the river he lay down whilst she filled the bucket, which she set amongst the bluebells. Then she also sat down, her long arms clasping her knees. Sitting thus, in repose, she looked like a longing, typified. As the dog whined, she started. It *was* Martin. He had just finished milking. Amos Trip had taken the kits down the hillside, on their way to Brungerly. Scott's eyes were heavy and red for lack of sleep. He had a miserable, draggled appearance. He was weary, worn out, she was fresh, fresh from a happy sleep—bought by his unrest.

Reaching her he threw himself down on the grass, on the other side the bucket that held the reflection of a branch of flowering currant. They spoke no single word, after that one look at each other—that look which said "I see you again!" Martin lay upon the cool grass, his face turned into it, as though he were half asleep.

His first remark seemed inappropriate to the morning.

"*The Decline and Fall of the Roman Empire* is a fine book," he said. "I read it till the stars went out. *I* didn't seem much, somehow—nor Four Gates. Before I had seemed all *I*."

Helen answered nothing. There was a smile in her eyes.

The wind went sighing through the wood.

"It's peace here," breathed Martin.

"It's struggle," answered Helen, "just like in the Roman Empire. The fish will want worms, but the worms won't like it."

Martin half turned his face from the grass to look at her. "What time is it?" he asked.

"Only six o'clock yet," she told him. "There's time to go to sleep."

"I might sleep all day," he answered drowsily.

"I'll sit and wake you," she told him, "in an hour."

He looked at her. An hour's rest! Soon the toil of the day would start. Twelve hours before he could close his eyes.

"If you'll wake me in an hour," he said, "and—stay where you are." She smiled consent. He heaved a sigh of relief, drew a deep breath, and closed his eyes. In two minutes he was in a dead sleep. Helen sat on the other side the bucket, watching him. There was a truce between them. She sat and looked at him, drinking her fill of the tired, sallow face. She talked to him, in a crooning way, very softly, as a mother might to a child.

"You have never to leave me, Martin," she breathed. "Remember. You belong to me. You mustn't be afraid. I wouldn't leave you—if you were ten times mad. You are ugly, Martin. Why should I care? That is not reason. You should not reason. Have I ever asked you to go back generations, Martin, and see that all your ancestors were wholesome and strong and good? You are a coward. My mind condemns you, sometimes—

38

and yet—you must never leave me, Martin, never go away where I cannot see you. Do you remember when you came to the farm at first? I liked to think you were as lonely as I, then. You must never go away, you cannot. I have stopped you for five years. You are getting tired. You will see that I am right, I who am nothing but feeling, I who you called selfish, once. I will not be miserable, Martin. I would sooner die. You cannot take yourself from me. Why did you come at all if you have to go away again? It is you who are mad—to imagine you can get away—from me."

Then she sat in silence, listening to the murmur of the river, to the wind in the leaves, and always watching the sleeper, brooding over him. She was pacifying a fear. At the stroke of seven from the church clock she woke Martin. He opened his eyes dazedly, blinked, and then said good-humouredly, "Been there all the time?" She nodded.

"It is not often you are—good," he said. "I'm tired, too," she answered.

He rose from the grass, stretched himself, and took hold of the bucket handle simultaneously with herself. The wind blew her hair against his cheek. It flushed, then paled. The two faces were mirrored in the bucket of water, the one tempting, the other struggling. The hour of truce was over.

"Why do you have your hair down?" he growled.

She did not answer. There was a look in her eyes as if she were laughing.

Her fingers touched his on the cold bucket handle. He let go and Helen set the bucket down. She turned and walked over to an oak, and sat in the bend of the trunk. He came over towards her, slowly, like one who is beaten.

"One kiss, then," he said, as one granting a favour. Helen laughed.

She held herself proudly.

"I can go without," she said. Martin started. He had never thought of that. The desire to chase that which fled him took possession of him.

"You could never withhold what I asked," he prophesied egotistically. She laughed. It was a tantalising sound.

"The old man will be waitin'," he said, nodding towards the house. "Helen—" He was humble now. The simulated pride that was only a decoy dropped from her. Their lips met. She clung to him—but he wrenched himself away. They picked up the bucket and proceeded towards the farm. As they reached a knoll Helen paused. The softened murmur of the river came to them, the chattering of birds, the rustling of the million leaves.

The woman's face was paler than usual, her eyes darker. The paleness and the darkness of her gave the suggestion of a passion-flower. As she paused her body swayed, as a blossom hurtled by a wind. Martin's look and hers met. His was sombre, veiled, and his mouth compressed into tight, hard lines.

"Martin—" breathed Helen.

Her voice was faint, as though speech were a mockery and a uselessness.

"Ay," answered Martin, taking the full weight of the bucket, and moving his glance to a leaf of hawthorn that had fallen into it.

The wind went through the hyacinths, the leaves murmured, and the deep undertone of the river came up to them.

"How can you fight—crush *It* down, always?" she asked, wonder in her eyes, her tone.

"It," she had said—and her hand had pointed down to the water's edge. She saw a spirit gliding amongst the gray rocks, the whispering rushes, the cuckoo flowers drenched with river spray. A townswoman would have said "Nature." The countrywoman breathed "It." With the perception of the power, the mystery, the glory of the priestess she had trembled before, like a child, her wondering look was fixed again on Martin's face, full of that question.

"I think," said Martin tersely.

"I cannot think," she told him simply, greatly, "when I am near you." They went up towards the house of shadow, the house where the old man would be waiting ghoul-like.

Abel Mason had not come down as they drew up to breakfast. There was no sound on the floor above.

"Tha'd better call him, Martin," said Helen, in the tones any daughter of a farmer might use to a man-servant. She did not even look at him as she spoke. Her gaze was turned upon the face of the tramp, who was sitting at the table with the easy unconsciousness of one who had a right there. She was taking note of his jaw, his mouth, his eyes, and wondering how long he would stay.

Martin rose.

"Like the look o' me?" queried the tramp boldly, insinuating something into his voice that said "man." Boldness was his chief note. That was why he could hold his own in the doss-house, why he would hold his own in a wider world and one as unscrupulous if more cultured, why he hoped to tame Helen, Helen who antagonised him with the fearless something that looked out from her eyes.

Helen turned to set the teapot down on the hob before answering his question. She looked at him again.

"Happen I do, happen I don't," she said cryptically.

"That's a pity," said the tramp, as if he read some hidden and unfavourable meaning in her words.

"What difference can it make?" she asked indifferently. "You'll only be here for th' day."

Was there some cunning attempt to get to know how long he was staying? The tramp could not tell. She could fence as well as himself.

"He's ta'en me on," he said.

"Eh?" she jerked, and he saw for a moment beyond the veil of her acting.

"He's ta'en me on for a goodish while," he said calmly.

"I expect it's just till we get th' fields mown," she said nonchalantly.

"Happen," said the tramp darkly.

Martin came back and drew up to the table.

"Is he comin'?" Helen asked him.

"He's ne'er answered," said Martin in a perturbed way. "Usually he's down first. It's strange, Helen."

Helen looked across at him.

"God'll not have gi'en stuff," she said carelessly. "Happen he's gone out. I'll go up an' see."

She left the room, closing the door after her.

"A fine lass," commended the tramp, much as one would admire points in a dog.

Martin nodded.

"Ay," he answered laconically. They heard Helen coming back.

"He's gone out," she said. "He'll ha' gone to look as the Corple Stones hasn't gone off in th' neet. He goes to look at 'em, betimes," turning to the tramp, "an' comes back lookin' like he's been in th' company o' Owd Nick. If he's been up to th' Corple Stones we'll ha' a storm when he comes back. He's a bit leet in his top storey, you know, so don't be surprised if he tells you he's changed his mind about you stayin' on to help a goodish while."

Martin started as she communicated the fact that the old man had taken Fielding on to work, communicated it in a subtle way that the tramp could not be sure how to take. It looked as if she were afraid of the door opening at any moment, her father coming in in a storm, and Martin unaware that he must be careful of his demeanour, as there was another worker in the field.

"Ay, we're all a bit touched, we Masons," she went on, covering up her tracks about the warning to Martin.

She spoke the awful fact as unemotionally as though she communicated that it was peculiar to the Masons to be born with a longer thumb joint than most people. She faced the phantom, pulled the veil from its face, stared into its awful eyes, and dared it to do its worst.

The tramp turned his look from those fearless eyes, that magnificent courage, to the face of Martin Scott. The labourer was looking at Helen with a glance of reluctant admiration. The tramp wondered that any man could be mad enough in his sane fears to think that a mind of such hardihood could be a seed ground for madness. It was as grim a joke as any he had ever heard—even in the doss-house. He could have laughed aloud to think of it all. Martin's fear, old Mason's hatred, Helen's love, all playing into the hands of the doss-house tramp, the man at the bottom, who was going to get up from down under, and climb up, up, and up over the dolts whose indifference had pinned him fast in a world whose limitations had ever irritated him, giving him no scope for his broad- winged ambition to get the best out of life.

It was just at this moment that the door was flung open. It banged terrifically after the old man. Silent, grim, looking as if he had been out all night, he crossed to his chair in the inglenook. The dog got up and crept towards his feet, then licked his boots dubiously. The next moment Nero flew to the other side of the kitchen.

"Give us my breakfast," he growled at Helen. He might have been waiting hours for it.

"It's ready," she answered.

"No back answers," he commanded. She was mute. "An' don't turn stupid," he yelled, "or by the gods—"

She met his infuriated eyes calmly. He meant trouble. "Will you ha' milk ower your porridge?" she queried.

"Don't I allus ha' milk?" he asked.

She poured a generous supply on his dish, without answering.

"Reach it here!" he commanded, with a snarl. She handed it to him. He flung the contents of the dish behind the fire, with a jeering laugh, and handed Helen the empty vessel. She took it calmly, set it on the table, and sat down to finish her breakfast. For two minutes there was silence in the kitchen. Martin and the tramp went on with their meal. Helen, too, with a callousness that showed of long usage to such scenes. Her eyes had a green glow. The tramp caught a look of warning that she flashed across to Martin. It said, "Be careful. We are in his hands."

Martin Scott sat with his impassive look longer than ever the tramp had yet seen it. Once more, as on innumerable occasions, he was to see Helen bullied. The hand that held the spoon shook. Again Helen looked at him, at the look with its strange absence of feeling that meant the keenest feeling. A gleam of fear shone in her eyes. She hurried to give him his cup of tea, and, taking it round to him, touched his hand as if by accident. He stirred in his chair, and cleared his throat.

"Haven't I to have any breakfast this morning?" shouted old Mason.

"Leave Martin alone, lass. Get summat cooked."

She was looking at him, feeling that he was coming round to Martin in his attack—and, eager to draw the storm down on herself rather than risk a combat between the two, she showed a stubborn front.

"I'll ha' it ready soon," she answered sullenly.

"Now," commanded her father. She got up from the table, and got the bacon sissling.

"There's a fence broken down, Martin," said Mason. "What's the meanin' on't?"

There was despotism in the farmer's voice—the despotism of a man who holds another man's living, and something still dearer, in his hand. The woman bending over the pan on the fire turned swiftly. Her father read a fear in her eyes—the first fear he had seen, the fear that he and Martin would quarrel, and that he would send Martin away.

"I—I'll see to it, I didn't know it were broken down," said the iron-proud man at the table.

"Tha'd better," said Mason insultingly. Again there was silence. Martin had not spoken. He had crushed his pride back into his heart.

He soon pushed his chair back and went out. Helen followed on the excuse of emptying the teapot. From his seat the tramp could see that she crossed over to the dark figure bent over the broken fence—there was a humility in her attitude. Martin raised his head, conscious of it, conscious that she realised what it cost him to tramp his pride underfoot. The two shadows met on the sunny field, then Helen returned.

"Tha's been a long time emptying that pot," said her father.

"I went to look at the sow," she lied. Never in all his life had Fielding Day heard a lie that sounded so truthfully. She lied with the magnitude, the thoroughness, of her nature; yet, even as he looked into her unflinching eyes, he knew that to lie came hard to her. She did it because she must. The bacon was set out on the table, and the old man drew up to it. He had barely eaten two mouthfuls when he jumped up from his chair, mumbled something about the bacon being burnt, and then—he had picked up a knife, and Helen had flown to the other side the table, as one well practised in such agility. She watched her father's movements with the alertness of a cat. His face was wild in its rage, his eyes glaring so fiercely they blazed, but whether the look of madness he wore was real or cunningly assumed to cause terror, the tramp could not tell.

"Now, Martin's not here to come between—this time," he chuckled, moving slowly round. She also moved, keeping the door at her back. Her face was no paler than its wont. She looked at the menacing knife, then at the wild eyes, but no cry left her lips for help. Her one idea was to keep the door at her back. The old man seemed to read this idea in her eyes. It was a combat between them, his one desire to get her away from the door, hers to stay there.

A swift movement and a nearer lunge of the knife drove her a little further than she had thought, giving the old man the advantage.

"Aren't ta fleyed o' me, now?" he cried. "He-he! Where's thy courage now? Call o' Martin. He's only two fields away."

"You dursen't murder me," she said, smiling. "You'd swing for it. Did you do like this wi' my mother?"

A change came over the face grinning into hers. The knife slackened in his hand. "Don't talk o' thy mother to me," he snarled. "Why doesn't ta call o' Martin? Isn't he th' bravest lad in the world? He dare face owt—owt at a', Martin Scott. Shout on him!" He saw by her face that this was just what she did not dare do. To call Martin in was to court what she feared, the snapping of the last link of the chain, of Martin going away—of separation that would be as cruel as death. He read her agony in her face now. He gloated upon it. Pang for pang he was getting from Tom Hinson's daughter, an eye for an eye, a tooth for a tooth, as the great law went. He mocked her with the weak indecision of Martin Scott, with the memory of the lad who had dropped her hand from his, all those years ago—with the knife shining nearer, yet nearer, and something in his look that made the tramp recall with a shudder the words that he had spoken so short a time ago—"I get afraid lest I kill her, and lose my revenge." The pale face grew paler now, yet the tramp could not think it was fear. The breath of the old man was now upon the white cheek, the two pairs of eyes looked into each other.

46

"Now," said Abel Mason. "Now—will ta defy me again?"

She uttered no word.

The coldness of the knife was at her throat. Something primitive stirred in her as that coldness pressed her warm throat. She flattened herself against the wall, her thin arms extended on each side of her. She shrunk more at the feeling of that primeval terror than at the knife itself. Her eyes darkened, her face paled almost to death hue. Her lips parted—and the old man stood there, laughing, laughing, in his horrible way.

"Why don't you kill me, an' ha' done wi' it?" she said in a low, penetrating voice. "Kill me, kill me, kill me."

Again the old man laughed.

The laughter seemed to goad Helen to distraction. "Kill me," she said fearlessly, "an' ha' done wi' it."

"What die so young? Go away?" he jeered, "where tha'll never see Martin again, nor the moors tha loves, nor th' sun—"

"I'm not fleyed," she said. "Why don't yo' strike? I'm not fleyed. Yo' shall never make me fleyed. Never. Not whatever yo' do." With a swift, unexpected movement she snatched the knife from him. Her hair showered about her face as she did so, and then—her quick ear caught a sound, a sound she feared, the footstep of Martin Scott. Before she could move, he entered the doorway—saw her, with the almost fanatical light shining in her eyes, inspired by her rising up against that terror of feeling the coldness of the knife at her throat. It was not difficult to believe her the branch of a mad family, now, with that ecstasy upon her death-like face, her dishevelled hair about her, and the shining knife in her hand.

"Martin!" she gasped, flinging the thing away from her.

He looked bewildered, horrified.

"What—?" he began. The word died away in his throat. She looked at him, saw the dull horror stealing into his eyes, and realised his thought. Martin thought she was mad, Martin, whom she had not called because to do so might imperil his staying at the farm.

"Doesn't she look bonnie?" jeered the old man, who was sitting in his chair in the inglenook. "Doesn't she look a reight Mason? He-he! I'm proud o' thee, Helen, proud o' thee."

"Martin!" half sobbed Helen. Before she could say more, the man had turned. He was rushing away, away, to shut out the sight of that look he had seen on her face as he had opened the door, the look that was of the courage of martyrs, defying animal-fear of the knife, the look of superhuman mind which he had taken for the wildness of madness.

"Martin—I'm—not—not—" she murmured. The words stuck in her throat. She sat down by the window. She was not weeping. Only her eyes were closed, as one enduring intensest suffering. Just at that moment the door was reopened. Martin Scott had turned back. He looked at her. He had forgotten the old man, the tramp, the outsider, everything but Helen. He walked over to her side.

"Helen!" he said. There was a look upon him of one snapping a fetter. She looked up with a sudden joy that was tragic.

"I'd only ta'en the knife off him," she said, pointing to her father. Martin accepted the explanation. Whether it fully accounted to him for the look he had seen on her face could not be told.

"Ne'er mind," he said, as a man who has made up his mind to something. "Ne'er mind, Helen." He took a trembling hand in his, standing with clear resolve shining through him, a village Hamlet who at last had left the inaction of thought.

She looked at him.

There were tears in her eyes—tears flung from the agony of an overjoyed heart.

"Martin!" she murmured.

Old Mason had half risen in his chair. There was panic upon his face, in his blue eyes, in his attitude.

"Fool!" he jeered. "Steve Mason, her great-uncle, killed his three little childer—just because 't were dark, an' he'd seen a woman go by the window wi' a white bloose on."

Martin was looking at Helen.

"She got that knife to me," said Abel Mason.

Martin still took no notice.

"Ne'er mind, Helen," he said tenderly. "Ne'er mind, whether it's true or whether it's not. It's all in a lifetime. I'll—stand by thee."

Old Mason was listening intently, watching Martin Scott's face. The panic faded somewhat from his own. He reseated himself in his chair, filled his pipe with tobacco, and winked towards Fielding Day.

There was the sound of steps coming up the flagged garden path.

"Th' Post," said Abel Mason. "Open th' door, Martin."

Martin Scott moved slowly towards the door, took the letter, closed the door. Then he handed it to Mason.

"Read it, Martin," commanded Abel Mason.

Something passed away from Martin, something passed into him—some subtle change—as he tore the orange note open. But Helen did not notice it. As a sun-worshipper might stand in ecstasy after any eclipse, she sat, believing, believing, because she had hoped so much, clinging because she did not dare but hope, though hope had cost her so dear.

Martin read it silently.

He murmured the words over to the old man.

"Tha'll ha' to take another journey," said Abel, as one reluctantly issuing a command. "Happen it'll be th' last. If that telegram's aught to go by, she won't last lung. It's not one o' th' pleasantest tasks, I know."

Helen started from her dream of happiness. She leapt from her chair, and across to the hearth. There was something almost menacing in the movement, in the look.

"Yo'll noan send Martin," she gasped. "Yo' can't send Martin, yo' shan't send him. What do yo' allus send him for? Go yoursel', or send me. I'm not fleyed. Let me go. Let me see it. Whatever it's like it'll not scare me. Let me go. Let me see my Aunt Milly."

"I'll go," decided Martin hurriedly. "I'll go."

"I'm sorry tha's to go, Martin," said the old man. "Reight sorry. But there's nobody else for 't. An' I want to know everythin' is done for her 'at can be done. Tha'll bring back full word, Martin?"

"Ay!" said Martin. "Ay! I'll not be long, Helen."

His glance met the challenge of hers. In his was the recognition of a certain danger, which he would face and conquer—of voices of fear that would call to him, to which he must not turn to listen. In her eyes was a look of hope, of trust, that was sadder than despair. She went and sat by the window, staring at the blowing green stuff in the garden. Two yellow butterflies were courting in the sunshine.

She sat there until Martin was ready.

"Maybe tha'll get back to-neet, Martin lad," called the old man, as he stood with the door half open, the sunlight streaming across the sanded floor, a scent from the wide outside world stealing in.

"I shall come back to-neet, sure," said Martin. He paused, waiting for something. Helen rose from her seat by the window and followed him out. The tramp walked over to the window, concealed himself behind the shutters, and watched.

"Sloppin' an' slaverin' about one another?" asked the old man sarcastically.

"She's pinnin' him a bit o' lad's-love in his coat," reported Fielding. The old man took a slow, luxurious puff at his pipe.

"He-he!" he laughed. "Lad's-love! lad's-love!"

The tramp came and sat in the chair in the other inglenook.

"Tha looks like a November mornin'," laughed old Mason. "There's naught to be downcast about. Thy two thousand is safe. Martin's done. What he were sayin' to Helen were what he felt he ought to say—so he said it, at last. 'T were more'n half actin'. He were deceivin' hissel'. 'T were th' reaction o' seein' her wi' th' knife— an' that mad look. He's been cavin' in for some time. A mon can only stand so much. There's a terrible deal o' imagination about Martin Scott. I saw it in him when he came here, a little lad. An'—he'll go away—an' the place will call an' call him—an' he'll hear it callin' till he dees. Did ta see how his hand shook this mornin'? His nerves is goin'. I've put extra work on him—an' shifted his sleepin' to that dark room wi' the photos o' mad folk in it, an' Helen's hung there among 'em—among my folk. It's not much sleep he gets. It's a' told. He's done. That were his last struggle, this mornin'. An' now he's gone to see Milly. She's terrible, Milly is. An' by that telegram she's worse nor ever she were. An' he hasn't slept none for a long time—an' how he saw Helen by the door with the knife will a' come back when he sees Milly, an' he'll remember that mad woman he happened to see when he were a child. Sometimes I think if it hadn't been for that, that memory, fresher because he were a child, he'd ha' just snapped his fingers at it a'."

At the white gate a woman stood, waving her hand to a man with a sprig of fragrant lad's-love in his coat.

When he had gone she did not turn into the house, where the two men sat. It was as though she could not face its oppression again. She was waiting for great news, and must wait outside. She sat down by the water's edge, and watched the wagtails fly to and fro. Then she fell to thinking of Martin, of just where he would be by now.

"I'm goin' to be happy, happy," she avowed passionately to the flowers.

"You're happy, growin' where you were meant to be. I'm goin' to be happy, like other folk. In a few hours Martin will be back. I'm goin' to be happy."

Her eyes were full of the burning tears of one who has seen heave through a loophole in hell.

For the first time she had the blasphemous feeling that it might be better not to love. She knew it for blasphemy. Opening her dim eyes she stared across a blaze of colour that was life—a green slope laughing in the sunshine, and saw a water-wagtail fly down to the water with its funny little waggling movement, its white marks gleaming in the radiance.

It was beautiful, with all its struggle, that world of nature, she knew.

She was part of it, of the mould, and the last year's leaves, and the moist bluebells.

"I can't stan' much more," she murmured. "But I've thought that so often. I'm so strong—so very strong."

Then she looked again at the beauty of the world. She thought of the days when as a child, as a lonely girl, she had soaked all that beauty into herself. After Martin had come it had never been the same. Human feeling had made her see less in the woods, the moors, the hedgerows. It had been a passion before Martin came. To find a bird's nest had been heaven. It was still sweet. But her pantheism had become humanism. Martin had even spoilt that. She rose from the grass, and went slowly upwards to the farm. She had not been in the wood more than ten minutes. It seemed ten hours. All the time she was waiting, waiting, as one between life and death, for the great sign. She was in the hollow of Martin's hand, subject to every wind of circumstance that blew across his sky, and the loneliness, the inhuman apartness of the sky, the shuddering feeling that it stretched over a world cast into being by a blind chance, even as her life, as Martin's, as the little wagtail's by the river was cast, terrified her. She turned and ran, ran staggeringly up through the wet, tangled grass, up to the horror-shrouded farm, where she had suffered so much, running to the company of those two whom she hated—anywhere, away from that great lonely void.

The gray shadow of Loneliness clutched her. The only thing she feared clutched at her. She was nothing, less than nothing, less than the little wagtail by the river, if she lost her mate. There was no meaning behind anything.

CHAPTER IV

MARTIN COMES BACK FROM HELL

MARTIN had come back from hell.

He was asleep beside a pool on the heights of Corple Stones Moor. Through the windy, starry night he slept, the moor sounds all about him, black shadows of sheep passing through the dimness, the little pool at his side shaped like a cradle and tumbled full of stars. He was asleep, now. Gethsemane was over for a spell.

Sometimes he half woke, a faint sorrow touching him, a sorrow for Helen's waiting. Then Sleep seized him again. Once he dreamed that he was a little lad again, running over Brown Moss with naked feet, watching a hawk. The dream changed, the loneliness of that boyish time merging into one of more awful horror. Helen was dead. He tried to cry out. He struggled to shout, to beat down the very gates of death, to reach her. Agony turned round and round in his heart, a burning knife—and then—he sat up, his eyes open, bewildered by the sight of the Corple Stones sticking up through the dawn. A world empty of Helen still crushed him with its barren weight. He stared up the Corple Stones, rubbing his eyes. Then he remembered how he had got near those familiar shapes jutting up into the blue and rosy sheen of dawn. It was only a dream. The whir of moorfowl's wings made a wind on his face, he heard the startled ga-bak, ga-bak, ga-ga-bak from a cloud of grouse, whilst away below him rolled a valley of opal mists shot through with the golden fires of a day that yet held a living Helen. Fool! He had been thinking not many hours before of ships and the sea, ships that carry men away from problems they cannot face, flying, eager ships that carry men into lands so far away that there they can start anew. Then the gods sent a dream of a dead Helen. The sweat of agony was on his brow. His resolves were gone.

Shakily the strong man rose to his feet. Self-contempt was in his heart. He steered his way across the dew-drenched bents, over the earth-bobs green enough for fairy-thrones, across the coarse gray grasses and fine rusty-tinted ones hiding water-holes, some of them man-deep. He was going back to Four Gates, and—no nearer the solution of his problem than when he had climbed those heights vowing never to come down till he had solved it.

He wanted to look at Helen with the others there, to let reality blunt that dream, until she had no advantage to reap from his secret recollection of it. She was strong enough, in her conscienceless pursuit that ran him down without shame, because her love was as shamelessly pure as the water seeking its own level.

For an hour Martin walked on across the moor. There was something monotonously soothing in the steady march forward, from earth-bob to earth-bob, through the tangled grass and whitened rushes, pressing the bents down over the water-holes with his boots, and hearing the sucking sound following his footsteps. He came to the edge of the moor. Another valley lay below him. Leading down to it was a steep path that ran through a world of fresh, uncurling bracken fronds. They clung about his feet. There was nothing to be heard but the cold tinkle of a northern rill, or the movement of little moor creatures scurrying away from Martin's feet. Once he almost stepped upon a tawny-backed frog. It seemed a world without problems. It seemed that he might put his problem by—here in this world of bracken and sky. Something of the morning gladness stole into his mind. And at the back of his mind, with every step, he was foolishly, deliriously glad that Helen was alive.

Then, the gods made him again their sport, flinging him from mood to mood. He heard a foolish, pealing laugh that brought him to a standstill. He looked all round, but only the waving bracken ranks met his gaze. Yet the sound was that he had heard once in the silence of the night.

Ss—sh!

The wind went through the bracken.

He watched the swaying, sappy stalks, the nodding tops uncurling to the sun. Then, in a flash, he caught sight of a great head, with a shock of thatch-like hair, a pair of vacant eyes, and the slobbery animal mouth. The face leered on him from a break in the foliage. He knew that face. He was looking at the idiot son of a poor widow down in the valley below. Silas was lying down in the bracken. Martin knew that he should pass the cottage door of the widow, but he did not call to Silas to go down with him. A dull rage against the gods took possession of him. He left the hill world, taking the sheep-track, hard and stony, but for a long time he heard that mirthless laugh ringing after him.

As he touched the road that was made by man, he paused and looked up at the hill. It was now a wonderful cloud of grey patched with moss- green where the bracken was, tinged with yellow where the bare clay was piled. His jaw was gripped. His eyes had the look the tramp had noticed in the inn, as if some crater in his soul were opened. He was thinking of that old-young face with the something missing behind it.

"God!" he mumbled from between half-clenched teeth, "what man could risk it? And Helen—" Then he went on, with bent head, amazed at the conscienceless way of women. He almost stumbled upon a pair of rabbits, that scurried through the briar hedge. They were happy in their world, happy, and without conscience, even as Helen. Martin, world-bound, was trying to think!

CHAPTER V

HELEN VISITS A STRANDED FEMALE

WHEN Martin had been thinking of Helen as waiting for him in the farm, she had not been there at all. After tea was cleared away she had sat by the table, till dusk fell, and the lamp was lit. Old Mason sat in the inglenook, his eyes closed, his legs crossed. He looked like some evil god. He was not asleep. At times he shot a loud and unexpected laugh into the stillness, to test Helen's nerves. But the pale woman, with her hand resting listlessly on the story of *The Decline and Fall of the Roman Empire*, did not start. The old strong stillness that had been rent from her, in the stress of the morning, had closed round her again. Her eyes, wide and dark, stared at a big, ash-coloured moth fluttering round the flame of the lamp. She commanded the tramp, who was sitting on the other side the table, to catch and put it out into the garden. He answered by dropping the insect on the live coals. From the shadowy corner that cross-legged giant had laughed again. Looking stealthily towards Helen he saw the listlessness of the pale woman broken by a flash of hatred, as she looked at the tramp. Then she had turned to her book once more.

A knock came to the door. Helen opened it. The scent of wet lad's-love came to her.

"Please, Miss Marsh is poorly, and says will you come?" piped the treble of little Agnes Trip.

58

"Come in, Aggie," said Helen, and led her in by the hand.

"Your bonnet's untied," she continued, and stooped to make a bunch under the little soft chin. The look of passionless endurance was gone. The curves of the lips softened. In the stoop of the slim figure was the ancient graciousness of the mother. Her glance devoured the soft little face, its childish colouring, then, carried out of her habitual reserve, she bent and touched Aggie's cheek with her lips. From his corner old Mason watched her. The gleam of a sudden idea shot into his half-opened eyes.

"Were't dark coming up here, Aggie?" asked the woman who had no fear for herself.

She was stooping again, arranging the ribbons on her bonnet; her voice had a croon in it, the croon that only Martin had heard.

"I'm fleyed o' th' lone," confessed the child, looking up into that pale face. "I don't like sleepin' by mysel'." She slid her hand into Helen's. The sight of the moss-headed old man in the corner scared her.

Again the old man laughed.

"Some are born to ha' bed-mates, Aggie, an' some to go wi'out, an' allus be i' th' lone, day an' neet. An' then when they're put to bed wi' a spade, wi' their heads on th' gravel, they go on sleepin' by theirsel's, i' th' lone an' dark. There's many such i' Four Gates Churchyard. Miss Marsh'll be one. There's many such. Eh, Helen?"

"There's nothin' to be fleyed on i' th' lone or th' dark, Aggie," said Helen.

"Then—you're not fleyed o' th' lone?" asked Aggie.

Helen did not answer. The old man laughed viciously from the chimney-nook. His daughter took no notice. She was watching the clock. She had moved to the table and leaned upon it. There was only the tick of the clock, the fall of a cinder, the growling of the dog from under the settle, in its old antipathy to the tramp.

"Arta goin', Helen?" asked the old man.

"Has Miss Marsh sent for the doctor?" Helen asked the child, ignoring the query.

She shook her head.

"Aren't any of th' naybours goin' in?"

"They've all fallen out wi' her," said Aggie.

"She were once a fine, givin' lass, Sue Marsh," continued the old man, as if speaking to himself. "She'd ha' gi'en Joe her soul, an' asked him what he wanted after that; but he were like th' chap 'at were told by th' butcher that th' beefsteak were tender as a woman's heart, an' axed for sausages. He he! He left her, Joe Gillibrand did, an' shipped to America. Wanted to get out o' her way. She liked him too much. It sort o' tired him. Men be built that way, Helen. Ay, queer fish we are. So Sue were left. An' she grew into a selfish, grabbin', crotchety, twisted thing—like she is now. Some women are so. Some goes out o' theirselves wi' bein' left lone, an' some goes in an' moulders there, an' th' stronger they are th' more twisted they get—unless they're Christians, when they take to dogs an' cats an' other folks' childer, an' meddlin' with other folks' troubles. But Sue was a strong, proud, axin' lass, as wanted summat for her hersel', summat a' her own— summat o' thy make, Helen."

His daughter stared back into the malignity of his eyes.

"I'd ne'er be left," she said, tonelessly. "Sue Marsh were to blame. What did she let him leave her for? If she couldn't howd him it served her reight, bein' left lone."

As she spoke she was moving towards the clothes-closet, and a moment later took out her black cloak.

"Tha'rt goin', then, Helen?" queried the old man.

"Ay," she answered.

"An' what about Martin's supper?" he asked.

"Martin mun get what he can catch," she said.

"When wilta be back?" asked her father.

"I'll be back by noon—whatever happens," she said, donning her cloak.

The old man was looking at her.

"Tha looks like a nun i' that, Helen," he said jeeringly. "Look at her," addressing the tramp. "Isn't she like a nun? He he, look at her, her e'en, her lips, her forehead! Doesn't she look like she could say good-bye to th' world an' fix her eyes on glory to come? He he!"

Helen regarded both the grinning faces.

Her own was calm. A faint smile was written upon it.

"If any took it into their heads to brick me up alive," she said, "they'd be fain to let me out."

"There'd be holiness for thee, Helen. He he!" said her father.

"Life, all on it, is holy enough for me," she said. "I'd hate to ha' a halo painted round my head, to set me up above the others. I'd sooner be buried in a red shroud than a white, wi' those little forget-me-nots at my breast, an' my hands crossed. 'Twould be a lie to send me to the grave so. I'd fight wi' my teeth an' my nails to be what Nature meant me to be! 'Twould be hard for them that bricked me up alive. Look at my e'en, an' my lips—an' don't think I'm ashamed o' 'em or ever will be. Nobody'll ever make me shamed O' life, all on it."

Taking Aggie by the hand she went out into the blue dusk. The laughter of her father and the tramp followed them out.

Old Mason left his seat and peered through the crack in the window-blind.

"She's carrying her," he said, with a fierce joy in his tone. "Carryin' her—an' thinkin' how 'twould be sweeter still if she were hers an' Martin's, thinkin' how she'd go through hell for sich joy, an' laugh at it a' the while. She were made to live an' love, an' give an' take, more'n most, as if to make her suffer more. An' she shall go down to her bed i' th' dark wi' empty arms, an' sufferin's barren o' fruit, an' th' love o' her heart dried up like burnin' sand was poured into it. Bricked up alive! She'll be fain to be that, an' won't ha' that peace. Thee an' me to watch her, Day, like she be a prisoner, to watch her i' her agonies—when she'd fain creep away like an animal. She's built to creep in a hole when hurt. An' allus four eyes a-watch on her, so that she cannot weep, nor pray, nor cry out, but we'll hear her. An' never a child's eyes to look at the sadness o' her face—an' at the end, for I'll live to see the end, for she'll break to pieces under it, to hear her wail at a life without flowers or fruitage—an' then—it's sad, but she'll get away fro' me, then. An' as she dees she'll think o' Martin, an' how she'll sleep i' thy grave, when she hates thee, an' thee an' me'll stand by to watch her, an' as she goes I'll tell her how Martin left her an' 'twas all for nothin'—for nothin'.'"

He sat down in his chair in the nook, laughing horribly. Then he looked across at Fielding Day.

"How much of a brute arta, Field?" he asked, curiously. "She has a way with her," warningly. "Martin has been struggling to get away these five years. She might beat thee."

A thin thread of fear was in his voice. Day, craving to be a tin god, was yet—a man. There were brute beasts that women turned into men, sometimes.

If this happened, his revenge became a broken thing. He looked at Day.

There were no signs of softness in that wolfish grin.

"I'll make her my slave, or I'll bray her to a mortar," said the tramp. "I've said it once before—I'll break her heart, or I'll break her neck."

Old Mason's eyes glittered.

Then a shadow crossed his brow.

"But," he said, "the mind o' her, mon, the mind that looks out of her e'en! The soul o' her, as parson would say, what about that? 'Twould escape thee, somehow, like quicksilver. I've bruised her flesh often, when she were a child—but her e'en allus stared at me so, like summat I couldn't get at. What about that?"

Fielding laughed shortly.

"When a boss had my body," he said, "he had my soul, if I've got one, damn him. She's never belonged to anyone before, remember that. It's only bin negative sufferin'. Wait till it gets to th' positive. Give me her body, an' I'll put her soul through hell-fire. But it's against human nature to do things like that for nowt—an' every time I put th' screw on I'll want some compensation for th' loss my moral balance has sustained."

He looked gravely at the old man.

Old Mason looked back at him steadily. Then he burst out laughing, and Fielding Day joined.

"To th' end o' my fortune, Day," said the old man, regarding him again.

"Let me see th' fear look out o' her e'en, th' fear I felt i' my heart, a' them years back, lest her mother leave me. Let me see't, an' I'll pay for it, twenty shillin's to the pound."

*

Helen left Aggie at the door of the Trips' cottage, and went on towards that where Sue Marsh lived. She was somewhat surprised at Sue sending for her. Except for comments on the weather the two women were not intimate.

It was the last house in Four Gates.

When Helen stood before the rickety gate she saw that the white blinds were dropped to the bottom. No ray of firelight or lamplight radiated the house. On the doorstep Sue's blind white cat, Mary, mewed for admittance.

Helen knocked on the door.

The sounds echoed as through an empty shell.

Then there was deep silence. At length Helen caught

faint sounds. It was a weird murmur of pain drawn from unwilling lips, mingled with a noise like the chattering of teeth. Helen pressed the latch down, but the door did not yield. Sue was locked in. She might be dying, but had not unlocked her door, lest she be robbed.

Helen knocked again.

Then she stooped and placed her lips to the keyhole.

"Sue, Sue!" she called. "Open th' door. It's only Helen—Helen Mason." But the moaning went on, mingled with the mewing of the cat. It was useless to appeal to the neighbours. Sue Marsh wanted none of them, nor they of Sue Marsh. There was nothing to do but sit down and wait for Sue to recover sufficiently to open the door. Helen sat on the doorstep. The blind white cat crept under her cloak. She was not greatly disturbed. The door would open, sometime, or it would remain closed. Her own agony was uppermost. There were some hours to pass before Martin came back, and all was won or lost. It mattered nothing to her where those hours were spent. She was on the rack. It might have been awful to some to sit on the other side of that door, in the gloom of the weed-grown garden through which the wind sighed, the shadow of a black tree hiding her from sight of the passers-by, if any came. But the awful had been familiar to Helen as far back is memory went. There was something of tragic harmony that the woman who might be left to face the "lone" should sit and listen in the gloom of twilight to the moaning of the woman who had been left lone twenty- five years ago. Whilst she sat there she was planning how to meet every possible mood of Martin's on his return. She became conscious at last that the moaning within the house had ceased. She attacked the door again. There was utter stillness, but looking through the keyhole she became aware of the glimmer of a moving light. It wavered from side to side. Occasionally there was the sound of teeth a-chatter. She could not see Sue, as some object partially blocked the aperture.

"Who's there?" asked a weak voice, tinged with suspicion.

"Only Helen," said the woman in the cloak.

"Helen what?" cross-examined the voice.

"Helen Mason," was the answer. There was the sound of several bolts being pulled back, creaking in their rusty sockets. The door opened. A skeleton-thin woman, taper in hand, shedding a light on a pallid, blue-lipped face, peered out. Sue Marsh had the face of a corpse, save for the gleam of the deep-set eyes, and the keenness with which she surveyed Helen.

"Come in," she invited.

A gust of wind blew out the light.

Into the darkness of the death-like house Helen followed the woman, whose movements she could discern by the yet lingering spark of the taper. Its smoky warmth of wax was further reminiscent of candles burnt for the dead. The smell of a house situated in a hollow, and warmed by few fires, greeted Helen like the mouldiness of a vault. A shudder went through her, not of fear, but that she had been called upon to view a fate that might be her own, even at the moment when it was trembling in the balance. Whilst in her proud heart was the crushing sense that she lay in the hollow of Martin's hand, for his tossing away, or keeping.

"Mind catchin' thy head agen th' rafters," warned the chattering voice. "Jim O'Brien hung hissel' on it through gettin' that lass i' trouble. They say he haunts it, but I've never sin him. I'm too owd for him, maybe! Too owd an' too ugly. No, I've never sin him." Her cynical laughter was checked by some spasm that clicked her teeth together. Helen passed from one dark room into a darker one. The mewing of the blind white cat went before her.

"I'm goin' to ha' another do," said the voice. "Shape thyself, lass." She evidently dropped into a chair, for there was the creaking of it; beneath her, and that rattling sound of shaking limbs, chattering teeth, and the low murmuring had begun again. Helen groped everywhere for matches, but could find none.

"Howd my hand," commanded the voice brokenly, "or I'll be shaken to bits."

Somehow or other Helen groped her way to that clammy, bony hand, and steadied its shaking. Then she found the other hand and held that, too. Whilst all the time as she knelt in the darkness it was to her like her own youth kneeling and holding the hands of her own old age—an old age lonely, dwindled, cold with suspicion and morbidity.

But at length it was over.

Sue Marsh managed to gasp out where the matches were. Helen found the lamp and lit it. The yellow light lit up the little kitchen, shining on the woman laid back in the chair, her eyes closed, her lips a blue line, her thin, pale hair shaken round her face by the violence of the spasms that had passed.

There was a bed in the corner of the room, and to this Helen dragged her almost helpless, strangely made friend. When Sue was laid on the bed, and half-undressed, she turned her face towards Helen. Her eyes gleamed in their hollow sockets.

"I think," she said grudgingly, "tha might kindle a bit o' fire. Tha'll happen be cowd." Whilst this order was carried out she watched her. Helen knew that each tiny cobble of coal was counted. Whilst the fire flickered in the cold chimney, the woman on the bed revealed glimpses of her contorted mind to the pale-faced girl fanning the flames.

She lay on her side, her face turned to Helen, who was kneeling on the fender. The cracked, blue lips might never have been warmed by a lover's kiss. They were clipped close, veritable purse-clasps. She had ripped her bodice open in her struggling for breath during the heart-spasm; it was still open. Lead-coloured, withered breasts hung like empty bags, misers' bags that had given nothing. The lonely shadow of herself was on the wall, as it had been these many years, moving when she moved.

It was a strong face, with good features, but it was ugly. She had stood alone, lived alone—and had that ghastly resemblance to a corpse.

"I've nobody to thank for nowt," she said gloatingly, her eyes fixed upon Helen's face.

"Not many can say that, lass, eh?"

Helen shook her head.

It was slightly bowed, that dark head with the hood slipped from it, almost as if she did not dare to look too closely at that pride-ravaged countenance. There was too much similarity between the fate of this woman and what her own might be, for her callous and dispassionate on-looking. If Martin leave her, would not that be the tendency of her own wild nature, to shut off her kind, want no pity from them, no love, no crust of bread? There were only one pair of hands from which she could take love, as a wild bird taking crumbs, and those were Martin's. There was an intensity upon her face as she fanned the fire. She might have been fanning the love in Martin's heart.

"No, nobody to thank," murmured the woman on the bed. "It's gospel truth. It's good to think of it. I say it ower to mysel', every neet, as I put th' lamp out. 'Nobody to thank, nobody to thank.'"

Helen listened to the ritual of a starved life.

"An' I say I've done very weel. There's them can't get along wi'out a chap o' some mak'. They be a lot o' trouble, fellies. An' what they bring. If men and women never come together there would be no trouble. An' what brass saved! An' childer—what are they? They tak' all your brass to bring 'em up into folk, an' then they start makin' trouble for theirsel's, an' them as nosed 'em. It's a' to risk. It's a' to risk. I've gotten along very weel. An' if I've gotten nowt, I've ta'en nowt. But some wouldn't like to be lone."

She was staring at Helen.

Helen was looking back at her. She had ceased to fan the fire. She was listening to this old age of hers speaking of needing nothing, giving nothing, unaware that its creed was that of those rotting in Four Gates Churchyard. A corpse lay there, its pallid lips speaking joylessly of taking no risks, no chances of change, morbidly thankful that it was left undisturbed in the dust. There was a fascination to her in looking at what she might become. She had always looked her fears full in the face.

"An'—when you dee?" asked Helen's voice. "Won't you feel like you're goin' away only knowin' half—like someone has only had feelin' down one side o' their body?" Her words trailed off into the silence of the mouldy house.

"It's only trouble I've missed, trouble an' toil," answered Sue. But her eyes gleamed. The voices of her departed youth called to her. "It's only trouble I've missed, an' poverty, an' things always in a toss. An' I've a pot o' brass."

"But never to have had a child close to you," said Helen. "To go down into th' dark without knowin' that— an' to know that the sun weren't shinin' on a face that had somethin' o' you in it! To have none to weep for you as you were put into th' earth. Just to be put into th' earth, like a stray cat, an' th' end on it, there. Seems like those who haven't had love haven't had a soul! To be buried—like a stray cat!"

The woman on the bed had raised herself on her bony elbow.

She looked resentfully at Helen. Through the dust that was strewn upon her came the tumultuous longings of life, the sound and clash of it, the laughter and tears of it.

"Tha'rt thinkin' o' Martin Scott," she said, so unexpectedly that Helen started back as if she had received a blow. "Tha'rt mad on him. All Four Gates knows on it. Even I know—shut off like I'm i' my coffin. For that's how tha thinks I am. I can see it in thy face."

Helen sat as if carved in stone.

All Four Gates knew.

"I saw yo' both stood under th' yew-tree, one neet," said the old woman. "Joe Gillibrand an' me stood there, just th' varra same, years agone. An'—he left me."

Then her tone changed.

She turned eagerly to the woman kneeling motionless on the fender. The fire was dying down, a fitful flame or two vainly trying to fasten round the coals.

"Tell me a' that's goin' on," she begged, cravingly. "Tell me who's courtin', an' who's to be marrit. I'm not as dead as tha thinks. I'm alive—burnin' alive, sometimes. A' this courtin' an' marryin' catches at me. It's th' only thing interests me, after th' brass I pour into my lap. I muffle mysel' up i' dark cloes, so nobody could tell me if they saw me, an' steal out o' dark neets to listen to lovers talkin' behint hedges—an' when I come home here I say over again all their silly passionate talk. I'm alive, Helen Mason, alive, though I'm buried. Who'd think an old woman like me would steal about like a ghost o' neets? Now, aren't I alive?"

Helen did not answer. She was clasping and unclasping her hands nervously. She felt sickened.

"What's ta think of it, lass?" queried the old woman. "Aren't I alive?"

Her hollow eye gleamed in its socket.

She seemed to challenge Helen, to challenge the dream of her own youth, with its healthfulness and proportion.

"Horribly alive," Helen answered, shiveringly.

"An' what does ta think on it?" asked the old woman.

"I'd rather dee," said Helen, passionately.

What she looked at was a corpse, with a corpse's contorted view of life, a corpse whose starved longing for human love had grown into disease, so that now there was nothing left to interest her but gold and sex.

"I used to think I'd dee," said the old woman. "But—I went on livin'. An' at last I got used to it, eatin' an' sleepin', just like it mattered. Think on it, allus th' empty house, an' th' echo o' my own feet, an' allus my shadow there, an' meals lone, an' the long lone neets— an' then I got used to it, an' clung to it, an'—ay, it's strange how we get used to things when we mun. An' when I felt alive, alive an' sufferin' agen, I would steal out an' listen to lovers. Am I awful, Helen Mason?"

Helen looked into the pallid face.

"Anyone that doesn't get bread thinks on it a' th' time," she said. "You've been a-hungered. An' you haven't deed—only half-deed—that's a'. Life isn't like you think. It's full o' things besides passion. An'—I don't think I care for Martin Scott as you cared for Joe Gillibrand."

She had confessed to Sue Marsh as she might to the shadow of her own old age. Sue Marsh had spoken as she might to her own lost youth. They looked into each other's eyes. Helen stood tall and pale, like something opposing a flood that was sweeping nearer. The old woman laughed.

Her laughter said that she thought Helen very young.

"How does ta like Martin?" she queried.

Helen paused. When the words came they rushed forth from the deeps of silent years. She was not confessing to Sue Marsh, but to that shadow of her own old age.

"How?" she crooned. "Why, th' ground he walks on, th' old coat he wears—when I see him far off, an' when

I see him near, when he frowns an' when he smiles, an' when he quotes from books an' thinks hissel' wise, an' when he thinks hissel' strong—an' a' about him. For better or worse, if he were a leper, or a murderer, an' a' against him. That's how."

Sue Marsh sank back on her pillows.

She was smiling.

"That were just how I cared for Joe," she said. "Lass! Lass! It's best for such as we be to wed wi' one we care naught for. Th' other would walk over us."

All night long Helen stayed with her, holding her shaking hands when the spasms came on, watching her fascinatedly as she slumbered between, when exhausted, listening to the talk of this starved woman, turning always in the direction of sex or gold, the two obsessions of her perverted mind, listening in sickly horror. When she left that house in the grey dawn she was years older. Something of the scene she had left had eaten into her. She cast fearful glances behind her, leaving that house of living death.

She peered in at the farm window and saw the kitchen was empty. Martin had not yet returned. Several things told her this.

She passed noiselessly out from the garden and down the hill-side, till she came to the wood, a-thrill with morning. The blue world of the wild hyacinths was a-dance. She saw nothing of it. The screws of her rack were turning, turning. She was waiting and listening for Martin, to catch the first glimpse of his face as he approached, with her destiny in his hand. She was waiting, desperately strong to fight for her very soul.

CHAPTER VI

ALMOST WON

LIKE a cat watching for its prey, Helen was watching for Martin. Her body was almost hidden in the long grass. Coal-black hair streamed wide on each side her face. Through the dark, shining meshes of it the bluebells burned. Out of the whiteness of her face her eyes shone with a light that would have had her burned as a witch in olden days. Her lips were vividly red. She was ever biting them. The black cloak was tossed over the bough of an ivy-strangled oak some yards away; it waved solemnly and slowly in the wind.

The old blouse of soldier-red, open at the throat to allow her to breathe more freely, gave her a look unlike the women of Four Gates.

She was looking through the round, deep-shadowed arch of the old lichen-lined bridge. The half-circle of the arch mirrowed in the water completed a perfectly rounded frame, wherein was set a vignette of the real and imaged world, shimmering green and golden glory, interspaced with springtime sky. If a bird flew from one bank to the other there seemed to be two, one in air, one in water. The wagtail on the still grey stone was preening its wing in the wave below.

Away beyond a pebble-white bank the river curved mysteriously out of sight.

She was waiting for Martin. She looked again at the still reaches of river at her feet, charmedly still like some crystal-gazer.

She was watching for Martin.

For seven hours she had waited thus. Twenty-eight quarters had chimed from the square, grey tower of Four Gates church. She had stirred slightly whenever that sound broke the stillness, until the last stroke. At the last stroke she had not moved at all, as if she had inured herself to wait till the crack of doom, if needs be. Many pictures had passed into that mirror at her feet, from school-children on their way to school, to old age, hobbling along with "one foot in the grave"; a pair of lovers had kissed there unwitting of one who watched them hungrily; a young mother had paused to rest there with her baby; the whole gamut of human life had passed over the old bridge to be reflected at the feet of the woman in the grass.

At last, into the mirror, stepped the figure she had waited for.

She did not start.

She was looking intently into the mirror.

Martin had stopped midway on the bridge. He was hatless. His face had its most enigmatic expression, and that dark sallowness of tint which in times of crisis was ever accentuated. He looked towards the farm once, then down at the waters. He was alone, and for aught he knew, unwatched. But no shadow of what he felt or thought crossed his countenance. He had wrapped himself round in sheet-ice. It was his most difficult mood. He would be sombrely cold, answering in monosyllables. Helen coiled herself face downwards in the grass. There was no need to look further. She had seen and knew. When she looked up again the bridge was empty. Martin had gone. Would he take the gap in the hedge and come down by the river, or proceed up the lane to pass through the farmyard? If he came down by the river she would know that under that enigmatic look was hidden some indecision, that he was taking the longest way round because he was afraid—afraid of her.

Placing her ear to the ground, she listened.

There was the soft, swaying sound from the bluebells, the fine, almost inaudible voices of myriads of grass-blades, the murmur of winged insects, and always the deep, solemn undertone of the river, like a great rich chord with which all the slighter sounds blended, aerial laughter harmonising with the chant of a god.

She heard the crackling of the hawthorn boughs pushed aside as he came through the gap in the hedge. He had chosen the river-path. She coiled herself more closely in the deep grass. Whenever she came down into that wood a wild, pagan faith always shot her through, from the memory of the spell she had cast there. She felt herself twice as strong in the wood, and Martin twice as weak.

She watched him advance. He was threading his way to avoid crushing the bluebells or any little life of the grasses. The paradox of the humanitarianism that could keep her soul on the rack, yet shudder lest the pulp of a bluebell be crushed back into the sod, gave her a wild desire to laugh. Never before had she felt like laughing at so unfitting a moment. Her throat throbbed, too. A pulse had sprung into it suddenly and feverishly. She pinched herself fiercely to shake off this strange feeling. She must be strong, strong as those who fight for their very existence. She must be alert, like an animal.

When he was within some yards of her she sat up unexpectedly.

"Martin!" she cried.

The blood rushed to his brow.

He stood looking at her. She was sitting in the grass, little bits of it sprinkled over her. The sun was shining full on her. She was laughing! She had said "Martin," like a child playing hide-and-seek. He wondered if she knew that laughter curved her mouth so that it drove him almost wild to refrain from kissing it.

"It seems a long time sin' tha went, Martin," she said, as he waited for her to fire the first shot.

She had *tha'd* him. He knew she was most dangerous, then.

"Ay," he answered.

He directed his glance towards the farm.

"How's my Aunt Milly?" she asked, formally sympathetic.

"Dead," he answered.

"Dead!" ejaculated Helen. He saw her soul in her eyes.

"Ay, dead," he said, with formal reproof. "Aren't ta sorry?"

"I never tell lies," she said, "if I can help it."

"There isn't another woman in Four Gates but would—"

He stopped.

"Tha should ha' bin a local preacher, Martin," she gibed. He opened his lips as to answer the taunt, then closed them again.

"I can't help havin' been brought to Four Gates," she added.

Helen went on: "I've never seen Aunt Milly. Blood's thicker than water,

I know, but fire's fiercer than either. Love's fire. How far can ta go back, Martin? Three generations at most— then a's misty. An' what's behind that mist? Disease; weakness, crime, happen. Do I want to look? When Matty O'Bill's wanted to insure her father for another penny, th' Insurance men came, an' axed questions. Is love such traffickin'? I'd dee before be on a par wi' such! I give a', an' want a', an' risk a'. If love isn't that, put it on a grocer's bill an' calculate what it'll cost an' if it's worth it. Martin! Martin! I'm a woman, but a better mon than thee!"

Her voice had run the gamut of fiery scorn, crooning love, hard cynicism, and the glow of the poets.

"Nay," began Martin.

He stopped. It was dangerous to "barge" with her.

"Martin," she called. With a swift movement she had risen, standing face to face with him.

She was stroking the sleeve of his coat, with an abandon of affection. "This isn't a play-house," he said. She ignored the taunt. Her lips had lost their colour.

"I'll dee if tha leaves me, Martin," she told him. "I may go on eatin', an' sleepin', an' talkin'—but I'll be dead. Promise me, Martin "

"Remember tha'rt a Four Gates woman," he said, as she still held him.

His voice was brutal.

But he had turned his glance from her face.

"Sit down by me, Martin," she pleaded. "I'm not goin' to fight. I've bin through Hell." Her voice caught. There was a sob on her lips, though she was trying to laugh. Her smile was the most tragic thing he had ever beheld.

"I'm i' Hell, yet," he told her, but his voice had lost its fierceness. As he spoke he tried to loosen her hand from his sleeve. It came away as if he had brushed a snow-flake off, strong though her hands were. There was a limpness about her that he had never seen before. After her passionate, virile outburst of a few moments back, it was the more marked. She drooped. It gave him a curiously elated sense of dominance. He so seldom felt himself her equal. She had cried out for truce from the long battle. He felt as the conqueror of some barbarian.

"I'll sit down, then, for five minutes," he compromised, and laid his watch in the grass.

They sat down together. Her hands lay idly on her lap. There was an abandon of fatigue in their pose. Her shoulders drooped, her head was bent, so that her face was half hidden. The cloud of hair about her reminded him again of the little girl who had looked at him so searchingly years ago, as if wondering what sort of play-fellow he would be.

He drew nearer to her.

She did not move or look up.

A gust of wind went through the wood, stirring the shadows at their feet to fantastic changes. The cloud of her hair was blown across his cheek. His blood tingled at the touch. One of her hands moved languidly and caught the recreant tresses, twisted them into a knot which she thrust inside the neck of the soldier-red blouse. A suspicion shot faintly through his mind that she knew that her close, silky cap of black hair lent to her the look of a weary boy pal.

But she was not looking at him.

He could look his fill at her, without meeting the disturbing magnetism of her eyes. She sat beside him, tame as the tamest woman in Four Gates. She placed one of her hands out into the grass and leaned upon the strength of her arm. It seemed nearly too weak to hold her up. Slowly Martin's hand travelled across the grass, reached that white hand, then covered it from sight with his own. Her fingers did not tremble; neither did they lock in his, in their old eager way. Again the conqueror's feeling surged through him. He had a consciousness that she was at his mercy, his to stay by or forsake; he was a god thereby, he, a common, toiling man to the rest of the world. He was stronger than she, now. He had thought her invincible. She was less than he at this moment. The knowledge felt to give him back some manhood which he had felt to be slipping from him in his indeterminate thoughts, of late. The wonderful Helen who had laughed where he had shuddered, who had seemed to defy the very gods themselves, was beaten. The rack of waiting for him had smashed her up. Her sullen determination, her aggressiveness, her almost inhuman boldness of staring fears in the face, her bright shamelessness—all were gone. She was on the level of the other women of Four Gates, the women who "would wait to be asked"; the women who wept where she would fight; the women who gained balm for their hurts from the sympathy of other women, whilst she smiled to hide wounds. The woman who was not afraid of the lonesome darkness of a moor in the gloaming, afraid of being bogged or beset by the barguest, was weak as any, after this long fight, and he who had sometimes felt out-manned by her, felt himself grow in stature as she had become understandable and weaker. Something primitive and ancestral swept him through, the subdued passivity of her mood gave him so keen a sense of her dependence on him. She had said she must die, if he left her. The crushing feeling of her magnitude was gone. Her boast that she was the better man of the two had been spoken almost before the lowering of her banner. He could not but be glad. It was right that he should be the stronger. This creature who sat so droopingly by him, by tireless energy, watchfulness, by every appeal save to his animal nature, had fettered him down in a hell of fiery unrest for five weary years. She had spoken words that were rivets of steel to bind his soul. She had made appeals that became commands because of their unanswerableness. She had grown to be something to wonder at and fear as well as love, whilst he had felt to dwindle and peak, to grow into a straw at whom the gods laughed. She had none of her disturbing words to say now; nor was her silence that strong silence more powerful than words.

This moment's dominance was his.

"An' tha'll dee if I leave thee, Helen?" he queried.

He had shed half his mail. What need was there of mail before so weak a thing?

"I'll dee, Martin," she answered.

"Tha loves me greatly, Helen?" he asked.

Yet even as he did so it seemed strange to him that he, the moment's master, should ask this of the lesser one, even as Helen, when dominant, asked it of him, in her jealous, fearful way. He was trying to think in his old way, but found it more hard; there was so little to fear in her.

"More than tha cares for me, Martin," she answered, droopingly. A wave of tenderness swept him nearer to her.

"Tha doesn't know, Helen, tha doesn't know," he said.

There was something trance-like in her looks. Her head rested wearily against his shoulder, where he had drawn it. Samson might have felt so sure of his strength before he was shorn.

He touched her cheek gently with his lips. The coldness of it terrorised him.

"Tha'rt cowd, Helen," he said.

She did not answer, but sat as if too weary to move. He had clasped the thin shoulders.

He was wondering if her lips were cold also.

He kissed them. She might have been out in the frost.

The whisper of the wind through the grasses was the only answer he got. Her body was close to his, so close that he might have felt the throbbing of her heart. But that was calm and dispassionate also.

"Tha'rt cowd, Helen," he repeated, shaking her arm a little.

"I feel cowd, Martin," she answered.

He could not tell if she referred only to physical coldness. In a moment a fear had caught him, octopus-like. His secure strength of dominance fell from him.

"Helen—" he called, tensely.

There was an awful stillness that seemed to lap him round like lead.

Some pulse had stopped beating—some pulse to which the grass waved, the sun shone, the birds sang. His cry was wrenched from him against his will. Up near the Corple Stones, some hours ago, he had wished that she might let him go. The shadow of reality was bitterer than the dream. Had the rack of suffering been too much? He remembered having read that the brightest fires burnt out most quickly. Worlds burnt themselves out, passing into darkness and negation. Human loves had their limits, so much rapture, so much to suffer, ere darkness fell and the coldness of a dead world. Helen's might have burnt out. Supposing that his dream meant that! Ages of superstition woke in his mind in a moment.

"Helen," he repeated. "Tha hasn't gone away from me?"

He felt to be struggling with death.

She did not move or look at him.

Then he clasped her to him. He was kissing her wildly as one who would galvanise a corpse into life.

"Does ta care for me? Only tell me that, Helen?" he reiterated.

"I care, Martin," she answered him mechanically, with that strange passivity. It sounded worse than any denial. He remembered the sudden coming of love, like a miracle. They were gathering May blossoms on their way from the Fair, and Helen had stumbled down from the hedge, floundering against him, the blossoms and thorns and her hair striking his breast, and love the beautiful, the awful, was upon them.

Even so suddenly, he knew, love could depart.

He shook her gently again, calling her name, whilst his repetitions sounded foolish in his ears.

"Tha lies, Helen," he said fiercely. "Them as love don't say it like that.

Let's have th' truth; whatever it is, I can bear it. Tell me. Why arta so cowd, so different wi' me? Helen!"

Then he fell to kissing her again, because she did not speak. But her chill hand freed itself from his, and motioned him languidly away, beating as if at his warm heart—to tell him that space to breathe, freedom, peace, were better things than the slavery and tumult of love. Even so, a love in its death-agony might cry out and beat for release.

She wanted peace.

She could love no more, suffer no more.

That was how he interpreted it all, this bewildering phase.

He laid her down on the grass, moving some paces away, and stood looking at the river. The spot had a mocking aspect to him. It seemed that places had souls and could laugh at human misery. The moment became tense with such fate that all his life might have led up to it. His brain swam. He hung on a dizzy bridge over the gulfs of Eternity, whilst yet he knew that this moment, this day, this agony would pass, this terrible Present become the tolerable Past. Helen had ceased to love. If he left Four Gates it would be as a homeless beggar.

No, it could not be true.

He would ask her yet again, call her this once more. "Helen," he pleaded, then stopped hopelessly.

He was kneeling down by her, in the careless blowing world of grass-spires.

Her eyes unclosed.

They were full of tears. Her breath came in little gasps, as one coming from some numbing spell, some semblance of death.

He took her hand between both of his.

"I thought tha didn't care, Helen, any more," he said. "Why were ta so strange wi' me?"

"I don't know," she answered. "I sort of gave out, Martin. The feelin' seemed to go away from me. 'Twere awful. I only wanted to lie still, an' be left alone. But it wasn't that I didn't care, Martin. I wonder if folk i' their coffins hear folks talkin' round them, as I heard thee?"

She looked back at him, with something of her old look.

"I thought I were stronger than that," she laughed, weakly. "Fancy givin' out like that."

She had come back. She had never gone away. It was only physical reaction, born of mental anxiety. He had taken it for the death of love.

"Kiss, Martin," she begged. Her voice came weakly, but held the throb of the old eagerness, with the croon of love that was half a laugh at its own folly.

"Tha couldn't stop lovin', Helen?" he asked, kissing her cheek. He was cautious now in his kissing. She was waking up to the situation.

She shook her head somewhat sorrowfully.

She had waited all these hours, to be strong in order to attack Martin, and a moment's physical weakness, that sense of life half fading from her limbs, had helped her more than her fiercest attack could have done. She felt again that almost irresistible desire to laugh. Weakness, not strength, won men, then. The gods had been on her side, this once. But she must follow up the advantage. Already possibilities were presenting themselves.

"Tha thought I had stopped carin', Martin," she said. "What did it feel like?"

He gave her an eloquent look.

His face had resumed some of its usual reserve, but his hands shook a little.

She nestled against his coat wearily.

"Tha's felt it once," she crooned, smiling faintly, that weakness wrapping her round with something pallidly beautiful. "I've had it near me, that fear, neet an' day, for five years. I've dreamt tha were gone from me an' Four Gates, an' wakened wi' th' pain, an' made myself sleep again, an' in the mornin' there it's bin again, like a shadow, followin' me. An' it's the first time I've given out, Martin. They made me strong, Martin. They say folk are made for their places. They made me strong. Happen that's how they make souls has to burn i' hell. Th' weak ones would burn away, an' stop sufferin' too soon."

He met her pale, wonderful look—the glory of her eyes. She had told him that this moment's agony under which he had cried out had been her companion, night and day, for five years.

"Lass—"

He bent over her. His lips were parted in some utterance great with fate for both of them. The breath of the words was on his lips. Helen felt it. Eye met eye. Martin's weakened under the challenge of hers. Martin was giving in. The gods had sent him to her, through the wood that knew her spell—that she might take him unawares, with their aid. She sat up, and clung to him, like a white flame.

A throstle was singing some yards away in a green bush.

Martin came nearer the edge of the gulf.

"Thy e'en are black as neet, now," he said. His own were shining with that rare softness that occasionally lit them up. Helen was waiting. She did not understand. She was afraid he was gaining time. She wished him to say something that would bind him forever to her and Four Gates, for she knew if he spoke it he would abide by it.

He saw it in her eyes. Her intense glance almost scorched his face. Her parted lips, her hungry look said, "*Now,* say it *now,* Martin."

Martin dallied, as if it were sweet to him. His expression was dreamy.

"I wonder," he said musingly, "why no other woman's flesh thrills me as thine does?"

"Why does th' quail o' the moor choose one mate and leave another?" Helen answered. The bare, scientific fact became poetry as she spoke it, and the clod of earth at their feet was shot through with more vivid glory.

"Tha'rt thin—pale, like a new moon," he murmured. "An' thy e'en are so dark, and thy hair. Helen—I believe tha'rt beautiful, that men would think so if ever tha left Four Gates."

"I'll never leave Four Gates," said Helen.

Her fingers were twined round his now, there was the crooning music in her voice, but the burning look on her face was still more marked. Was Martin never going to speak?

"Tha'd never leave Four Gates?" Martin asked, studying her face.

She was waiting for him to pick up the broken threads of five years ago, whilst he was asking foolish questions, making comments on her looks, and what others would think of them. She frowned. A sense of the indignity of it irked her. Out of the long patience of her waiting came something fiery and impulsive that urged her to say, "Take me or leave me, Martin—but don't be long about it." Then she looked full at him, seeing a look that she had never seen since that evening five years ago. In a flash the truth burst upon her. In this tender conning over of what was to him half a miracle, Martin Scott was already picking up the threads of five years ago. His had been a brief tenderness, revealing itself only as they had crossed the spaces of two moonlit fields. Then he had said soberly, "We mun ax thy father." That father had laid bare a horror-shaded future, and the tender lover had become the saturnine man. The door had been shut on that joyous tenderness for five long years. He was going back now—and she had only just perceived it. It was lad's love he was giving her at this moment, sweet-scented, happy lad's love that had lived somehow through storm, iron restraints, struggles between them.

She leaned against him and listened to the voice of the river. She wanted to realise it. She felt even younger than when she was a little girl, for she had been lonely then, and loneliness is aging. She was young, young, young! The throstle seemed to sing it. Martin and she would both live years yet—in one house; grow old together, and sleep in Four Gates churchyard together. They would fight for, and sometimes with, each other. It was not an earthly Paradise she wanted, it was only life; toiling, suffering, joy-veined life, with Martin, that she wanted. The glory of life was rushing towards her, darkened though it might be by the clouds of her destiny. She was sailing through blazing seas of splendour after leaving the greyness of valleys barren with negation. The deepest cores of her hopes opened, sunned by the look in Martin's eyes.

"Why wouldn't ta ever leave Four Gates?" he was asking again.

It had been a long pause.

Both had fallen upon their own dreams, listening to the throstle.

Helen had travelled far since he put the question before.

She looked into his face, seeing the look still there.

"Because I've suffered so much here," she said. "An' now—I am goin' to be happy here; happier than I've ever been before, eh, Martin?"

Helen looked questioningly at Martin, a proud humility in look and voice. That voice was pitched half a note lower, a sign of disturbance. She not only knew herself to be in Martin's hands, but she was going to tell him so, and ask him what he meant to do with her. The courage, the love that was greater than Four Gates, was held in bondage by the pride that was of Four Gates. The colour had flamed into her cheek.

85

"Am I going to be happy, Martin?" she asked.

Even so a savage might kneel prostrate before some god, head in the dust.

The god bent his head nearer.

"How can I say?" he answered, very humbly.

The colour had fled her lips again.

"Am I, Martin?" she persisted. "Am I? I want to know—now."

There was a swift movement. Martin had laid his cheek boyishly against hers. Something of adventure was in his expression. The very air about them seemed aware that at last his indecision must go. There was a hush—a stillness. Martin's lips were parted for words for which Helen waited thirstily. But they were never spoken.

Before they came, the air was beaten by discordant cries, the growling and yelping of the dog, the swish of branches being swept aside behind them, and a mad party, headed by old Mason, swept down towards them. His hair stood almost on end, his eyes rolled in frenzy. He was making cries more akin to the beasts than to men. His head was lowered, his arms swaying like the sails of a windmill to sweep any obstacle from his path. It was a sight terrible to see. Nature had loosed a ghoul upon the beauty of the springtime noon. The lovers had risen to view it. Martin was looking on it with re-awakened loathing. He watched old Mason's movements with dull horror.

"He's goin' to pitch hissel' into th' river. Stop him, Martin!" yelled Teddy Trip. Fielding Day, axe in hand, called from chopping timber, was some yards behind Teddy.

"Martin!" exclaimed Helen, plucking his sleeve.

"I'm off," he said, in an undertone. Faint as it was, she heard it amidst the din of voices. She faced him.

"Where?" she asked sharply.

86

There was an odd determination on him as he faced her.

"Anywhere—out o' this," he breathed. The next moment he had taken to his heels, "as if old Nick were after him," to use Teddy's phrase. Fielding Day and Teddy Trip wrestled with the old man. But Helen stood looking after that fleeing figure.

"It's knocked th' lass a bit giddy," said Teddy to Fielding as they got the old man quiet between them. He had suddenly become passive as a lamb. "I can manage him. Look to th' lass."

Fielding Day dropped behind.

Helen had not moved a foot from where Martin had left her. She looked dazed. The tramp touched her on the arm. She started nervously. Her eyes reminded him of a trapped hare's he had seen.

"We shall want some dinner," said Fielding Day.

She looked at him, but did not answer. He repeated his remark. "Ay," she answered, and swayed a little.

Day put out his hand to steady her.

He had caught hold of her elbow in his great hand as she set out for the farm.

"I can walk—by misel'," she said curtly. She dragged her trembling limbs towards the house, trying to walk straight. They were getting her father up the stairs as she entered. Helen set Fielding's dinner on the table, then sat down. When he came down with Teddy he moved to the table and commenced to eat, inviting Teddy also to sit down. Helen moved towards the doorway of the kitchen.

"It's Brungerly Market Day," she said. "I shall go in ten minutes. If Martin comes to his dinner it'll be set ready under a cloth, in th' larder. My father'll be a' reight wi' a bit o' watchin'." She commenced to get ready.

She went upstairs and returned some minutes later in her Sunday attire. She had a basket on her arm.

There was hardness on her face belied by something of panic that stared from her eyes.

"Keep th' fire in," she commanded Fielding. "I'll mayhap be back i' time to bake. An' Martin'll want a fire if he comes." She moved to the door. She moved with sudden decision. Fielding Day pushed his chair back as he heard the door close behind her. He watched her from the window. There was the same definite movement as she went through the yard. The dog followed her, but reluctantly went into its kennel at her bidding.

"Could ta follow her without bein' sin?" Day asked Teddy Trip, suddenly, turning from the window. "I'm bothered about her. She's upset. I want to know which way she goes."

Teddy Trip shook his head.

"I've known Helen sin she were so high," he said, holding his hand a yard from the floor. "I'm noan goin' to spy on her—not if Jesus Christ Hissel' axed me."

"I'm fleyed she may be goin' to do hersel' mischief," said Fielding. "If tha'll not go—I will. But, nay, I dursen't leave th' cow. It's due any time."

Teddy pondered.

"Tha thinks she's goin' to—" he stopped, and shuddered. Then he said,

"What shall I do?"

"Follow her to th' road an' see which way she takes," said Day, sitting down at table. "Then come back an' tell me." He spoke masterfully, easily, with his eyes on Teddy. After giving Helen time to get a little way ahead, Teddy went out. Fielding Day commenced his dinner. Teddy Trip puffed into the house just as he was finishing picking a bone.

"Well?" he asked, sucking out the marrow.

Teddy sat to recover his breath before answering.

"She's stuck her basket in th' hedge—hidden among th' hawthorn," he said. "An' I followed her on, till she took a field-path an' I saw th' fells i' front. An' I should ha' kept after her then—but I sees Martin Scott i' th' front, an' she starts peltin' after him. So I came on here, just to relieve thee."

Fielding Day flung the bare bone down on his plate.

"It's a' reight, then," he said indifferently.

"It's a queer do when women takes to chasin' chaps," Teddy said meditatively. Fielding laughed.

"Doesn't ta think so?" asked Teddy.

"It's out o' th' common to do it openly," admitted the tramp.

"But as it happened—they were nobody about— nobbut me—an' I've known her sin she wor so high—" His voice was perturbed.

"Say nowt o' this in th' village," said Fielding. Teddy looked at him curiously.

"She'll be Mrs. Day in less than three months," said he in reply to Teddy's look. "I can do a bit o' chasin' mysel'. An' she'll ha' forgotten a' about Martin soon after."

His voice was very sure. Teddy's face lightened.

"She'll be that happy-like," said Teddy.

"Ay," answered Day. "She'll noan bother about what's gone before nor what's comin' after. She'll ha' quite enough to go on wi' day by day." His voice was pleasant, almost amiable.

"Well, I'll be movin'," said Teddy, the disturbance gone out of his voice. "I'm glad to hear what I have heard. An' good luck to thee. Tha'rt a likely lad. An' of course, I'll say nowt i' th' village, for I've known her sin she wor so high—" He went.

Fielding heard the gate close soon after.

There was the sound of tapping on the floor above. He went upstairs, standing outside the door of that room where they had locked the old man for safety.

"Let me out, Field," came Abel Mason's voice, sanity in every tone. "It were a' actin', Field. I saw 'em fro' th' windows. An' so—How he ran, Field! How he ran!"

Fielding turned the key and let him out.

Briefly he told old Mason what had happened.

"It's gettin' near th' death," laughed he in answer. "A day or two now—at most—an' Martin's gone. I've watched her fro' bein' little. She's prouder nor her mother. She'll take thee. Everything's strong in her. He he! If she'd bin mine—she couldn't ha' bin o' stronger mak'. They only cast them o' that mould once in a while. Tha'll ha' summat on, Field—to tame her—" Again he spoke testingly—with that shadow of fear in his heart. Then he laughed. The wolf-like look had shot into the eyes of Fielding Day.

They tramped down the stone steps.

After dinner old Mason sat looking at the clock. There was a sultriness about the day that presaged a storm later. At three it broke. They could see it from the window, travelling round the countryside, by town and hamlet, louder and louder peals of thunder signalling its approach to Four Gates. Day went to get in the frightened cattle. He drove them before him, whacking them to get them on the run. Already he looked on them as his.

Old Mason got up from his chair to watch the black clouds swoop past. "Storm—storm!" he murmured once. "It's bin a' storm. Grand! Grand! If we can't ha' love—storm's th' next best thing—force, destruction, ruin, terror, blight, an' earthshake."

A blaze of lightning illumined his features.

There was something majestic in his expression.

Just then there was a terrific clap.

"Th' bolt's fallen, somewhere," said Fielding, out of the hush that followed.

"They're allus fallin'," said the old man.

He turned from the window, crossed to his chair, and sat down. He relapsed into an evil, cross-legged god again. But whenever a deeper peal shook the house he laughed, gleefully, as though it were some expression of his nature.

CHAPTER VII

MARTIN CALLS ON HIS SAINTS

"WELL?"

Abel Mason turned from the fire to look at Martin, who had just entered, drenched to the skin.

"How were Milly?" he asked, giving no sign that he had seen Martin that morning by the river.

"Dead," answered Martin, beginning to unlace his soaked shoes.

The old man's pipe crashed upon the floor. His exclamation sounded like grief. It was consternation. If Martin tided over the burial of Milly, his scheme might fail. Milly had been very useful.

"So it were as I said," the old man murmured. "Th' last time tha'll need to go."

"Ay," acquiesced Martin.

He kicked his other boot away like a part of life he wished to be rid of.

"Now, whear mun we put her?" went on Abel Mason, with that note of grief in his voice.

"Put her!" ejaculated Martin.

"She's comin' home to th' only two i' th' world wi' her blood—to be buried," said Abel. "Ay. A drop o' blood goes a tarrible long way. She mun be browt to her own kith an' kin."

Martin did not answer.

"Tha could shift back agen, i' three days," said old Mason, to let Martin know he wanted his room.

Martin stood erect.

"I shan't need th' room," came tersely.

"Eh?" The grating of the chair-leg and his heavy shoon drowned the joy in his voice.

"I shall want my wages," Martin told him. There was impatience in his tone.

"I can't be left i' th' lurch, a' on a minnit's notice," grumbled Abel Mason. He could not spare Helen these three coming days of exquisite agony, though it was sailing near the wind to risk it. Three days of terrible hope for her, that would exhaust her, then she would be washed up to Day's feet, by the tides of despair.

"How long?" queried Martin.

His hands were clenching and unclenching.

"Three days." And as a guarantee of good faith, Abel Mason penned out an agreement to give to Martin Scott his three months' wages in three days, provided he stayed the time.

Soon afterwards he sat down to a meal, the first he had touched fortwenty-four hours. It tasted good. He was going away. He must get fit. Already the fact that he had taken the first step had half divorced him from the oppression of this grim house. In three days he would have shaken the dust of its threshold from his feet—forever.

Just then the gate creaked.

It was only Day come in with a harness to mend. The false alarm served Martin as a warning. He crammed down the rest of the food, only half hearing Mason's directions about the coffin and Milly's arrival.

When his feet were set on the road he swung along, wanderer's freedom entering his heart. The wind in the branches made nomad-music. "I'm going away," it seemed to now shout, now whisper, then rise to a clarion note of triumph.

"She's not beaten him," said Mason to Day, after his departure. "She'll never drag him past Milly. But Helen is deep, tarrible deep—like aught that's feightin' for its life. She'll fight reight to th' end, like a trapped rat. That's how it is she suffers so."

"What could she do?" asked Fielding. Helen was not back. Her chase across the moors had been all for nothing.

Old Mason sucked his pipe-stem.

"It's not what will she do, it's what won't she do," he said. "She's proud, but she worships Martin. She'd live i' hell wi' him an' laugh, an' mortify i' heaven wi'out him. The nearer he gets to goin' the fiercer she'll get. It's my opinion she'll fairly chuck herself at his head—so's if he does get away it'll ha' to be reight brutal, like chuckin' her away, body an' soul. Now, Martin's not brutal—not so much so as most chaps. An' he likes her that weel he daren't look at her sometimes. An' besides—if I'm not mista'en, Helen's never played her hussy-card yet."

"Her what?" queried the tramp.

"I don't know what tha'd ca' it. I ca' it her hussy-card," continued the old man, as if he liked the sound of the word. "It's not flirting. She could flirt no more nor a wild cat could flirt. She's savage. But fro' Eve up'ards every woman has had a hussy-card in their pack. Some's hardly known it were thear, an' never used it. Some has. Some has bin too proud—an' Helen's proud. It's showin' a bit too much stockin', i' some, an' showin' too little, in others. It's wearin' a ribbon to flap i' somebody's eyes just when it shouldn't. It's owt—an' it's nowt, in a way. It's stickin' to him with both arms when he's chivalrous, so as he can't get away. Lot's play it wi'out knowin' it. But Helen—"

There was the creak of the gate's rusty hasp.

"She's here!" they muttered simultaneously.

Fielding was chopping up wood when she entered; old Mason was refilling his pipe.

"Were there a good markit, Helen?" asked her father. "Field said tha'd gone to th' markit."

"Fairish."

She sat down in the first chair by the door as she spoke. Old Mason poked the fire up. Her hat was crooked, her face almost blue-white, her sopped garments clung to her. After a time she came nearer the fire and sat down in Martin's chair.

There were dark shadows under her eyes. She had been weeping tears of blood. She had been to a queer sort of market.

"Tha looks cowd," said her father sympathetically.

She moved resentfully in her chair.

"I'm a' reight," she said. "But I do feel cowd to th' marrow." A slight pause. Then: "Where's Martin?"

She had taken the bold, direct way of getting to know.

"Gone to th' town to wire for thy Aunt Milly bein' fetched hoam," said her father.

"Fetched—here?" ejaculated the woman. This last blow had sapped her strength. She sat down again. She had risen to stand over the fire for a moment. For a long time she did not move.

The choppety-chop of Fielding's axe came to her, the murmur of their voices going on about farm things.

"Tarrible quare, wild things, ferrets," drawled the old man, spitting into the fire. "Th' females has got to be mated, or they dee. Tarrible savage things."

"Ay, ay," she heard Fielding say; then she was lost in her own thoughts. How long they had gone on talking she did not know. But a word from Mason reached her. She leaped from her chair. The red light of the fire shone on her rigid countenance.

"What did yo' say?" she asked her father, her voice scarcely more than a breath. "Goin' i' three days. Goin'."

Fielding went on chopping.

She turned on him. The sound was too much.

"Stop!" she commanded, as if his blows fell on her heart. He laid his axe down.

The old man was looking at her with simulated surprise.

"Why shouldn't the lad go if he wants to mend hissel'?" he drawled. "Is there a law agen it?"

She sat down.

"Ay, why shouldn't he?" she asked, struggling to hide herself behind a forced calm. "Is th' kettle boilin'?"

"Ay, ha' a cup o' tay?" said her father.

"Ay, I'll ha' a cup o' tay. A cup o' tay is varra comfortin'—after bein' out," she finished. There was irony delicate as a thread of steel in her tone.

A cup o' tea to console her for the loss of Martin Scott! There were some in Four Gates, she knew, who took a cup o' tea when in sorrow. It was a womanly and orthodox beverage. And she—she was a Four Gates woman. She sat stirring her pot round and round, that smile on her face that was like moonshine on a field of polar ice. Amos Trip rattled into the yard with the empty kits. Helen dragged them in, and scalded them—ready for morning.

The long hours trailed by. From twilight-grey to sable turned the sky. It was a starless night. The storm had passed over Four Gates, but still raged in distant towns and hamlets, as faint openings in the sky sometimes showed. Fielding Day went to bed. Old Mason went to bed. Helen said she would wait up for Martin. She sat in Martin's chair, in the ingle-nook, the candlestick near her. She was trying to read *The Decline and Fall of the Roman Empire*—trying to make sense of the words. Ten o'clock. Eleven o'clock. Half-past eleven. She put the book down, mended the fire, blew out the candle. For some minutes she sat over the flickering blaze, her knees almost touching her chin. She was murmuring broken words over and over with dreary monotony, trying to suck faith from them still. They were the words of the spell she had spoken in the autumn wood. They were spoken differently now. Some of the fire of faith was gone. What they lacked in fire they had gained in the ferocity of despair.

She drew the long settle up to the fire, placed a cushion made from an old garment for her tired head— and lay down. The dog was nosing about amongst clothes hung in one of the corners. She watched him begin to lick one of the hanging sleeves. It was Martin's old coat. Rising, she went to the corner and lifted it down. Jealously lifting it from reach of the dog she pressed it against her bosom.

"Maybe I come o' mad folk," she murmured to the dog. "Maybe it's a form o' madness to love—as the dogs love their masters." She pulled off her bodice, with its Sunday look—and lay down, wrapped in Martin's rough coat. The touch of it on her bare neck and arms was a sweet agony. She smelt at the sleeves, and crushed the roughness of it closer to her. The dog came scenting it, too.

"We're savages, thee an' me," she said to the dog. Then, more quietly, "I mun sleep. It'll take me all my time to beat him"—then she fell to stroking the coat again. Soon she was asleep—asleep even with the doom of Martin's going hanging over her, asleep because sleep was strength, and she willed it to be strong, to go down, if she went down, a fighter.

A low growl from the dog wakened her.

The tell-tale gate had creaked.

She heard Martin's funny little cough—somehow characteristic of the man—short, brusque, cautious.

Then the door opened. He came into the glimmer of the kitchen. The shadow was on the dark settle; the darkness of his coat hid Helen, and she had turned her face to the settle-back—only her black hair streaming wide. His own thoughts made him unobservant. He fumbled about for matches, but found none.

A movement of the dog's led him to see that Helen was laid upon the settle. The last time he had seen her she had fallen exhausted on the bents, giving him his chance to lose her by going into a curtain of trailing mist.

"Aren't ta goin' to bed?" he asked.

His tone held a civil friendliness that struck on her ears with a death-like sound of farewell.

He was so sure of himself that he could greet her without either bearishness or aloofness.

"No," she said, without stirring. "What is there to sleep for?—to eat for?"

There was a short silence.

"Tha'rt goin' away, Martin," she said.

"Ay," he answered, with pleasant openness.

"So'm I," she said.

"It's no good usin' threats," said Martin. "Nowt'll stop me now. I'm just goin'."

"I'm not threatenin'. I mean it. I shan't eat, Martin," she said.

"Well, I'm goin' to eat," he said callously. He stirred about, lit the candle, made his supper ready, and sat down. When he had done his meal, he pulled off his boots, stood them neatly together under the table, took up the candle, and was moving away with a quiet good night.

"Art takin' th' leet away wi' thee?" she asked.

He came back.

"Where shall I set it?" he asked.

"There!" she told him.

He placed it on the chair drawn near to the settle. The light fell full on her face, now turned towards him. There was a wretched sickliness about her look that startled him.

"It's like to be, Helen," he said. He was going to sit down by her side and argue rationally about it. She turned her face to the settle-back again, with a slow movement of despair.

"I shan't eat—any more," she said.

Martin sat down on the chair and held the candlestick on his knees.

"That's silly," he said.

"Silly to stop eatin' when th' sun's gone out?" she laughed.

"I don't want thee to dee, Helen," he said, god-like.

"But tha'd leave me to be buried alive, i' Four Gates— to dry-rot—me, a live woman, wi' blood i' my veins! Tha'd leave me to starve an' hunger an' thirst—an' curse the stones beneath my feet as if they were a prison-yard! Tha'd leave me to go on year in year out, like a leper tha dursen't touch—an' be glad I *lived*! Till I grew old an' leaden, an' thin as a shadow, a passionate shadow, a ghost wi' a' th' cravings after life, like they say folk are that are killed i' th' back an' loiter round places! Tha'd be comforted, away wi' some other woman, an' childer to climb on thy knee, to think poor Helen still went on eatin' an' sleepin' an' doin' odd jobs here i' Four Gates, an' thinkin' o' thee—till Death came—or what tha feared! But tha shan't ha' that comfort, Martin Scott. It's only custom to go on eatin' when th' best has gone out o' life. I've not had aught to eat for a day. Tha goes i' three days. Six days after tha leaves Four Gates I shall have gone further." She ceased. Martin had listened to the changes in that low voice as a bird might listen to the whistle of the fowler.

"Tha couldn't do it," he said, with knitted brows.

She turned the daring beauty of her eyes on his.

"Why not?" she asked.

"'Twould be wicked," he said.

"Tha's to fa' back on what th' parsons say," she said. "What they've allus said to crush down th' desire to be happy—like birds and beasts are happy. Say summat out o' thy own heart, Martin—don't parrot th' parsons."

"Tha'rt a liar!" said Martin. "There's no parson about me."

"Tha'll leave me i' Four Gates, Martin?" she asked.

He did not speak.

But his lips were locked.

"Tha'd leave me here—me, that am all thine, Martin, thine! Every bit o' my body, every corner o' my soul, every pulse o' me. Tha'll go away from me—as if tha'd had no responsibility for me an' tha'd naught to do but go away. I wouldn't leave a dog so—a mangy, miserable, whinin' cur—that wanted me, that had no one else. Coward! What did ta come to th' farm for, an' stan' in' look at me through th' white gate?"

She was sitting up.

Her eyes were ablaze in the wretchedness of her face. There was a terror in her voice that he had never heard before.

"Woman!" said Martin. There was terror in his tone, too.

His voice was quivering.

"Ay, woman!" she repeated. She had crystallised in her tone the scorn of the platitudes tossed to woman in place of happiness, all through the ages.

She beat at her breasts with her pale hands.

"Tha'rt hysterical," began Martin.

"Happen," she smiled, cold as glass. "Happen. Th' sea when it craves, th' wind when it sighs, th' rain when it weeps—it's hysterical. It's a custom to tell women so—like it's a custom to keep on eatin'."

"Tha'll hurt thyself," he chided, catching at one of the hands that still beat at her breast, even as some savage woman might rock herself, and beat her bosom at the coming of death to take from her all she loved.

"Why shouldn't I hurt myself—when tha can hurt me?" she asked.

"Why shouldn't I beat breasts that aren't fit to nourish? Why should I have to hold to a life that's not fit to pass on, like a torch is passed on—forever an' forever?"

He bowed his head.

"Good neet, Martin," she said. "Good neet. Go an' sleep."

He rose and stood up by the settle, looking down on her, candle in hand.

He felt guilt upon him as he bent down, a plea in his eyes.

"Kiss a coward?" she laughed.

Then, whilst the agony was hot in his heart, she made a sudden movement. The candle clattered on the floor, guttering out into darkness. She had drawn his head down to the softness of her throat. Her kisses were in his hair—the coat had come unbuttoned at the neck, and his cheek was prisoned against her bosom.

"Tha'll not go," she was saying over and over, like a frightened child.

"I shall go—go—nowt can stop me," said Martin mechanically, as one repeating a litany. He was trying to unclasp her fingers from the back of his neck, trying not to think of her, her touch, her voice, the words she had spoken. He dragged himself from her clasp, trying to think all the time that in three days he would be away. The blood was beating in his brain.

Then he got free of her arms.

She looked at him as one who had fought for her soul. The old terror of her power swept over him, and made him cruel.

"Look! What would Lizzie Trip an' a' o' them think o' thee?" he asked, pointing at the open coat, the bare gleam of her neck. He averted his eyes.

Slowly the woman's eyes travelled down to that strip of bared flesh—the flesh she had forgotten, in her elemental purity. Her gaze travelled to Martin's averted look—to his bent head of shame—to his standing there in the red light like a grim rock.

All the blood of her body swept into her face. Red-hot needles of shame seemed to stab her through. The sob of a helpless child came into her throat, whilst she cowered down into the coat.

Martin was looking at her.

"Jesu Maria! Save us from women and wine!" he said suddenly, and staggered away. They were old words from broken memories of a child of poverty and religion. He had shouted on the hosts of bloodless angels to help him. He had invoked Heaven's aid—whilst she had only her own strength! He had assigned to her the place where priests and stern moralists have stood women from time immemorial—the place somewhere between angels and demons, according to convenience. He had asked to be saved from her as men asked to be saved from drugs.

Helen sat stunned.

She heard him open a little window in the passage—a window that looked out on a bed of white pansies. He was standing to let the wind blow on him, she guessed.

He heard her low voice from behind the closed door.

"Coward!" she said. "Coward—to shout to Heaven. It's waur nor gettin' drunk. Coward! A' men have been cowards sin' Adam. Cowards! Beasts!"

There was deep silence. Then she heard his steps move along the stone corridor and up the stairs where Milly Mason would soon be carried.

She sat over the fire.

There was something cowering in her attitude still. It reflected her mind. She clutched the coat up to her throat. But there was only the dog, the great, loving, unquestioning soul clothed in hair and flesh, to look at her. Martin had cried out on the immaculate mighty ones—to protect him from her—at the sight of a bit of flesh. A power she had never thought to use was laid bare to her. It was the card in the pack which she had never played. It lay there, powerful, come up through the ages, having broken the hearts and crazed the brains of mighty men—Anthony, Nelson, Napoleon—ay, even the gods themselves. She stared at the fire as if she saw it there, potent, magical. She laughed, as she had felt like laughing before—at the discovery that her physical weakness was a keener weapon than her strength, her courage, her defiance and attack.

She opened the coat and stared down at that strip of soft, white flesh.

"Dust to dust," she murmured, touching it. The dog came and laid its head on her knee.

She stared into the soft amber eyes that could blaze with the fires of hate on stranger and enemy.

"Tha's no soul," she said to the dog. Nero blinked.

"Nobody tries to shame thee—o' Life," she said, stroking the soft ears. A croon came into the dog's throat at the touch.

"Tha never asks questions—tha just loves," she said. The stub of a tail wagged. Her voice was very soft.

"If I were God," she said, "I would only give th' animals souls, because they're not ashamed, nor fleyed, and ne'er ax questions."

Then she lay down again on the settle.

The fire flopped into its centre. All was gloom. The tick-tick of the clock seemed thick. Sometimes a window-sash rattled, then the dog would growl. A sound came to him once that made him start—then steal to the settle. He began to lick Helen's face. He was licking tears away in the darkness—such tears as only the calm, strong weep when the lonely darkness wraps them round, and prop by prop their strength has given way.

Even as one savage soul comforting another the dog licked those tears away.

She got up, pulled off Martin's coat, and sat shivering before the almost dead fire.

"Jesu Maria!" she said, reproducing Martin's tone.

Then she laid herself down on the hearthrug. "Let me live wi' th' beasts of the field." The night wore on. Her voice counting softly up to ten and back again, went on monotonously, as to induce sleep. But even sleep had gone. When a blue bar appeared under the blind she rose. The dog at her feet stirred also. She lifted up the blind and stared out upon the garden. Another morning had broken over Four Gates.

CHAPTER VIII

THE END OF THE WORLD

HELEN was alone in the shadow-filled kitchen. She was lying on the old settle, before the fire, listening in a dull fascination of horror to the ticking of the clock.

There were only two hours now, then Martin was going away. The milk-kits were to scald yet. She had gone on strike.

She had played the trump card of feminine helplessness, much as it had hurt her proud spirit to do so. For two days she had feigned illness, starving under Martin's eyes. She was parched with thirst, and afire with hunger. The smell of food from the table behind her, where Martin had spread her a meal before going out, came to her like a temptation. But to eat meant to bring back the colour to her lips, to eat meant therefore to make it easier for Martin to get away. She was treading down the regal pride of her heart; she was appealing to him as beggars, lepers, children, mangy animals appealed—to the human pity in the human heart. Oh, the pain, the ignominy of it! To be crying out to Martin's pity! To be saying literally, "If you leave me, I know not what I shall do!" Her hands clenched together under the coat that covered her. The indignity, the helpless futility of it! To be proud, yet to have to throw pride away! To be courageous, yet to learn the meaning of fear; to be sane, yet to fear that one might go mad; to know oneself greater even than the thing it loved, in all these things, yet to have to plead to that thing as a cripple pleads at a cross! The mockery, the spite of it! Surely the fires of hate were as heaven to the fires of love!

Martin said he was going. She had begun to believe it. He had only to come back for his wages, and his box. That box stood near the settle-end strapped, labelled, ready for his going. The blasphemy of it shuddered through her. He was leaving her—her to whom he had said in that moonlit field with the hedge of foam-white blossoms—"I love, forever, forever, forever!" She had believed it then, she had believed it since; but to say that, then to go away. There were some who said it and forgot, some sooner, some later—but, Martin! Did it come to every one who loved the most, so, with such a horror of surprise and dull ache—that the one they loved could be unfaithful? Love was for glory or shame. But—Martin was leaving her as people left infected houses, as rats left sinking ships.

He had kissed her, he knew the taste of her lips, he; and none other; he knew the croon of her voice, he had seen her proud, wild soul in all its nakedness. She had followed him across the moor—calling his name until strength had given out. Had he called her so, she could not have gone a yard. That was the first incense of her pride, that she had cast on the fires of love—odorous with sacrifice. Since then, she had starved—starved to make herself pale, that the paleness of her lips might strike to his heart. She had given him the key of her heart. There were women who only gave to men the key of their faces—but she, Martin knew her heart. Wherever he went he would carry the key. And he was going away. He had said so. All Four Gates had rung with it, by this. It seemed that every stick and stone in the lanes must know that Martin Scott was going away, that she was being left, even as Joe Gillibrand left Sue Marsh all those years back. Sue Marsh's body had been found dead that morning, behind the door, the blind white cat licking her face—the face Joe Gillibrand had once brought the colour to with his coming and going.

Whenever Helen opened her eyes she saw the ghost-like animal that had belonged to the dead woman, crouched inside the fender. Martin had brought it to the farm, to be cared for. Martin was kind to cats.

She put out a weak hand, touching the box. A half-scream left her lips as she touched it. It was real. It was Martin's box, with the key of her heart inside it, to be carted away. She fancied that something must happen to stop him, then it crossed her mind that Sue Marsh would have had the same thought, years ago. The gods were not to be trusted. She must do something. Yet—She stared helplessly into the fire.

Across her memory came the recollection of that little scene two nights ago, as he had stood hypnotised by a little white dust. Here in Four Gates she was fighting for her soul. Might she not play that white magic of dust once, for her soul? To be greater than the gods! Her cheek flushed. She was laughing tremulously. What was a little pride? Throw it away, the last sacrifice. But she frowned into the fire. She was proud. The narrow tenets of Four Gates hemmed her round, at times. It was so little, that pride—yet losing that—what was she? No, no, she could not lose Martin. She was a savage. There were no pale, beautiful saints with halos of dim gold in her childhood. Her friends had been will-o'-the-wisps, witches, barguests, creatures of power, who could raise the quick and the dead. These breathed to her "Win, win"—that only defeat was ignoble, these earth-bound spirits who hovered over the blowing bents, the wind-paled rushes, those creatures who had stirred the potion in the black pot that had the force to overcloud the stars. Like Martin's childish saints, these also were bloodless, but they had in them the breath of the hills and moors. They were close to the earth and of it, whilst his saints were remote and cold.

What was it?

It was only to play the spirits of her childhood against his—earth against heaven, life against death, love against reason. It was only—but Four Gates sat in judgment in her heart. It was so little that was left. But if she threw it away—she would be nothing, nothing any more; no roots to her. So she felt. She would have plucked herself up from the foundation, and then—

The creak of the gate came to her, the sound of a step.

She listened, hoping that it was not Martin. For once she, too, wanted to think, time to think.

It was Martin's step.

She sat without moving.

He advanced into the circle of firelight.

He stood with his back to the fire, looking at her. The firelight wove a spell about her. He had barely looked at her for two days. In two hours he would be away. He might look at her now. That memory should be the only thing he would keep of Four Gates. Everything else, every thread, his old clothes, should be flung away. But that little memory he might keep. He was leaving Four Gates. Never again should his eye glance upon it, on the hills around it, the trees in its fields, the places where he had hedged and ditched. He was leaving Helen. On both he might let his eye wander lovingly, for the last time. On neither must he look too long. He knew that.

He was looking at her now.

It had always seemed to him that there was something about her in the firelight that he never saw at any other time. One might have expected her to make passes on the air, and do what she would, as she sat with the shadows about her, and her long hair, black as night. It was hard to believe that she was like the rest of mortals, limited in strength and powerless to mould her own fate, struggle as she might.

"Well," queried Martin, looking down at her. "Nowt to say?"

She moved her head from side to side.

Her eyes were hidden. They were looking down at Sue Marsh's blind white cat.

"Won't ta wish me luck, Helen?" asked Martin.

She laughed, without looking up.

It was a little mocking, weary-toned laugh.

Then she looked at him.

Her eyes had that vivid greenness that reminded him of a cat's.

"I wish thee luck, Martin Scott," she said, very slowly and deliberately. She spoke in the same tones as those that had struck fear to Andry's heart, in that wet red wood, years back. If she had not the power, her desire, her willingness to play with elemental fires, was as great as that which had burnt in the heart of the wildest witch in the county.

"Ay," said Martin uneasily. "But there's all sorts o' luck."

"Why should I wish thee ill?" she asked, in a way that made him wonder whether or not she spoke in bitter jest or quiet earnest.

"Why should I wish thee ill? That would be wicked. Besides, were wishin' any good tha wouldn't be goin' away now."

Martin was silent.

Then he said, as one who answers some accusation: "No—why should ta wish me ill, Helen? I never did thee any harm."

"No," she said, very simply, and looking away from him. "Tha only came—an' went away again, Martin."

She was looking at the cat.

The curve of her cheek, the fullness of her mouth, the sheen of the black hair touching her waist—he could drink it all in.

"Folk are free to come to a place an' free to go away again," said Martin, a thin note of antagonism, of self-defence, in his rational tone. He was thinking of a tragedy that had happened at a farm on a hillside not distant—of a moment's passion in a man for which a woman must pay dear to the end of her days. The man had gone away.

"I never harmed thee, Helen," he said proudly. "Folk are free to come an' go, aren't they, when they leave a lass as they find her, an' leave no trouble behind?"

Her eyes turned from their survey of the cat, with its peculiar blind stare and hungry licking of its chops with the red tongue, to rest on Martin's face. There was a consciousness of moral strength stamped upon it. Her look passed over it, in lightning scorn.

"Tha feels an angel compared wi' Tim Green," she said, reading his thoughts so well that he almost started. "Evil be wrought by too little thought—an' sometimes—by too much. Tim took Matty and left her. It were a' the possession he knew. When tha goes away—who is there I could wed straight, Martin Scott, wi' thee in my e'en an' my ears, ay, i' my very dreams o' neets, i' my very blood, as the air o' Four Gates is part o' me. What tha's left is hardly worth th' takin'! 'Leave no trouble behind! Leave a lass as they find her!'" She laughed. Through the orthodox moralities of Four Gates and all other places like it, she shot a shaft of ridicule. Martin was pondering what to say to her.

"Wilta leave me as tha found me?" she asked. "Wilta? Can I get back to that place where I were before tha came—before I thought o' thee? Can I tear thee out o' my life, just because tha's gone away, an' has done me no harm, i' the way Tim has harmed Matty? Are there no other bonds than flesh bonds, no other debts of honour but those? Aren't there looks, an' words, an' thoughts, that be forged i' fire, as much as if parson muttered 'em,—are there no childer women noss i' their dreams that belong as much to some men who left 'em as any that go clothed i' flesh, an' able to suck th' longing from a woman's breast, just because they are flesh?"

Her words came out in a torrent.

It was an iron creed.

It was so old that it seemed startlingly new. It was the creed of the sacredness of first love, such as a tribal savage would have held, ere the complexities of modern life placed a barrier between body and soul, gave leave to love and depart fetterless, if that the law said that no harm had been done.

Its narrowness, its amazing claim took away Martin's breath.

"But—" he said, then paused for words. Then he went on rather haltingly: "How many men an' women are there i' Four Gates, or any other place for that, who wed th' one they first thought on, an' kissed?"

She did not speak.

Like a sullen savage she sat on the old settle, stubborn, unconvinced by any arguments he could pour.

A wildness of something near despair shot through him. Why was she not more like the women of Four Gates? Why did she always make it so hard, so uncomfortable, for him? Why could she not put herself on one side, as many women might, smile, and say, "Go and be happy, Martin. It is right"?

"Tha's th' curse on thee," he said, in a hard tone. "Tha forgets. Can ta pass it on, and on, and on, forever—to put others through all this we're going through, to leave it all to be fought over? Tha'rt th' last o' th' Masons. Can ta not be brave enough to say, 'It shall end here'?"

Helen looked at him.

Flint met flint.

From the collision sparks were struck. The little kitchen faded from the ken of both. They were fighting each other now, fighting in animal self-preservation—Martin's fear of staying and its consequences, Helen's fear of his going and its consequences, wrestling with each other.

A savagery flashed into Helen's eyes.

Martin's held the cruel tolerance of a modern judge, dealing with reasons.

"Curst, am I?" she cried, with a rebellion against the decree of gods and men alike blazing through her. "Why? Because I might ha' a child that were gladder or sadder than most, at th' comin' up o' th' moon! Or because it might fancy itself a prince, when its pockets were empty? Or because it might, in some minute, plunge a knife into what it loved? Sane men do that last, every day i' th' calendar. Mean men an' weaklings an' cowards are bred every day o' th' week, an' walk th' streets i' th' sun an' aren't ashamed. What if I bore an idiot? Somewhere between man and dog his mind would come. Would he be less happy? Would he be less loved? Curst, am I? I defy the curse. If I weren't born to be happy, let me dee. I were born to live, to love. Who shall say to me I weren't? Thee—tell me if tha can—tell me, this once, an' I'll say no more words—say to me, i' th' face o' these woman's breasts, that I were born to be treated like a leper! Call on thy saints, an' what th' priests told thee, an' what folk gabble to mock th' livin' sun i' the sky an' th' flowers i' th' fields—an' tell me, a livin', breathin' woman, to go down to my grave i' th' lone dark, like a curst creature! Tell me that, Martin Scott, if tha dur'st."

She had torn open her bodice—savagely.

She was far away from Four Gates and its tenets now. She might have been some high priestess of Nature's—imbued with the holiness of life and its aspirations,

111

and scorn of those who ran from its battles. From every tone, look, from every inch of her tall form, issued a majestic pride, defiance, and dignity. Her look said, "Blaspheme, now, if tha can."

They stood looking at each other.

It was the cry of the human heart against the bondage of custom's ethics, against the fears of the human mind.

She was daring his cold saints to protect him now.

Slowly, like a man beside himself, Martin moved towards her. Her hair showered about her like a veil, but through it came the moonlike gleam of her breasts. Her arms, their whiteness hidden by the ugly bodice sleeves, were crossed over her breast, so that there was now a look of primitive shrinking in her attitude. But her eyes met his, filled with a look of scorn. The pure shamelessness of her cast a radiance about her. The little hollow under her proud throat, the dusky holy veil of woman's hair flowing over those gleaming breasts like a cloud half hiding the moon—they made her look fair as the Mother of God. But never had any painter painted a Madonna of so valiant a look. It was as if she had declared her right to be the mother of men by the rare and simple virtue of courage—courage that would dare all, risk all.

"Can ta tell me—now—to go an' dee an' rot—content an' christian-like? Can ta, Martin?" she asked.

Martin groaned.

"Helen—" he pleaded.

His voice shook like a reed in the wind.

He was looking in awe at what he had prayed against two nights before.

It was not Helen that he saw before him, asking him to tell her to rot and lie in a lonely grave, accursed. It was Life—warm, pulsating human life, shut off and thrust aside by some whim of fate, crying out and calling, calling louder than the voices of iron laws, social customs, priests, philosophers, and schoolmasters, saying, "Why? Why? Why?"

She had put him in the place of the judge, the Pharisee—but before he condemned her she had bidden him look at her.

"Hush!" he said in torment.

"Tha can't leave me, Martin, tha can't," she was saying.

He was trying to get back, back to the firm strand of reason on which he had stood during these last days, back to the peace that had been growing in his mind. He was looking away—and his eyes fell on the niche in the wall where Abel Mason had once told him that his grandfather had put the bloody rags he had ripped from his throat—the grandfather on the maternal side, from which the madness sprung, the grandfather whose name had given no clue for years that this Abel Mason was a branch from that old man who had died cursing his destiny.

"Martin!"

The agony of the cry pierced his brain.

Had he turned his head he would have seen that the thick hair was covered over the swell of the white bosom, eclipsing its beauty. Under the old bodice her heart was beating in a woman's panic of agony and fright. She had come back to Four Gates. Exultation was over. She was no high priestess. She was a woman—her cheeks hot and cold with wonder as to what Martin might think—if he would understand. She belonged to Four Gates. It claimed her remorselessly. Courage was big, but Four Gates soil was round her roots. Fear was upon her. She had dared, she had walked over burning ploughshares, to open the eyes of Martin's soul—she had used white magic, but she had used it as a priestess, not a courtesan, because she was a Four Gates woman who had lived from childhood

with the storm-rack of the moor and of destiny. But—
Martin might not understand. She had tried to snatch
fire from heaven. To get it she had walked through hell.
She had risked all.

"Martin!"

It was the child's cry of terror at the threat of darkness
again.

Their dual voices rang together now. In them both
was still the sound of the struggle. In their voices was
the sound of Martin listening to his pale saints, and
Helen crying out from the tabernacle inhabited by
spirits of earth, moulded out of the red clay and the
salt seas.

"No, no—" she could only mourn, as though against
the dark.

Her voice was faint.

Her arms had fallen to her side. Her chin was sunk
on her breast. Martin did not look at her.

"Better sorrow now than in twenty years," he said.
"Helen—tha'll thank me sometime, when in years to
come—"

"When we're dead," she moaned. "Martin!" But the
thought that he could leave her—now—stunned her.

"It's like deein', Helen," said Martin. "Oh, it's hard.
But—my son might ha' this to fight, to stan' just here,
like this. It's sin we dally wi'. I'm only a man, Helen. I
dursen't look at thee any more. 'Twere sin to tempt me.
For three generations, Helen, it would be—on an' on,
an' on—a mad race, cursin' us when we're dead—think,
Helen—"

She was standing like something in marble and
ebony.

She saw him—saw his shadow on the wall, crossing
himself, the man who in those two moments of crisis
had been compelled to return for sustenance to the
faith of his childhood, against the spell of life and love.

114

She saw him open the door, saw him through the mist of this bad dream, in which she could not cry out. Not only her tongue was dumb, cleaving to her mouth in a great panic, but her very brain had lost its function. She tried to think of one word to say, only one word to cry aloud, to keep him from going through the doorway. It seemed as if she had never known words, never heard them, never learnt even the simplest. Something whispered to her in a formless sort of way that perhaps she was going mad, was joining that long and shadowy line of the accursed whom Martin had thrust her with. How long she stood thus she did not know; it might have been only a few seconds, it might have been an eternity; but when the sound of the closing door came to her a galvanic shock went through her, something woke up in that dumb brain. She rushed to the closed door.

"Martin! Martin! Martin!"

The cry rang out with a fierce intensity that made the air quiver again. She was beating with pale, helpless hands against the door. Quite suddenly she perceived that all she had to do was to lift the latch and then she could get outside.

She was still calling that name, but almost without knowing it, and running down the hillside through the long, wet grass, heedless of who might hear her. She was not conscious of anything except that Martin was going away and that she must stop him. She was running, stumbling, crying, shouting for her soul to come back. Once she thought she saw Martin, that he had turned at her cry—and something of a perception that, if she were not out of her senses, she was very miserable, came to her dimly.

She ran more quickly.

It could not be true. Martin could not be leaving her. Nothing so awful could be true.

That was what she told herself. Surely that was Martin, away down the hill. Only, there was a strange, heavy mist upon everything, on the earth, on the trees, in the sky. She must hurry. She could overtake him before he reached the bottom of the hill, or entered on the road that ran past the houses where curious faces could peep. She remembered that she had not fastened her bodice, and tried vainly to fasten it with one hand as she ran. What matter? Martin was going away, and she could not let him go for what Four Gates might think of her.

Then the whole sky seemed to turn to a hellish blaze of red. Her sight was bathed in blood. Through the red blindness she heard the evening birds piping. Again she wondered if that was how people heard the sounds of life when they lay in the tomb. The red turned into pitch-black—pitch-black everywhere, through which she groped dizzily, trying to clutch at something to hang on to, but her hands only clutched that empty air, all weird and black. Martin was going away, and something was happening to her—her heart had missed half a beat, maybe. She was swooning, like any weakling woman who wept by the fireside. A rage against herself tore through her brain.

"Weak fool!" she stammered, condemning herself, and bringing all the force of her will to bear, struggled against it. She stood quite still—then tried to find something solid again. Her hand touched something—a man's coat.

"Martin!" she cried.

He had turned back, then.

He could not leave her.

She began to laugh, chokingly, now the terror was past. Things were dim yet, the sky far away, but the birds did not seem as if she heard them through grave-loam. She clutched the man's sleeve.

The mists began to clear from her sight. The wind blew her hair about. Something of ecstasy stirred in her. He had not gone.

To-morrow she must punish him. Not even Martin could go unpunished for putting her through this agony. But now—just now, she held him with a lost child's panic.

Then, with the suddenness of a sword-thrust, she heard Day's voice say callously, "A bit of a mistake. Scott's gone. But—blast it!—I'll do as weel, won't I? Tha mun shut thy e'en, like they're shut now, a' th' time, an' think it's him."

Helen's eyes opened wide, staring into his grinning countenance. They had an uncanny look, those eyes, appearing to gaze into boundless darkness.

"Gone?" she said tonelessly.

After that dizzy joy she had felt, the waters of despair rushed over her. She went deep under them with a hopeless shudder. She would never come up again. She knew it.

It was worse than pain.

It was death.

"Ay," said Day's voice, a long way off. "He's gone. But—I'm here."

She heard herself laugh. She ought to be weeping, weeping tears of blood. She was laughing instead. The sound reminded her of a broken whistle Martin had played on when first he came to the farm. Something had happened to it and all the music had gone, though the note-stops were left. What a queer pain it was to die suddenly, and hear the world go on.

"Ay, I'm here," she heard Day's voice. "An'—one chap's as good as another, isn't he?"

His arm went round her, drew her close to him. He was kissing her lips. She had once felt that she would die of shame if any but Martin kissed her. She had been mistaken. It didn't hurt a bit. What was that he had said? One man as good as another? She heard herself laugh again. She had lived all these years and never thought of it.

"I'll take thee," Day went on, as if she were in the Left Luggage Department.

She laughed once more.

Even if a man is taking a woman for financial gain, it hurts his vanity to be laughed at. It hurt Day's.

"Stop thy damned laughin'," he said, shaking her by the shoulders. "I said I'd take thee, does ta hear?"

Her eyes stared into his.

There was laughter in them beside which tears would have been light comedy.

"Wilta? Tha'rt very good," she answered, with something finer than scorn in her tones. It stung the tramp through his coarse rind.

"All ower Four Gates it's said tha's hung thysel' on Martin," he said, still holding her by the shoulders. "When they look at thee through their windows, as tha goes by, that's what they'll be thinkin'—how he's run away fro' thee."

There was a quiver about the lips. The pride of her stirred. She withdrew herself from his grasp. Her gaze fixed itself on the evening sky, with the moon leering vacantly back at her. She was thinking that Four Gates, and particularly this hillside, had once seemed beautiful to her. Now it seemed that she were caught here in this bowl of the darkening hills. *She* could not run away from Four Gates. She was of the breed who live and die in a place. Four Gates was her world. She could no more step out of it than she could have deserted Martin. But Martin had gone away, from her, into that unknown beyond the hills.

"I'll take thee," said Day again.

He was stuffing his pipe with tobacco, and leaning against a tree, whilst watching her narrowly. She had flung herself at Martin—all for nothing. She was tasting bitter waters.

"Well?" he asked her, at length, betwixt pipe-stem and teeth.

"If tha likes," she answered.

The apathy of the tone was in striking contrast to the white flame of her face.

"Tha means it?" he queried.

She nodded her head in assent.

"Why—?" he began.

She was beginning to move slowly up the hillside to that house emptied of joy and torment now.

She turned her head sideways. Her eyes, set in that strange smiling stare, met his.

"Because tha'rt th' first asked me," she said. "An' because I don't care. I've done a' th' carin' I can. I've got through it. An'—I'm not goin' to wear th' willow."

"Tha understands," he said, facing her grimly. "Tha'll be mine."

"Ay," she acquiesced.

He still regarded her in a bewildered way. He had expected some struggle, a longer chase. She had fallen into his hand with no more resistance than a dead thing.

He gripped her by the arm suddenly. Brute-passion was in his eyes.

"Mine, body an' soul," he said, savagery in his voice. Conscienceless as he was, something urged him on to set the case before her.

She drew herself up with a gesture of pride.

"'Soul', " she laughed. "Nay—how much does ta want for thy money? Women sell their bodies at Brungerly, I've heard. A parson once talked of 'em sellin' their souls, these painted women. He'd ne'er bin a woman. That was why. He'd have known they had none, else. What they sell is flesh—like they throw to tigers at Brungerly Fair."

"Well, flesh, then," said Day, grinning.

He drew her to him.

Her passivity reminded him of a woman he had once seen dragged from a canal. There was something of the same stare on her face, too. His kisses had the unrestraint of a savage sucking at a bone.

"Give me th' body, an' I'll take chances on th' soul," he grinned, releasing her so suddenly that she almost fell.

She regained her balance, looking at the evening sky, and did not answer.

"What's ta get out of it?" he asked, as they moved on again through the long wet grass.

"There were some folk in Brungerly got sick o' sellin' stuff cheap," she said, "so they threw it away, to go rotten—to make sure it shouldn't be offered at twice," she smiled. "What I get out o' th' bargain is just that—security."

"Agen Martin comin' back?" he asked.

She nodded.

"He'll not," she remarked, with the tone of an outsider, contemplating the whole from an impartial standpoint. "But—"

She stared at the sky again.

"Tha could ha' committed suicide," he said.

"An' folk guess," she smiled. "An' him be sure. That would be stupid. Besides, I have committed suicide, only there'll be no coroner's inquest."

"There may be hell after," he grinned.

She was silent.

Her face said that she did not care. Her end was a barrier, a barrier of flesh and blood, the more devilish the more of security it gave against any weakness of hers for Martin Scott.

"I'm a sort of insurance against fire," grinned Day.

She nodded.

They were nearing the gate. The sharp scent of lad's-love came to them.

As they passed it she bent down, in a casual way, and tried to pull it up by the roots. It was the bush Martin had set years ago. Kneeling there on the flagstones she tugged at it until it came up. She hurled it from her as if it had been some loathsome thing.

"Somebody's comin'," said Day, as she rose. "Fasten thy bodice. It might get thee an ill name," he grinned.

Up the hillside came the sound of drunken singing.

Passing into the farm kitchen, Helen covered the bit of bared white neck.

Her father had come in, and was curved over the fire. "Where's Martin?" he asked, looking up.

Helen was on the hearthstone now, fastening up her hair. He poked the fire into a blaze to see her face better.

"Gone," she answered, without turning into the kindly shadows.

Her voice had its ordinary tone, save that it had fallen half a note. But he watched her hands, empty of the hair now. They were plucking her dress restlessly, with a little monotonous movement.

Her lips were white, and her teeth caught them at times.

She drew a chair up to the table and began to eat.

"Tha'rt hungry, aren't ta?" he asked.

"Haven't I bin eatin' naught?" she asked, clattering cup and spoon about. "Haven't I bin ill?"

He watched her.

She was eating, actually eating bread that must taste like dust, swallowing life down emptied as it was of joy. What a creature the gods had given him to torture. Men could eat with their hearts torn out, he knew, but women—he watched her, pushing mouthful after mouthful down by sheer will.

"So tha'rt better," he remarked.

"Ay, I'm better," she answered, reaching for the salt dredger.

"I'm fain," he said. "Whear's Day?"

Helen did not answer, for Day had opened the door.

"Here!" he said. There was a note of triumph in his voice. He passed round to the back of Helen's chair. The light from the lamp lit up the rigidity of her face. There was a ghastliness about her before which a lesser man might have trembled, awed into a seemliness towards something great as death. It was weird as if that coffined corpse upstairs should essay to eat.

Fielding Day looked over her head towards the old man in the corner. He winked coarsely and meaningly, then laid his finger and thumb on the nape of the white neck.

"She's goin' to be wed," he told the old man. "Aren't we, lass?" He compelled her to turn that wan face up to his by the pressure of his thumb. There was something in his attitude that reminded Mason of the handling of a hare.

"Eh?" jerked the old man.

Then he burst into laughter.

"I don't believe it," he said.

Helen turned her gaze upon him.

"It's true," she said, reaching out for another piece of bread.

He rose from his chair.

"Let's see thee kiss her, lad," he said, with simulated tenderness.

Helen pushed her chair back from the table.

Day caught her by the arm. "A good neet kiss," he said.

She submitted passively to the indignity of the coarse caresses such as she had received on the hillside. Then, as she was turning away, Day pulled her back to him, and kissed her again. He left a blotch of tobacco-slaver on her cheek, and laughed.

"Has t' finished?" she asked quietly.

He nodded, letting her stagger again. Without wiping the brown spittle from her cheek she took her candle.

It was at this juncture that a loud thumping fell on the door.

"Go, see who 'tis, Helen," said the old man.

She went to the door with the candle lit, and opened it.

"Somebody to screw up in their wooden suit, isn't there?" said a stuttering voice. "I've bin told she lives here. Whear is she? What I says is, 'Have a good time. You'll be a long time dead!' Whear is she? This is Mason's farm, isn't it, whear that dead woman lives?"

"Come to-morrow," said Helen. "You're drunk, Jabez."

He stared at her, suddenly realising that the door was open.

"Drunk!" he said indignantly. "Drunk!" and he lurched in through the doorway. "An' if I am? Shouldn't them as is drunk fasten up them as is sober? Which room is she in? All reight. Everything's in order. Everything's in order."

"Show him th' way, Helen," said old Mason. "He can't hurt Milly, anyhow."

Jabez was staring at Helen, in one of those lulls that come to drunken men.

Candle in hand, she was looking at him. The stillness and whiteness of her seemed to hypnotise him. Then he let out a yell like ten thousand demons.

"She's got up!" he shouted, and dashed through the doorway.

Helen closed the door after him, and went up to bed.

Abel Mason stretched out his hand to Day. Then he went to a drawer, taking out a fat bag, and emptied its contents on the table. The gold shone in the lamplight.

"Twenty, to be goin' on wi'," he said.

His lips moved as he counted. Day's moved also. They had to count over again, as he said Mason had given him one too little.

"Ay, there were but nineteen," said Mason.

He watched Day scrape it into an old purse he had brought from the doss-house. Then he leaned towards him across the table.

"What's ta think on her?" he asked, leering.

Day's eyes met his with the same look. The old man's eyes narrowed. It was as if he would pore into the tramp's very being. The fear was on him again. He was afraid that this man, gloating over the little pile of sovereigns, and with the wolfish face more wolfish still in its double lust, might so far awake to Helen's spell as to be an inefficient tool of his revenge.

"Did ta *ever* love a woman, Field?" he asked.

Day started, looked up, the bestial expression of his face shattered.

"Ay," he said jerkily. "My mother. She shut th' door on me whenever I went—an' she ordered I'd not to go to her funeral, an' she left me her curse in her will. That's th' stock I come on."

"Tha'rt a'reight, Field," said the old man meditatively. "But did ta notice her eyes, Field? Did ta notice her eyes?"

Day left him, shaking with laughter, over the fire.

He had to pass Helen's room, and listened for any sound from within. The silence from that other room where the dead lay was not more deep. Creeping stealthily, he placed his eye to the keyhole. He saw her. She was sitting by the table on which stood the candle. She was biting into her own flesh—biting into that bared white arm to discover whether she were really dead or only in a trance. Those eyes, with that look that made Mason laugh, were closed. Her lashes fluttered once. He moved cautiously away. Then he shrugged his shoulders. Just for a single second he had felt fear lest she should unclose those eyes, and know he looked at her.

BOOK II

CHAPTER IX

SNOW

ACROSS the barren purity of the snow-covered moor, with above it "the wide open eye of the solitary sky," the wind made that whinny of unutterable sadness which is born of its having nothing to wrestle with. The earth-bobs, the runnels between the bents, the tufts of fine, blood-tinted grasses overhanging dark water-holes, the mounds tossed up by the moles—all were covered by that shroud that is as the symbol of sanctity to the ascetic. Under it were furze-bushes, their gold ready to shoot sun-like pomp on the face of the world. All that was seen of them now was a bloomless jag here and there pricking through the snow at its thinnest fold, like cypress bloom in a winding sheet.

It was one vast, blinding track of whiteness.

No footprints lay upon it, save those made by the feet of moor-fowl, or the dragging of their wings as they had flown low across it, or the soft indents of the pads of a baby hare's feet, born in these wilds of March, on this height of desolation. Across the monotony of the sky a hawk went, its wing like the sail of a ship forlorn on an ashen sea.

It was even as a world where the foot of man had never been.

Whilst ever, seeking vainly for something to struggle with, the wind wandered, crying.

Into the desert of grey sky-space projected the Corple Stones, ebon-dark. No snow clung to their smooth, age-worn surfaces. But gaps between them were filled with it in man-high drifts.

Far below those black figures, dumb lookers down on the muted valley, the trees in distance—dwindled field and hedgerow were sheeted phantoms, and away in the unbroken whiteness that might smite the onlooker with a sense of ice-ages gone by, the reservoir was black. It was hard to think that life had ever pulsated here, or would again.

The hill-stair by which Martin Scott had ascended to the moor on the night of his dream by the little cradle-shaped pool, could now have been climbed by no human foot. It was sheet-ice. Thaw-winds blowing at intervals, had brought streams of snow-water over the sharp moor-edge, only to freeze them into icicled daggers. The valley path was abandoned by the cautious. Snowslides from the heights were feared. As across the moor, so the valley below the Stones showed no human footprints; if such had been they were now covered up by the last downfall. In a drift the board of a farmer's cart thrust itself through the snow like the prow of a foundering barque, and upon it might have been read the name of one Edward Trip, farmer, of Corple Moor Farm.

Under that virgin snow were likewise buried lambing sheep overtaken by the blizzard i' the dead o' night; in those shrouded trees were the deserted half-built nests of birds who had travelled oversees, restless to reach one little lane in the wide world, maybe one bush or tree in this now lost valley. Life and hope had sunk under this polar purity, and the wildness of the overhanging heights, with what Lizzie Trip termed "their God-forsaken look," was indeed something to make the timid shudder.

Yet, toiling through the lonely vale, naked of growth, empty of sound, save for that low, tired intermezzo of the wind, was a human figure, its garments sombre against the snow. Occasionally it paused, as if looking behind and before, then up at the Stones, with some sense of freedom in the sight of these uninhabited wastes of snow and silence—then, it would come on again, dodging the drifts. Something in the way the snow was flung up again after each step, and in the sagging of its garments on the powdery carpet, suggested its being a woman. Her appearance on the dumb and barren aspect of the vale lent to her a tragic loneliness, with something of dignity borrowed from the gloomy heights above, and from the whole scene she wandered in. She had the appearance of a wanderer rather than of one who travelled to any given place. But when she paused, looking backwards, as if to measure the distance behind her, it might be said that something of melancholy pleasure tinged that pale face, as if she wandered away from, if not towards, some definite object or place.

She advanced until she reached a gate that looked upon an upland field. Against the white crest of this hill-field a ghost of a moon flickered wan light through the ashen sky. In the smooth snow of the upland were footprints extending from a cote in the middle way of it, near a little farm. Leaning against the gate, the woman surveyed the marks of these human feet, leading to the farm, with an expression of weariness, amounting almost to distrust.

From over the hill-crest came the barking of dogs. She looked back along the path she had traversed, then at the heights above. There was a wistfulness in her glance, as though, were it possible, she would never again turn into the haunts of men.

Wanner than ever in its moon-pale charm, with the hood of the same old cloak drawn over her dusky hair, it was the face of Helen Day, wife of the now locally famous Fielding Day.

It was scarcely changed, save for a subtle, restless crave that had gone out of the eyes. The whole expression of the face, now, had in it an almost inhuman remoteness from ordinary life. If asked to define that expression, a psychologist would have been baffled to say wherein lay its power of fascination. Sweetness it had none. It was hard, chill, pallid, with a soullessness that repulsed and attracted, this face upturned to the spectral moon hanging in the oppressive sky. Its beauty was stone-like. But it was a beauty haunting in its elusiveness.

After a few minutes by the gate, she put out her hand, unhasping a rusted chain.

The sound of the chain startled a hen and her brood. The startled mother hustled her chicks towards the cote, and watching the picture, a dim misery passed over the stoicism of the woman at the gate, like mist over an ice peak. Fastening the chain hurriedly, as one who chains down her mind, at the same time fastening up some dreadful thought within it, she passed into the field, walking straight ahead, edging as far as possible from the farm. But it was all in vain.

The bright eyes of little Aggie Trip had spied her. They disappeared quickly from the window-pane; the farm door opened, dogs barked, and Lizzie, blue-aproned, bare-armed, almost crushing in her matronliness, with Aggie's curly head at her stout waist-line, called across the interspace of snow, a note of reproach in her northern burr:

"Helen Mason! An'—passin' our door!"

There was no answer to that hurt surprise but to advance to meet her, as she crossed the farmyard, with its snow-swathed outbuildings and lean-tos.

At the gate they looked into each other's eyes, Helen's with that shrinking in them that might be interpreted as some wild longing to escape from human inspection.

"Tha need'st say tha were turnin' in," said Lizzie bluntly. "If Aggie hadn't seen thee, tha'd ha' gone by.

Happen we're not class enough, seein' thy husband—
tha sees we follow th' world, if we're out on it. We've sin
his picter i' th' *Brungerly News* last week. An' then—
thee tryin' to get past our door."

Helen smiled. Her smile and the clear look of her
were sufficient answer to Lizzie's suspicion. The latter
was convinced that whatever madness had made Helen
turn to those lone snows rather than to a cup of tea
and chat in a cosy farm kitchen, it was not that of
snobbishness. There had always been a good deal she
had taken for granted in Helen Mason.

Helen followed Lizzie into the black-raftered kitchen,
full of rosy lights on polished steel, and on shining
pewter vessels that hung on the old-fashioned wall-
shelves, whilst the smell of nettle-beer a-brewing and
bread in the baking, filled every nook and cranny.
Before the fire was Aggie's baby-chair, now too small for
her, but holding the dilapidated form of a wooden doll
that stared crazily into the caverns of the fire.

Aggie took Helen's cloak and made her smile faintly
by stroking the silk dress, now unveiled, with reverent
touch. Lizzie set her chair near to the fire.

"It's hot enough here," said Helen, taking Teddy's
chair in the shadowy ingle-nook.

"How do I like livin' here?" sniffed Lizzie
contemptuously, in answer to a query from Helen.
"Deein' here, tha means. How would ta like buryin'
alive? But tha doesn't know! Nobody can know, till they
come to it. Nowt to see but them gret black Stones,
fleysome as if they were sittin' i' Judgment—an' to
see a bird go ower th' sky, an' wish tha'd wings to be
back i' Four Gates. An' nowt but th' sound o' wind, an'
water, an' when that thunner-storm were on, Helen,
this valley reminded me o' hell, like what hell might
be—that black an' dismal. Why folks ever leaves Four
Gates is a mystery to me. But a bigger is how they can
go, an' ne'er come back."

Helen looked at her as she slapped a lump of dough into shape with a plump hand.

"Tha doesn't know what it is to be lonesome," said Lizzie. "Tha never lived away from Four Gates."

"No," said Helen, a small pale smile hovering round her mouth. "I've ne'er been away from Four Gates."

"An' how's thy father?" asked Lizzie. "Has he gotten his use back yet? I shouldn't ha' thowt he'd have had a stroke."

"He can trail hissel' across the floor to th' window an' back agen to his chair in th' nook, an' that's about a'," answered the woman in the corner. "His speech is a bit twisted like, but he makes me understand. An' it's as good as havin' hands an' feet, a'most, to ha' Field, for he does all for him 'at he can't do for hissel'."

Again that pale smile flickered round her mouth.

She was staring down at a blue mark on the back of her hand, a mark half-hidden by the shadow of a cunningly arranged frilling of black net.

"It's nice when it's like that," said Lizzie. "A sort o' son to him. Aggie, get me that fork to prick this cake o' thy dad's, or he'll think its noan reight. His mother allus pricked 'em like this—three little fork marks— just to let th' witches out, an' so we go on prickin' 'em, though nobody believes i' witchcraft, now."

She set Teddy's cake on one side, then looked up swiftly.

"There's a letter thear—agen th' clock, on th' dresser, Helen. Happen tha'll like to see it, seein' it's fro' an old friend o' thine. Teddy an' me thowt Martin had nigh forgotten there were a place on th' map o' the world ca'ed Four Gates, or else 'at he'd ta'en some mak o' spite agen it. Just reach an' read it—for my han's aren't fit, for flour. Sin' he writ Teddy when he'd bin landed i' America a month, an' sends back th' brass he'd borrowed—we'd ne'er had a wimp o' him. An' there's nowt much i' that letter. Not a wimp o' whether he's wed an' worried yet—nowt nobbut axin' if Teddy could let him ha' enough brass to bring him back to Four Gates an' 'at it's a matter o' life an' death. An'if Teddy can't—But thear! Reach it."

Helen sat looking at Lizzie.

Through the chill remoteness of her look flashed another, for a moment. But it was gone so quickly that Lizzie did not see it.

She was stirring milk into a sweet-loaf for Sunday, when she expected visitors from her beloved Four Gates.

"Get it," she repeated. "He didn't say we hadn't to show anybody, an' he wouldn't mind thee seein' it, anyhow. Ay, that's it."

Helen had risen and was crossing over to the dresser.

She had re-seated herself, opening the letter out, Lizzie's spoon clicking, and her comments made a running stream of sound to which Helen read.

"Ay, an' him used to be so proud," puffed Lizzie. "Aggie, open th' oven-door for thy father's cake. But I know—I could go on my knees, my bare bended knees, to ax to get back to Four Gates! But as for Teddy goin' to that priest he mentioned on—Aggie! Aggie! Why, of course tha's brunt thee! Here. Shut that blubberin'— an' I'll put thee green salve on."

Whilst Lizzie was salving Aggie's burn, Helen was reading the letter. She broke up a cob on the fire to get sufficient light. As the flames leapt up she looked not unlike the wild-eyed girl who had sat in the red autumnal wood with the dead leaves swirling about her as she drew to her the soul of an invisible man, setting upon him the spell that should bind him to her though he fled to the uttermost corners of the earth. He was coming back! Martin Scott was coming back to Four Gates. He was coming back as she had willed it that he should come back, on that storm-riven day. He was coming back—beaten. She also was beaten—wrecked. The big tides that had washed him out from Four Gates had not been able to keep him, to make him forget. He also was wrecked. He must get the money, be able to come back. She wanted to see him—the man who had thought he had only to get away, to leave Four Gates behind him, forever! The fool who had held her in the hollow of his hand, and flung her away, anywhere, to anyone—the coward who had kissed her and left her. He had taken the way he had thought without responsibility, without risk, and he had to beg Teddy Trip to send him the money to bring him back, a burning crave written between the reserved brevity of his letter.

"What's ta think on it?" asked Lizzie, fixing the staring doll in the arms of the sobbing Aggie, to console her for the smart of the burn.

"Will Teddy lend him th' brass?" asked Helen.

"Teddy can't," said Lizzie austerely. "For he's got none to lend. It's a' gone—i' this farm he's dreamed o' so long! Allus talkin' of a farm on th' slope o' a hill—an' gotten it, an' a' our bit o' brass swallowed up. So it's no use Martin lookin' to us—an' as for Teddy runnin' after that owd priest on th' strength o' his rememberin' Martin, if Teddy couldn't spare th' brass—well, Teddy said it's the craziest thing he ever heard. Martin mun ha' changed—"

With which she opened the oven door, popped Teddy's cake in, slammed the door to, then sat down, her broad back to the window, her face shadowed, but her eyes glinting as she looked across at Helen. Aggie was sobbing in an undertone now. The wooden doll was comforting her.

There was silence then, save for the loud tick of the clock, the fall of a cinder on the snowy hearth, the crackling sound of Teddy's cake in the oven, and from without the sound of the wind over the snow.

Lizzie moved restlessly in her seat, then leaned forwards. The sheen of the fine gold chain round the neck of the woman in the dusky silk dress held her glance—and seemed to give her courage.

"Thy father ne'er paid Martin them wages—fro' that day to this, I believe," she observed.

"Nor ever will," said the woman in the ingle. "Not if he waits till th' Judgment Day."

"Dead robbery, I call it," said Lizzie.

"Martin should ha' waited till my father came home, an' paid him," said Helen. "He'll ne'er get it now—unless he goes to law."

Whilst the bare supposition of a man who had to borrow money to get back to Four Gates going to law with a wealthy farmer made Lizzie shake her head with a "Nay, nay, he'll noan go to law. But I thowt—"

"Ay, there's some thinks because my father has had a stroke 'at it would soften his heart. But that would never soften—though his marrow ran away! He's harder nor ever, now. Nobody'll stick cannels round him an' make out he deed sorry for this an' for that. He's isn't the sort they make tracts on."

Helen's eyes met Lizzie's squarely.

Despite herself, the latter's silhouette against the window drooped disappointedly.

"Well," she said philosophically, "if he'll not, he'll not. An' now—ay, put it down on th' table. I'll put it on th' dresser agen. An' now—tell us all th' news o' Four Gates."

The telling did not take long, not even with the inclusion of the sow that had had a record litter,—of Andry the weaver being about to summons the new brewery people for pouring stuff into his stream that made his hens drunk every Monday morning, and of his being about to take a drunken hen as chief witness to Brungerly old court. During the recital Lizzie listened with a holy look. She wiped her eyes on the corner of her apron, as one moved by some religious ecstasy. Then, the tear and smile still lingering in her eye, she looked round the corner of her apron at Helen.

"Hasn't ta left summat out?" she asked, with tender slyness.

She saw Aggie leaning against Helen, and called her off with more sharpness than the occasion seemed to warrant.

"An' tak' that bucket—an' fill't," she commanded. "Th' well frozen? Well, that were yesterday, mayhap it's thawed now. An' let's ha' no back- answers."

Thus admonished, Aggie set out across the snow with her bucket.

Helen was sitting, somewhat rigidly, in the corner.

There was an alertness, almost painful, in the dark eyes, if the shadows had not woven a kindly obscurity over her face—a strained, shrinking look, almost akin to one of shame, of spiritual shuddering from hearing something she dreaded cried aloud upon the public air.

"Teddy stopped to talk wi' Andry about his sow litterin'," began Lizzie again, taking up the thread of conversation with an assumption of being casual. "Ay, that very day his cart stuck i' th' drift, yon, on th' way back. Andry's wife came out, as they barged, an' she gave him a wimp o' news, an' I says to him, as he sat where tha sits now, 'Teddy Trip—Helen'd ha' told me, I'm sure—an' how should Andry's wife know? But the next time I see Helen, I'll ax her.' "

"Ay?" said Helen.

There was something as antagonistic in her tone as on her face. The sound of it seemed to fluster Lizzie.

"Andry's wife said—" began Lizzie.

Then she broke off. The silence of the woman in the corner was embarrassing. Lizzie rose, and walking over to where Helen sat, stood before her, looking down at her in a tender, searching way. Their shadows on the wall stirred. From a snow-covered field at the back of the farm came the shrill cry of a curlew. Lizzie stood smiling in that tender, motherly fashion.

Helen's hands gripped the chair-arms that were dented with Teddy cutting up his tobacco. Her face was alabaster-white, her eyes had darkened in their old way when excited.

"Is't true, Helen?" asked Lizzie.

"Ay," answered Helen.

"Tha'll get through," cheered Lizzie. "Tha'rt strong."

"Ay," said the woman in the chair.

"It's a wonnerful thing," said Lizzie. "A child born o' two folk as loves—"

Helen smiled.

A soul in torment might have smiled so.

Lizzie was too taken up with the news to notice.

"When?" she asked softly.

"I' the fall," answered Helen. She was staring drearily into the fire at a coffin-shaped coal. A little beyond it appeared to be a miniature wood, and when the wind blew down the wide chimney red leaves were falling there—falling, falling, even as they had fallen around her when she had cast her spell on the wet wind, so that she had fancied it would meet Martin, whichever way he tried to escape her.

Lizzie's lips were moving, her plump fingers counting against her apron. There were visions in her eyes.

"Next year at this time," she said, "it'll be after feelin' its feet. We couldn't hold Aggie at *that* age."

"It'll happen dee," said Helen.

The icy drip of those few words caused Lizzie Trip to start back.

"Helen!" she gasped. She poked up the fire again, to see that shadow-veiled face.

In every line of it was stamped loathing, a sense of degradation. The eyes stared wild and black.

"Isn't there any way out?"

137

Helen had risen from her chair, and stood up.

In her black attire, with dead-white face, she seemed some outraged goddess. Her words stabbed at the air. From without came the sobbing of the wind over the snow, and between it came fragments of "Rock-a- bye, baby" in Aggie's treble, with that thin, sad thread of the curlew's cry filtering through it.

"Helen! *Thee!*" ejaculated Lizzie, and flopped into a chair.

There was silence. Then Lizzie said, as one thinking of a scene beyond a scene, "Tha'rt not poor." Some of her ruddy colour had paled a little.

A cinder dropping made her start nervously.

"It isn't like you hardly knew how to keep a roof ower your heads, an' hadn't a rag to wrap it in," she said. "Or—as if 'twere a bastard!"

"It's a bastard," avowed Helen tonelessly. "A real bastard—gotten in loathin', growin' i' loathin', and it'll see it writ on my face. Those they ca' bastards are holy compared wi' 't. Jesus Christ's mother couldn't show no marriage lines when she went to th' inn. But—*this!* *Me*—to come to this! A bastard thrust on me, an' to ha' it put i' th' papers, an' a presentation, maybe—an' a' th' time to know it comes into th' world lower than a dog, because—I'm agen it all th' time! To struggle to give it life, when it's *him*—a' *him*, an' noan o' me, an' to hate it more for that, though it should make me love it more if—if he hadn't been a tally- husband!"

Her voice trailed off into mute misery.

Lizzie stared dumbfounded.

"But you're wed," she said feebly.

"Folk think so," said Helen. "Like they'll think it isn't a bastard."

Lizzie shook her head hopelessly.

Helen had a half-mad look to her.

"*I've* nowt to wrap it in," said Helen, thinking of Lizzie's past words. "Not a rag o' love to welcome its limbs. I'm givin' it every drop o' blood wi' a grudge, an' then, to ha' its hands fumblin' an' creepin' round my breast, an' it smilin' up i' my face wi' *his* eyes, maybe, whilst every cell i' my body shrinks away from it, or I'm clay-cold to it—*me*, to ha' come to this."

"If I hated a man ever so," said Lizzie, "I couldn't but love a little innercent child—when it sucked me."

Helen laughed.

"My father didn't bring me up like a turtledove," she said. "An' I'd no saints wi' leets round their heads, an' faces like they'd no blood. But there are some women like their men because they happen to be th' child's father. It's only th' other way wi' me. I'm made the other way, somehow—allus th' other way—runnin' after what should run after me, runnin' awa' fro' what I should run to. I feel like creepin' into a dark hole, an' ne'er comin' out agen—like I were *disgraced*. A' these years—dreamin', an' growin'—an' th' fruits—a bastard! I—I can't face it, Lizzie. Tell us—"

She had thrown out her hands before her, as if to ward off some terror. From outside came Aggie's joyous voice, singing:

"All in a row,
Gath-er-in' snow,
Some said Yes,
An' some said No."

Lizzie rose from her chair, and went towards the cupboard.

"Teddy's cake's burnin'," said Helen.

"Shall I take it out?"

Lizzie nodded, climbing upon a chair to reach that top shelf. From the duskiest corner of it she took down a canister. Her colour was still paled, with the gust of some old pain. Teddy's cake was clean gone from her mind. She marvelled that Helen should think of it.

"It's spoilt," said that black-robed woman.

"Ne'er mind," answered Lizzie.

"Leet that cannel, Helen," she said, climbing down. "An' ne'er mind scrapin' th' cake."

Helen obeyed.

The candle shed its lustre on the two heads bent over the open canister, and upwards on the two pale faces, one quivering as with a backward look, the other proud and firm. Once Lizzie looked into that countenance with shuddering wonder.

"Aren't ta fleyed? Hasn't ta no conscience?" she asked, almost in a whisper.

"I munnot ha' been there when they gave 'em out," answered Helen.

"Ginger cake," said Lizzie, tossing an old paper away, after a second's scrutiny. Helen picked it up.

"There's summat on th' back," she said, and then read out a name and address.

"That's it," said Lizzie. Then she sat down by the table.

"It's a long way to Thorn," she observed. "Tha'll not go to-day, an' it's darkenin' for more snow."

"I'll go to-day," said Helen. "I suppose she'll live there yet."

"She were there a year back," said Lizzie. "But I've not sin her fro' that day to this. Billy were twenty last Thursday, an' he were only a babby then—just walkin'. 'Twere to save his life I went to see old Betty, at Thorn, an'—I hoped 'twouldn't be written against me, bein' so. Th' doctor said he'd fade away if he hadn't nourishment—an' if I didn't keep at th' mill I couldn't get 'em, an' I ne'er could keep there when I were carryin' my childer, an' then Teddy lost his work—an'—'twere just a draught or two o' herbs." A pause. Then she said, shakily:

"'Twould ha' been a lad."

Her voice died away.

She was staring at the candle-flame, with a drawn look on her naturally plump face. Her hand was beating a restless tattoo on the table.

"She'll be nigh on eighty," she said, after a moment's silence. "An' I expect she'll be above greaund—for such like don't dee soon, them as traffics wi' th' devil, for she said she'd witch it back into th' neet agen—an' them herbs 'at she gave me ne'er grew i' th' sunleet, I'm sure."

Helen smiled sceptically, and got up to put on her cloak.

When she was fastening it, the door opened and Aggie tumbled in. Her hair was white with snow. She had been lying down in a field, she said, to make the shape of herself. Then she ran and picked up her doll from the chair.

"You've never looked at my babby," she said, with a matronliness quaint and touching. "When I get twenty-one years old I'll have a real one—instead o' a ring like Glen got when it was her birthday."

Helen smiled.

"What is she called?" she asked gravely.

"Helen," said Aggie. "Mr. Scott brought her me fro' Brungerly before he went away in the big ship." She began to sing and croon to it.

Lizzie followed Helen to the door.

The wind was blowing more wildly now. Sometimes it raised a ghost-like curtain of snow over the landscape.

"Tha'll let me know?" asked Lizzie.

"Ay," answered Helen, drawing her hood more closely over her brow. Then she said, looking at Lizzie, "Thanks!"

Lizzie drew back.

"Look!" she said, and pointed to a signpost which stated that trespassers would be prosecuted. A single magpie, ink-black against the snowy background, was perched on the pole. As they looked, he flew over the wastes of snow.

"An ill sign," shuddered Lizzie.

Helen laughed.

"It's iller—to be beaten," she said, and set her head towards Thorn, walking swiftly over the snow. There was somewhere to go to now—to Thorn—to that desolate hamlet where Martin had spent his unhappy childhood, near the wide, wild Moss where he had watched the hawks travel across the sky.

After two miles, during which the afternoon light had waned considerably, she came to the meeting of two roads. A vehicle came along one of these. She waited.

"Want a lift?" queried the driver.

"Ay. Thorn way," answered Helen.

"I'm goin' that way," he began, then hesitated.

"I can pay," said the woman in the cloak.

"It isn't that," he said. A short conversation took place between him and someone within the coach.

"Let her get in," said a clear voice, at length. "Let her get in."

Helen climbed up into the dimness of the old coach.

"Cold travelling weather," said that peculiarly penetrating voice from the furthest corner. "And Thorn is a wild place."

Helen saw white hair under a black cassock, a long, thin, pale face, with a pair of intense eyes, and from the blackness of the priestly gown she saw two thin, tapering hands in restless motion. They might have been trying to catch invisible birds—or perhaps they were only chafing against the cold.

"I'm going to see a friend," said Helen. Even as she spoke she had a sense of doing so against her will, and drew further into her corner, where she looked out on a backward vista of the Corple Stones.

"I know every soul in Thorn," said the voice. "What did you say your friend's name was?"

"I didn't say," said Helen, her eyes meeting his now, that he might see she was no fool. "But she's called Haggus—Betty Haggus."

The old priest came out of his corner and seated himself opposite to her now. The full light from the coach-window was on his face, that remarkable face eaten up by the intensity of those eyes. Helen remembered that she had seen him once, when walking with Martin in a Four Gates lane, and how Martin had told her, as he caught up with her, after talking to the priest, that he had been after catching his soul. This was Martin's priest. This was the man who had taught him about those pallid saints with their halos—the saints who had ranged themselves on Martin's side, against her, and the red earth, and the lawless winds, and the spirits of the moors and the cloughs.

The old man's hands were clutching and unclutching in their restless way. He leaned across the coach, looking at the strong face.

"Then you'll be sorry to hear that your friend died last night," he said. "I gave her sacrament. Perhaps it is now no good your going to Thorn—"

Helen half rose from her seat.

"No," she said. "I must get back—to Four Gates."

"There is a road a little further on leads straight there," said the priest. "Yes, I will stop the coach when we reach it. Four Gates, did you say? Four Gates." His eyes seemed to scan some mental register. At length they lit up with a fiercer glow.

"Then you might know Martin Scott," he said. "I— that is, the Church has lost sight of him for some time, but she never forgets. No, she never forgets. She is like a woman who has once loved and held. She waits. Do you know Martin? Is he there still? I should be glad if you would bear me a message to him."

"He left Four Gates three years sin'," said Helen. "Went abroad. He has no money, and wants to get back."

"Do you remember his address?" asked the priest.

Helen gave it. It was stamped on her brain from seeing it on the letter.

"You have a good memory," smiled the priest, taking it down. It was a long address.

"Like—the Church," she smiled back at him.

He looked at her intently.

"You are not—?" he began eagerly.

"No, I don't belong to you," she said rudely. "You would have bricked me up alive, a bit back—burnt me, or hung me! Your saints—they've no blood. I'd rather ha' th' smell of a moor clod than your incense, or a body smell from an old clout of a coat. I don't like your saints wi' their pale faces. They look tired. An' they blaspheme so. If I'm not to be happy, I'll not pretend. But—you might get Martin back. I should think you would be almost sure."

She rose to her feet.

The mocking pagan smile met the eyes of the old priest.

"Thank you," he said, as if she had given him something. He was folding up the leaf he had written on. "I shall write Mr. Scott. Perhaps I could mention your name—"

"He would scarcely know it," she smiled. "We are— almost strangers. I just happened to know where he is, and that he wants to come back. In small places folk know all about, even if they don't know, each other."

Then she got out as the coach was stopped at the road leading to Four Gates.

When she reached the village it was pitch dark. But along the road, lit by the fitful light of a lantern, a flock of sheep were being driven along to Brungerly, to the slaughter.

The red lights of the farm greeted her, shining down the hillside on a swell of snow. Creeping up to the window she peered into the kitchen.

Fielding Day was bent over his books, at the table, the red-globed lamp beside him making his wolfish look more keen. Old Mason was in the bed brought down into the kitchen for him since his stroke.

"Tha—gives her—too much string, Field," she heard him growl, in his twisted way.

Fielding Day looked up, across at the clock, then at the figure on the bed.

"String!" he snarled. "I'll string her, when she comes. I'll—"

Then he bent over his books again, his lips moving as he counted.

The twisted laugh of her father came to the woman outside, the woman who, following on after that flock of bleating sheep, had decided, with primitive loathing, or with weariness, that the gods were too much for her—that she could not set her hand against anything so helpless as an unborn child. Her father—Fielding— Martin—the gods! These she could fight, the fierce. But—a child!

She pressed the latch down noiselessly, and was in upon them before they were aware.

"I've come," she announced, smiling.

Day snapped his books together. He was weary of struggling with unfeeling figures. The light of battle was in his eyes. He had that half-laugh on his countenance which, with the whiteness of his teeth, made him so like a wolf at times.

"Ay," he said, straightening himself up. "So I see. Well, come in. Don't be fleyed."

"Fleyed?" she laughed, and advanced into the middle of the kitchen. Fielding Day stood watching her as she leisurely took off her cloak—watching and waiting, like something about to spring.

CHAPTER X

A CHAIN OF FLESH

AS Helen turned from hanging up her cloak, Day faced her. "Where's ta bin?" he snarled.

Helen's eyes did not move from his. They were watching each other like animals that do not trust each other enough to dare glance away for a moment.

"I've bin out," she told him, with cutting brevity.

It would be useless and humiliating to avoid a quarrel. Weary as she was she took up the challenge.

From the bed in the corner came a cackling laugh.

"O—out!" the old man mimicked, watching darker passions sweep over Day's face. He had been promising Day more share capital if he turned the screw a little more.

The savage beauty of Helen's eyes were like a laugh at Day. Terror, defiance, murder—thoughts he could bring there, but two things never—appeal, or love. She was strong. He had a delight in trying to break her. She was no reed, but a bar of tempered steel.

"Where's ta bin?" he repeated.

There was finality in his voice.

His hand shot out, catching her wrist in a vicelike grip. "*Now*—whear hesta bin?" he urged, smiling. "Tell thy devoted husband whear tha's bin th' livelong day whilst he's toiled and moiled and pined for thee. Or—shall I gie just another twist?"

"'Th'—thy lovin' husband,'" spluttered the old man, pulling at the bedclothes, his frame shaken by the silent laughter. "He he!" He was thinking of the dark scenes that had been enacted in that kitchen.

A little moan of pain came from Helen's lips.

"Not yet?" There was demonic pleasantness in Day's query. He moved his thumb upon the spot that communicated with the nerve centre.

Agony paled Helen to death-hue. But she was silent. After that moan she had set herself not to cry out.

Then—Fielding Day let out an oath.

For the desperate woman had set her teeth in the flesh 'of his hand, as she half-sank with pain upon her knees.

The blood of a savage race surged into Day's face. A woman had bitten him. A woman! The insult of it! His slave had turned upon him. He looked down at the blood on his hand—the blood she had tasted. From the bed came the laughter of the old man. The wind shouted defiance outside.

"I'll show thee for them tricks. *I'm* not Martin. I'm not one to run away from a woman—" The words came between his teeth, clenched with pain.

He grabbed a handful of black hair and began to drag her to her feet.

Two pale hands pressed against the roots to numb the pain. The wild eyes stared upwards into his. Hatred was in them—but no appeal.

"I'll break thee in," said Fielding. A fiercer throb shot through his wrist. His face was livid. With his free hand he reached a stick from a corner, still dragging her with him. They jostled amongst the empty milk-kits yet to be scalded.

She looked upwards at the stick with horror at the insult. To be beaten—like a dog! She had been beaten before, but not with a stick. Of course—she could go away, leave Four Gates, and thereby confess to Four Gates, and to Martin Scott, the fact that she was not happy. Happy! She had never thought to be happy.

But to be beaten—with Martin's old stick!—She looked at the stick. No, she would never leave Four Gates. Never. They should never know. Besides—this was her place, hell, maybe, but still—her place. She would not be hounded out of it. Besides—she had only five shillings. Martin Scott had run away, away from Four Gates. She would fight her fight out here, go down here maybe. And the farm, it was her birthright. If only the man would strike—and have done with it. Perhaps—it would not hurt very much. She closed her eyes against the sight of the stick—against the sacrilege of it. It was her naked soul that the stick would weal. Like an animal, she feared a stick—feared it in every corner of her heart. And *that* stick—! Martin's stick!

"Field," she breathed.

Her eyes were still closed.

With the cruelty in him he was not striking at once.

"Axin' for mercy!" he jeered. "She doesn't like th' stick, dad." Old Mason laughed.

There was a gleam in his deep-set eyes.

"Th'—the harder tha strikes, the more tha'll be loved," he said. "It's th' devil's truth, Field. He he! They be like dogs. Like dogs." He stared away and beyond the two, yet his eyes missed no single detail of what was going on before him, though, like a companion picture, behind it he saw the heights of the Corple Stones, and another Helen beside him—faltering the words that were betrayal. The pale beauty was like hers, the eyes were the same as these—these staring upwards with almost mad repulsion against the stick, Martin's old stick, made from a fifty years' old ivy vine.

"I'll not be struck wi' 't, Field," she whispered. "I'll not. I'll kill mysel'—if tha touches me wi' 't."

Long shudders of physical loathing against the contact of the stick ran through her.

Fielding Day laughed down at her.

"If she talks wild like that, dad," he said, "we'll ha' to send her to that big house in its own grounds, wi' rails round—"

Their dual laughter rang out.

With a sudden movement she sprang to her feet, though Day still held her by the coils of her hair, and the wrench of it was torture. Spectre-pale in her black attire, and almost spectre-thin, she looked at them.

"An' what is't you'd send?"

Vibratingly her voice mocked them. Her frail body that could be bruised and broken she granted them. With every cell of it shuddering back from, the stick, she denied them all else, strong once more, her soul girded for the blow to come, by the bitterness of their taunts.

A fiercer cruelty shot into the eyes of the younger man as he heard the mockery that answered their mockery, the mockery of the soul against what they could do to the body—the mockery such as had sustained heroes, martyrs, and the pioneers of all ages.

"Tha'rt fleyed o' th' stick," said Fielding, "an' tha'rt goin' to get it—unless tha says whear tha's bin. Come! If 't had bin Martin, now, tha'd ha' bin sloppin' an' slaverin' in his ear-hoyl whear tha'd bin—if tha'd had th' heart to leave him i' peace a minute. Now—out wi' it."

Even whilst she nerved herself for the insult to come, with the maddening picture in her mind, confused though it were, of how she would have returned from a walk in the snowy solitudes to tell of it to a faithful Martin, she wondered why Fielding should refer twice to Martin at such a time.

Then—the stick had touched her cheek, giving her a sickening, shuddering feeling. Her flesh shrunk away from it, with the insane passion that a savage would feel, knowing it a desecration. It was next door to Martin Scott beating her, whilst he laughed at her. That quivering woman's flesh shrunk away from it, even as it shrunk from Fielding's brutish kisses—more intolerable than blows. He, looking down into the hell of her look, had discovered another means to punish her. Foot and fist she had grown used to. Now he had found Martin's stick. The primitive in her, akin to the beast under the settle, loathed, feared, and hated a stick. Another thought ran through her brain, galvanising her from the stupor of horror the touch of the stick had brought.

"If tha strikes me where folk can see, Field," she panted, "I'll ha' thy blood." She was a white incarnation of terror and pride.

"Tha could say 't were the cupboard-door. Two lovely black eyes—" he said, just switching past her cheek again, making the air sing. "I'll noan lie," she said. But she cowered at the thought of apologising and lying openly to Four Gates. There was murder in her glance. Her eyes swept the table for some missile. Fielding Day laughed. As her glance went over the table she saw her father. The bed shook with his laughter. Then a cruelty shot into her eyes. Any reference of her mother always went through him with the hurt of a sword.

"My mother'd turn i' her grave to see you sat without a word to say," she said. The old man started.

"Mention thy mother to me—" he snarled threateningly.

"You cannot strike me, now," taunted Helen. Then her face flushed.

"I'm sorry," she said. "Yo'—yo' are makin' me vicious as—yoursel's—" Her voice died away into the lament of the wind.

"I can allus strike thee," said old Mason. "N—ne—'er forget it." S—wish!

The stick whistled past her head.

Then the old man started again, a smile of gloating triumph overspreading his face in place of the savage gloom it had worn for a moment. A terrified woman's scream rung through the dark house, a scream not born of physical anguish, but of fear and indignation against the threat of a deeper insult. It pierced the silence weirdly, echoing along the dim, cold corridor that led up to the room that had been Martin Scott's, that led up to the room that had seen Milly Mason laid between the pallid, flickering candles. The old man heard that sound as a high priest of Moloch might have heard the shriek of a belated sacrifice ascend vainly to the skies. In his glee he leaned down over the bedside, patting the dog. The caress from that hand was so unusual that the beast whined with terror.

Helen was not noticing her father.

Through every corner of her brain her own scream rang. The rest was Fielding Day's countenance—that of a tamer of wild things—and above her, mesmerising her, the stick. Martin's stick, the stick he had found as they came home from the fair on that blossomy, moonlit night which was surely part of some other life. In the back of her brain, behind the fear, was a curious, cold wonder if she would go mad, were she beaten oft enough with that stick, as some were driven crazy in the olden times, by strange tortures. Whilst she knew, with shuddering expectancy, that he had not struck her yet. He had only touched her cheek, then whirled it past her head, and still threatened. Therein lay the cruelty of the man. She was getting like Martin—Martin who had run away, afraid, not of what was, but of what might be.

They were breaking her, changing her, strive as she might. She knew it in this moment.

They had made her scream, like any tame woman of Four Gates who feared hell, and death, and judgment, and was good from fear. They were making her—a coward.

The long body quivered with fear and loathing at such a thought.

A coward!

Looking upwards she saw the laugh in Fielding's eyes. She took possession of herself.

"Strike!" she taunted. "Strike!"

Something that the stick had made her forget came back to her, as she heard the low sobbing of the wind over the snow, soft as a child's cry now. That crowning indignity might serve as a barricade against these lesser ones. She faced Fielding. She had unexpectedly found a weapon.

"Strike!" she repeated, with a laugh. "An' when tha strikes—mind tha only strikes me, beast, and not that which is thine—thine—all thine—none o' mine—mind thee. If tha hurts it, it may serve thee as I do, now, some day."

Remembering the barricade, she laughed again, a very savage, and spat upon him.

Day's arm was raised to strike—there was murder in his eye. Then—her words suddenly gave him a lightning shock. He stood, his arm falling to his side, staring at her in bewilderment.

"What's ta mean, she-cat?" he asked.

"Strike me!" gibed Helen.

Old Mason, in puzzled disappointment, was trying to solve the mystery of the change in the scene.

"What's ta mean?" asked Day. He jerked her to her feet, but in such a manner as not to hurt her too much. A fear was written on his face.

"Strike me—and mayhap thy son will curse thee for it," she flung at him. The simple words might have been a thunderbolt dropped on the silence of the kitchen.

The old man had raised himself in his bed.

"He he!" he laughed. "A child—a Cherubim, an olive-branch, to come here—to this h—house!"

He fell back heavily, his brow like thunder.

"Olive-branch," echoed Helen. At her tone both men started, so full of concentrated misery and hatred it sounded. "Olive-branch!"

She met their eyes.

Her own conveyed a message that electrified them. That which would have melted some other had enraged her—savage that she was, barbarian who felt only that hers was a motherhood without meaning.

"Conceived i' hatred, born in hatred, suckled on hatred!" she said. "'Twill come into th' world like a fiend! My curse upon it, Field—on all on it that's thine."

She went, a rushing cloud of black across the kitchen, and into the shadows of the corridor. Through the little window where Martin Scott had let the wind blow on him after his blasphemy and invocation of the saints to save him from her spell, she saw the stars shining, as she had often seen them through the boughs of the yew-tree.

Then Fielding's voice rang after her.

"We'll call it—*Martin*," he shouted mockingly.

She returned, and stood in the doorway, regarding him.

"Why does ta speak so often o' Martin?" she asked.

"He's deein'—that owd lover o' thine that ran away," he said, whilst the old man chuckled. "I've sin one has sin him—out yon—an' th' earth'll be atop o' him, ay, he'll be pushin' next year's daisies up, Martin Scott will, i' th' spring. Turnin' religious, too, they say—but not till he's supped deep o' life, ay, dregs an' a'. A wreck he is, Martin Scott. We'll ca' th' kid after him, for owd times' sake. Happen tha'll warm it i' thy breast then. Ay, Martin's finished. Tha'll ne'er clap e'en on him again."

"I shall," said Helen. "He's comin' back."

For the second time that night she electrified the two men.

"Comin' back!" they echoed. "To—Four Gates?"

"Ay," she answered. "Whear else should he come to? Don't folk allus creep back to dee whear they've loved?"

Fielding Day and Helen looked into each other's eyes. The old man was looking at them both with fierce satisfaction. The child he had feared was to be another torment to Helen. Her old lover was coming back. The old struggle might begin again—anyhow, she would see Martin die, know he was dying, as the leaves fell, and be unable to breathe a word of regret—would have to act as if he were any other Four Gates man. On the rack of the boss, bearing life that she had cursed, with the tide of death creeping up round her lover, she must let him be washed out without a word. She was a Four Gates woman.

Helen was regarding Day in wonderment.

She had caught a note in his voice new to her. Then she started.

"Tha'rt ne'er jealous of a deein' chap, wi'out brass—a coward 'at ran away?" she gibed.

Then she saw by the look in his eyes that he, also, had received the shock.

"Jealous!" he growled.

But she knew the truth, even as he perceived it, in that moment. She turned and walked away into the shadow of the corridor, away from that horror, her very lips blanched. Not content with her body, with the carcase Martin Scott had left behind him, the tyrant now wanted the very essence of her, the soul of her, the love of her, that which had died on that evening when she ran down the hillside calling vainly on a coward's name. Her body he had made his. After a long struggle he would find out that she was only that—a body, with certain physical repulsions and fears, a thing that ate, and slept and walked about, counterfeiting life—but in reality, dead, these three years, the soul of her gone these three years, and only to be invoked, like a spirit passed away before its time, violently, by spells—such as Martin's stick, Martin's name—Martin she hated most of all.

Her father had brought her up like a wild cat, yet teaching her to respect Four Gates, to give it power over her. Love he had never given her. Fielding Day had tortured her—kicked the corpse Martin had left behind, stirring it to the malignity that the dead might feel at being disturbed.

Martin Scott had loved—and left her. This was the worst insult.

She hated him for it.

Like a Four Gates woman she would hide hate as love beneath a matronly calm.

She sat in the dusk of the room that had been Martin's, looking out on the stars. Her black figure was silhouetted against the window.

"Comin' back! Comin' back! To dee!"

The little words fell on the vault-like gloom with wild ecstasy. Then there was silence.

"'Some day, Martin,'" she said, repeating words spoken half in jest under the yew-tree, "'some day, tha'll beg for a kiss—an' I'll let thee dee—without it.'"

*

Fielding Day's steps came along the passage.

"Open this door," he demanded.

"It's noan fast," answered Helen, out of the heart of the blackness.

"It stuck," he said.

There was a note of hesitation in his voice.

He entered the room, sitting down on the bed. He could see her woman's outline black against the stars, weirdly beautiful.

"Tha's got to ha' that child, curse it as tha will," he said, out of the darkness.

She laughed—a low, vibrating laugh.

"It's th' inevitable," she said.

155

"Not allus," said the man.

"It's th' inevitable," she told him again, with elemental passion and disgust—as if she shook something from her. "Besides—it's all o' a piece wi' th' rest."

"Tha's got to care for it—an' for me," he said. She laughed as if she heard one commanding the tides.

"What's thy price?" he said. "Everybody has one! Some go cheap, some go dear. What's thy price—the price o' what tha's ne'er gi'en me."

"I've got no price," said the woman.

"Tha'd ha' gi'en thysel' once," said Fielding, with that mixture of sneering brutality and tradesman's coldness. "But Martin wouldn't ha' thee. Most folk are taken at their own valyation. Even God—they say—won't ha' gi'en stuff. Thy price, Helen—the price o' what tha chucked at Martin—an' got back i' th' face."

There was silence.

Then she rose—her figure a black pillar against the star-littered window space.

"Take me away fro' Four Gates, Field," she said fiercely. "That's—that's my price."

He went towards her swiftly.

"What for?" he asked.

"I want—"

Her voice trailed into the silent darkness.

"Tha wants to start afresh—to forget—like Martin did," said the tramp-boss. "Well—I can't pay th' price. I promised thy father allus to stop i' Four Gates."

There was silence again.

He was frowning at the stars.

He had come to the place where he stood between two gods—the god of Love, the god of Ambition, serving the god of Hatred. To go up he must torture the thing he loved, loved after himself, not before, for so he could only love, but it was sufficient to shake him. In that moment when she had taunted him with being jealous of a man almost dead, a man at the bottom, he had realised love.

A savage antagonism to having this barrier thrust across the path of his ambition rose in his heart. He began to struggle—even as Martin Scott had begun to struggle. Martin had got away. Fielding Day was stronger. But Fielding Day was more of a savage, less of a complex modern.

"It's too high a price," he said. "I can't pay it. Thy father wants to stay i' Four Gates—an' it pays me better to suit him. Anyhow—tha'rt mine. I paid seven and sixpence for thee."

He strode nearer, taking her in his grasp.

"I like summat wild," he said.

He laughed, in his old brutal way.

His lips neared hers.

Then from the window he saw the starshine falling on her face. That strange beaten feeling that had been his as she taunted him with jealousy came on him again.

He let her go.

The futility of it was borne upon him.

"Suit thysel'," he said, with an assumption of callousness.

He went out, banging the door.

"Thy father wants thee," he called, some minutes later. Helen trailed downstairs.

"I want some bread an' milk," growled Mason. He was exhausted physically, lying back on his pillows.

She made it, put the napkin under his chin, and fed him with the spoon.

Afterwards she washed his hands and face. All the time his eyes glared fury at her. His helplessness was borne in upon him. The something he had not understood in the scene between Helen and Day haunted him, bringing the old fear.

"Field!" he breathed.

His tool approached.

"Kiss her!" he grinned.

He stared up into Day's face. To his excited imagination there was something of the shattered look it had worn as he had once mentioned his mother.

"Kiss thy l-lovin' wife!" he commanded.

Day took Helen by the shoulders and raised her face to his. The wincing look met him out of her eyes.

He kissed her in his brutal way.

Mason was watching—the fear going.

Behind his back Day's hand was twitching, as it had done once when the mill had lost an order.

Helen shook the old man's pillow up.

"Is it comfortable?" she asked gently.

"Comfortable as—h—ll!" he gasped.

As she was bending over him he struck at her breast. She put her hand to it, in agony for a moment.

"I'd forgotten th' kits," she said, ignoring the hurt. "Tha might ha' washed 'em for me, Field, bein' such a lovin' husband!"

"I could kill her—when she bears wi' me," Mason confided to Day when she had gone to bed. "She m-makes allowance for me, now. Why?"

Day shook his head. He was back in his figures. As Mason watched the old lust of profits creep into the man's face, he sank back on his pillows—and slept. The fear slept with him.

CHAPTER XI

WHEN THE DEAD COME ALIVE

LIZZIE TRIP, red with raking the fire, spattered with whitewash, her chemise peeping through the bursted armpit of her red bodice, almost flung the moggi out of the dish in her delight to see Helen.

"I've kept thinkin' o' thee," she exclaimed. "I said tha'd come," picking up the spoon she had let fall. "Eh, come up, an' pu' thy things off, an' tak' Teddy's cheer, for he'll noan want it yet. Two o' th' ewes were due, an' one's ta'en off to th' tops, an' he's had to go traunchin' after her i' this blanket o' weet an' mist, an' th' greaund on yon tops'll be like sponges 'at's been soakin' sin th' Flood. Serves him reight, for buryin' me alive. That's it, put thy feet on th' fender. Eh, dear, I believe I've getten too much ginger in, now, an' he said th' last welly brunt his guts out. Chaps is bad to please. They sort o' don't know what they want, an' when they've getten it they're wrong. It comes o' th' Lord makin' Adam without axin' poor Eve, I think, an' it's too late to alter it, now. Just make that cat come off that fender, Helen."

Here she saw Aggie stealing currants, smelled something at the burn in the oven, noticed that the cat was sniffing at a collop of bacon cooking in a saucer before the fire, and made a dash across from the table. She was, as Teddy said, "like a flash of greased lightning." In a trice she had banged the oven door open, removed the cake, clouted Aggie with the oven cloth, and made the cat fly into an obscure corner.

"Thear!" said the woman who was buried alive, jubilantly, and leaned back in the chair into which she had flopped after her exertions. She looked across at Helen, ghostlike in her black dress, as she sat with pale hands lying still in her lap, amidst the shadows.

The eyes of the two women met. Each knew that the other had gone back to their last conversation in that room.

"Well?" said Lizzie.

The sniffing of Aggie, nursing her grief under the table, came to them.

"Betty Haggus were dead. So I never went," answered Helen.

"Oh!"

Lizzie's ejaculation was eloquent.

"So tha'rt goin' for'ard?" said Lizzie.

"Ay, I'm goin' for'ard," answered Helen drearily.

"Tha mun look after thysel'," said Lizzie. "But tha looks warked to death. Tha's a' to do for thy father, I'll bet."

"Ay."

With that one little word, cold and hard, Helen closed the door on the topic, once and for all.

"Martin isn't comin' back," remarked Lizzie, watching Helen's face. Since that last visit she had suspected something.

"Oh," said Helen drowsily. There was a remote sound in her tone. The heat of the Trip kitchen was inducing the sleep that had deserted her for a week. Through that shadowy world closing around her, she was conscious of Lizzie's suspicions. She was amused, in a sleepy way, at Lizzie's transparency when she thought herself most deep, and at the queer fact that there was nothing to hide from Lizzie, no emotion, no regret, no ghosts conjured up at that name of Martin Scott.

She had reached that place where feeling is not, where no insult sullies, no love-bond enslaves, no rack wrings groan or prayer. The past week her father and Fielding had been devils to her. One kept her softening his pillows, paying her by spitting at the pale face, the other had hounded her with his meaningless passion. But she had felt nothing. Feeling was dead, at last. She had peace. But sleep had gone away. She was glad to creep into Teddy's old chair, now—and rest.

"Why—she's dropped off to sleep," said Lizzie. "S-sh! Be quiet, Aggie. Worn through she looks, poor lass."

"It's th' fire," apologised Helen, and half-asleep as she was, drew closer into Teddy's chair, to get away from any human pity. Lizzie threw an old blue apron over her.

"Thy father's had time enough to gether twenty lambs up," she remarked to Aggie. "Eh, he's a grand un. He's in th' ale, somewhere."

She kneaded into her dough angrily, as if it were Teddy, and looked irritably at the darkening sky.

Helen did not hear her voice any longer.

She was startled awake by the yelping of a dog, mingling with a sad, trembling cry, and Teddy's boisterous laugh rolling a rich chord in with it all. The door slamming to in the wind, rattled the ornaments on the dresser.

"Break my granny's lustres, wilta, tha great foo'?" was Lizzie's greeting of the dripping wanderer.

"Daddy, did yo' find th' babby-sheep?" queried Aggie; then, seeing it, she gave a shriek of delight that made the rafters echo. He had slung it over his shoulder, where it gave forth that timid appeal. Staggering into the red circle of firelight, Teddy toppled his burden on the hearthrug, smiling at his wife, and saying foolishly, "We're allus at hoam when we're wanted, aren't we, lass?"

Lizzie viewed him, her hands muffled in dough.

161

"Wet inside an' out," was her verdict. "If ever a woman wed a foo', I did. If I'd bin tied to a cow's tail I'd ha' come off as weel."

"Th' owd ewe's dead as a door-nail," said Teddy, ignoring her anger. "Ay. Stiff yon at th' back of a rock, among that blasted snow that hasn't a' gone yet. Look after th' orphan, Lizzie, when I'm gone. For my days are numbered."

"Shut up, tha foo', or tha'll waken Helen," said his wife.

Teddy peered round the shadowy kitchen. At last he found her.

"Waken her?" said Teddy. "I'll kiss her, ne'er mind waken her. I've known her sin she were so high." In trying to fix the height from the floor he almost lost his balance. Lizzie helped him up.

"Go an' tumble on th' lamb," she scolded.

Teddy was looking at Helen, and scratching his head. She reminded him of something. He was staring over at her, where the lanky-legged lamb had crept near her, bleating in forlorn fashion, all legs and shivers.

"I've a pal outside," he said to Lizzie, sobering for a moment.

Lizzie pushed him down into a chair.

"He's whear he'll stop, then," she observed.

"But—" gasped Teddy.

"Tha fetches no drunken pals in here," she assured him.

"He's sober," stuttered Teddy, trying to shake himself free. "He's allus bin sober."

"Ay, you're a' sober, but it's when yo're dead," snapped Lizzie.

"But it's—" began Teddy despairingly.

"He's no good, drunk or sober, if he's a pal o' thine," said Lizzie conclusively. Teddy found out that he must be drunk. So soon as he got up, Lizzie pushed him down again, like a jack- in-the-box.

"'Tisn't ale makes a chap drunk," he informed her. "It's th' change o' air. I wor reight as rain outside. Lizzie, let him in—"

"No," said Lizzie.

"It's Martin," protested Teddy.

Lizzie let him go so suddenly that he fell back in his chair as though he had been released from elastic.

"Tha great foo'! Why didn't ta say so?" asked his spouse. She began to struggle with the remnants of dough left on her hands. Most of it was on Teddy's wet coat.

"He were on th' tops," said Teddy. "Eh, ay. Th' poor old ewe's gone. When they're dead, they're dead, a' reight, an' for a long time, too. Helen! Waken up! Eh, I knew thee when tha were a little lass, wi' big, hungered eyes, an' black hair like rat-tails, so straight. An' tha used to say 'Tiss Helen.' Helen, waken up."

The woman in the chair sat stiffly white. She had awakened. She heard Teddy's ravings without knowing their meaning. She had awakened, she who had imagined herself dead. She could hear Lizzie's voice calling outside through the wet greyness—"Martin, lad, Martin"—in the distance. She was alive, but buried—horrible truth. The stoical world she had built around herself when the living earth had turned, to dust and ashes had, in its turn, crumbled away from her.

Martin had come back. His footsteps had awakened her. He was only a few yards away. She wanted to rush to the door, hurl herself against it, keep him from entering. To have to meet him—like this! Outside, she could hear Lizzie's voice, talking, talking. Her own tongue stuck to the roof of her mouth. She had all the fear of going dumb that had been hers as Martin rushed away from her. She had gone back to that evening on the hillside, when she had staggered blindly through the wet grass, shouting his name. But she must sit still and smile now. What agony coming alive was! And she must not cry out, must not let them know that she was fastened up, alive. The gate creaked to the touch of those hands that had let go of hers in her need. The sound shuddered through her. She was fighting down a thousand years in herself, wrestling with the desire to scream, scream, and scream, till the air shouted back. She was beating with passionate hands against being walled up, alive, away from Martin, remembering all the time that she must smile, as dead women smile behind their veils in that still, tranquil way. That was his cough—abrupt, characteristic. Only—it was more hollow. His feet were on the flagstones now. They seemed to walk on her heart. It began to beat, great heavy strokes, sledge-hammer wise. She was holding herself down in Teddy's chair. The knuckles of her hands were whitening in their grip. She was strangling the self that was coming alive, as she sat there, trying to twist her white lips into a smile; the firelight became a dull, red blur. The heart-beats were thunder in her ears, now. Through the surging sound of it came the cry of the motherless lamb. The throbbing of her heart shook her to the centre. Always as she struggled against its agonised desire to burst, the scream would threaten to escape. Teddy was singing a country song, about two young lovers and a new moon.

The earth was rocking. A queer mist dimmed material objects. Then—Day's child stirred within her. Her nails bit into the wood of the chair- arms. Trapped! A rush of tears came to her eyes—the first drops of a tide washing slowly up from black caves of grief. With them came again the desire to scream till the hills shouted back the voice of her misery and shame. Panic came as she felt the stinging wet on her cheeks. She was—crying. They were coming. He was coming. The lamp would soon be lit. She must—smile.

"Come thee in out o' th' weet, lad," Lizzie was saying. "An' get that drippin' coyt off."

He came in. Helen could see nothing else but that dark figure. She was struggling frantically with her heart now, holding it back with clammy hands, fighting with it as with some desperate animal, that was mad to live. The sweat broke out on her brow, in her torment. She had to wrestle with the scream once more.

He was leaning against the dresser. Even in the uncertain light there was a broken look in the whole figure. The tides of chance had washed him back to Four Gates—a wreck. He had done this to himself, whilst to her—She was trying to hate him as fools and cowards should be hated.

"Here's another friend o' thine," said Lizzie, motioning towards Helen's corner.

Helen tried to lick her lips with her tongue. Both were dry as dust. But behind her eyes that tide of grief came creeping nearer to the brink. She had that to fight, also.

Martin's eyes were looking at her.

Teddy suddenly started up, saying, "Let's ha' a leet."

"Go an' break th' glass, wilta?" said Lizzie. "We're millionaires, we are."

"I'll leet that lamp or dee i' th' attempt," vowed Teddy.

Martin was still regarding Helen. He had not yet recognised her. But he soon would. She must speak, or he would think—he might think she cared a little. As the thought came to her she wanted to laugh; a great wave of laughter flowed through her. Cared a little! She was one great empty ache that she had to sit there in that chair, divided from him by a few yards. He was a wreck, but he was hers.

As she tried to find words the child within her moved again. She had an intense desire to strangle it, but the crying of the lamb on the hearthstone tore her betwixt rage and pity.

"How's ta like this sort o' weather agen, Martin?" she heard someone ask. Why—it was herself. She had really managed to speak. Her voice sounded, though, to have run miles ahead.

"Helen!" exclaimed Martin Scott. He was off guard. The word came to her telling her all. He spoke the word with the trembling eagerness of a starving man. Then, conscious of being too bold, he said, "It *is* Helen Mason, isn't it?"

"Helen Day," she corrected him, hearing her own laugh come back to her ears strangely. What a world of liars and hypocrites it must be, when men and women could act so, laugh so, with their very reasons swaying, their hearts breaking! The blood was singing in her ears, that intolerable desire to scream and to laugh was on her again.

In the background she could hear Teddy and Lizzie squabbling about the lamp-glass.

Crash!

"Thin glass, that," he grumbled.

Lizzie sat down.

"There!" she said despairingly. "I knew tha'd do it. Another sixpence gone bang. Chaps are noan content unless they're smashin' summat."

Helen heard herself laugh. Then she was conscious that Martin was coming to sit in the chair beside her. It was occupied by Aggie's doll. She removed it for him. To do so she had to half rise from her chair.

Her knees felt to shake under her. He sat down. The dampness that had come down with him from the tops rose from his old coat and touched her cheek. She could smell the tobacco on his coat.

"I'm sorry I broke th' glass, lass," came Teddy's voice humbly.

"Chaps is allus sorry when th' damage is done," sobbed Lizzie. "Sixpence!"

"I'll go to bed, lass," said Teddy penitently, and stumbled off upstairs. "It were th' ewe deein' made me get drunk."

"Tha didn't like America, then?" Helen heard herself asking.

"No," he answered.

He was looking at her with conscienceless hunger, eating her up with those eyes of his. They were on her hair now.

"You're thinner," he remarked.

"So are ta," she said.

"I'm as good as dead," he told her.

The tears and laughter struggled in her again. Lizzie was still sighing about the broken lamp-glass.

"Get away," she heard her voice running on, "Field thought he were done for, last winter. He'd a cough. But I made him honey an' butter, an' stood o'er him till he took it."

She was lying magnificently, her invisible self wondering, yet applauding her own cunning artistry, which conjured up to the lonely man so tender a domestic picture. She perceived his looking at her in puzzled fashion. He was not more surprised than she was. But he made no reply. His hand tapped restlessly on the chair arm.

"Now we'll ha' a leet an' some tay," said Lizzie, getting up from the floor. Aggie had held the candle whilst she swept up the broken glass.

Lizzie asked Helen about her way of jam- making.

Whilst she undressed Aggie, Helen and Martin sat in silence. From outside came the wind blowing from the hills.

"Good neet," said Lizzie to the little night-gowned figure. "No, tha doesn't take that nasty doll a-muckying th' clean pillows." Aggie went off sulking.

"Childer!" said Lizzie. "Eh, dear! They're like husbands. Them as hasn't got 'em can bring 'em up best. Tha'll know about it, Helen, soon—" She stopped, conscious of having let out the secret.

Helen's heart was breaking her to pieces almost. She could not see Martin's face. But she sat trying to smile, her nails at the wood of the chair again.

"Tha can help me to make tay," said Lizzie. Helen forced herself to walk, her limbs trembling under her. The rest of the scene—the lighting of the lamp, the tea, Lizzie pushing the cake across for her to cut Martin a piece, the gossip of Four Gates, her own laugh and voice far away from her, was all a nightmare. She even asked Martin how many lumps of sugar—as though she could ever forget. At last it was over. Lizzie got her to sew him a button on—they laughed because it was "sewing sorrow to his back." At last she was ready to go, standing cloaked, by the half-open door, eager to run, to get away—like a hurt thing wanting a hole.

"Martin'll take thee to where th' trap comes," said Lizzie.

Helen pushed back that sweeping tide of tears again. Relief was not to be yet.

Then they were out in the shadowy wetness. The Corple Stones loomed down on them, crushingly dark in the mist. A watery moon tried to pierce the clouds at intervals.

"Th' birds'll be back soon," said Martin's voice.

"Ay," she replied.

"Noan i' last year's nests," he said.

"What's th' good?" she asked rationally.

He was looking at her again, amazed at her calmness. She knew it. It sent that wave of laughter over her again.

He stood still. She paused also. He was going to mention that other life of theirs, those miserably sweet days in that dark house.

"Helen," he said huskily, "I've come a' these miles to see thee before th' earth's on top o' me. Say summat." He paused a moment. The skirl of the wind from the tops came to them, a solitary cry. He went on hurriedly. That dreary sound drove him on.

"I'm not axin' much," he said, standing with bowed head. "But—say summat, Helen, just that tha hasn't forgotten, that tha wouldn't wipe it out."

She was choking back those tears, wild to come to her relief, fighting that desperate heart of hers again.

Far off she heard her voice obeying that proud mind of hers, giving him the lie.

"I'm a respectable married woman, Martin Scott," it said, whilst that laughter tried to shake her again. A respectable married woman! The irony of it.

She saw him looking at her with hungry bewilderment of unbelief at this coarse stamp of hers on that old love of theirs. He had asked her for a crumb of remembrance. She had told him it was not respectable.

With this look, which seemed to last an eternity, he left her. "Good night, Mrs. Day," he said.

She moved away, dragging herself along by force. The passionate desire to rush after him, to make it up, as after their old quarrels and struggles, was tearing at her. But—she could not. The gate banged after it let him through. He was gone. She walked on a few yards, gagging herself with a mouthful of the cloak. Her limbs were tottering, the last bit of strength oozing, but she dragged herself a little further. Under a hedge where last year's leaves were drifted, she sank down. Her finger-tips clutched at the mist-sodden earth, clawed at it even as she had been clawed, the poor, bruised child of it. Convulsive sobs, ending in more convulsive laughter, tore themselves upwards from the heart to those pale lips. The whirlwind went over her. Then the sobs came slower, and yet more slow. The pulse of outward grief ran down. She lay with tear-blotted face, staring hopelessly up at the darkening sky.

After a time she arose, shaking the leaves from her cloak. She was talking to herself, with the habit of those estranged from their kind.

"It's a lie!" her lips writhed. "Nobody dees o' grief."

Far off she heard the wheels of the trap that was to take her back to Four Gates. She looked at the misty heights of the Corple Stones. But she had to go back. Four Gates and her man were awaiting her. Cowards ran away. She had been dead before. He had a live thing to torture now, but she must go back, to her own place, hell that it was. She was a respectable Four Gates woman, going home to her honest wedded husband, and to her little world, which she had made to eat its words that she had been mad on Martin Scott. As she went along she was straightening her dishevelled garments, pushing back the wisp of hair that hung drunkenly over her brow. She had been buried alive, but Four Gates must not know.

CHAPTER XII

DOCTOR GREAVES IS SORRY

IN the wood by the water red leaves were falling. Teddy Trip had asked Martin to stay on at Corple Stones Farm. He had been a good help. Teddy could get away oftener. Besides, Martin had made a clear forty pounds in the summer, for Teddy, at Brungerly Cattle Fair. Martin was fine on a farm. But he looked so ill that Four Gates was always rumouring his death. He was going up to Mason's farm now. He was going for his wages. He stumbled against a man half-way up the hillside.

"Which way to Day's?" asked a weak voice.

Martin told the man, and followed in his footsteps.

But Jim Brett travelled too fast for him. He wanted to get back to Sally, and had heard in the inn of the good luck of his old pal, Day. It was like a beacon in his misery. The hatred of Day in the village, mingled with admiration of him, had scared him not at all. Day and he had dossed together. He went on.

Martin followed.

Those wages of his were really an excuse for getting into the farm. Helen, so he had heard, was at death's door. He was crawling up the wet hillside to be nearer her, crawling ignominiously, with that cough shaking him, to be near the woman who cared nothing for him, who was bearing another man's child. He was going up to the farm to ask for his wages. As if he had not got them, to the full! In the inn he had heard from Andry, who was blind drunk, of how Helen had once tried to wed herself to him, Martin Scott. He hadn't even minded the publicity of the thing.

He was going up the hillside in answer to that call from the past. A gust of coughing seized him on the crest of the hill. Whilst he struggled in its grip a string of curses fell on his ears. It was the man who had preceded him, coming back, hope knocked out of him again. Day had laughed in his face and shut the door, saying he didn't know him.

Martin gave him a sixpence.

It was one Teddy had given him, with a cautious look not to let Lizzie know. He had taken it in irony of spirit. Cursing, the tramp went down the hillside—back towards Little Moreton.

Martin reached the white gate.

His hand felt the familiar notch in the third paling.

The dog was in its kennel. It sprang up, the heavy chain clanking at his approach.

He spoke its name.

It growled, menacing him.

It was a bad omen, he thought.

Even the dog had forgotten him.

If a dog forgot, how should a woman remember— remember and forgive everything? The lonely blackness of the night coiled itself round him, an inky, cold snake.

He placed his hand on the dog.

The growl in its throat grew deeper, then changed into a croon.

At that sound from the almost blind beast, the door opened. The old man had trailed himself to open it. It was one of his better days.

"Oh, it's thee, Martin," he said. "Come in."

For there were only three folk in the world brought that croon to the dog's throat. The sound had announced Martin.

Martin entered.

"Hello!" said Fielding Day, sitting by the hearth. He nodded coolly.

Martin nodded back, and sat down.

The sight of Day sitting in his old chair brought a maddening jealousy to him.

"I've come for my wages," he said, in his old monotonous way.

Mason grinned.

"Thy wages," he said pleasantly. "Well—tha'll get 'em if tha waits long enough. Most folk do."

The hollow man sitting at the back of the kitchen cleared his throat. Blast it! He was going to cough, going to exhibit his weakness before this strong, handsome husband of hers. He tried to stem it, but on it came, shaking him to bits. He struggled against it all the time, hating it like something human. At last he shook it off.

There was absolute silence in the kitchen.

Then he heard, from the room next the kitchen, his old room, the room in which he had slept on that first night at the farm, the voice of the doctor.

"Now, Mrs. Day—"

The feet of Andry's wife going over the floor went over his heart.

Fielding Day sat, trimming his nails.

Mrs. Day!

The title jabbed at Martin.

He heard Andry's wife tramping about the room again.

Then she came out, with a cup in her hand, and filled it from the kettle.

"How goes it?" asked old Mason. "Tarrible quiet amang it, isn't she?"

"Some is an' some isn't," she remarked.

"Ay," answered the old man. "Tarrible unnatural-like, it seems to me."

His hands were clutching and unclutching at the arms of the chair.

"She'll noan dee?" he questioned.

"It's bin a struggle, but I think it'll be a' reight," she said.

The clutching at the chair ceased.

"Seems queer she doesn't cry out like others," he said restlessly. Under cover of being anxious that all was well he was longing for screams of terror and agony.

"Some's doomber nor other some," said Andry's wife. "But most flesh an' blood cries out at th' finish. Some ca's o' their mothers, poor things, an' some ca's on th' Lord as has ne'er thought on Him for years."

She hurried away with the cup.

The three men sat in silence.

The whining plea of Nero came to them—somehow conscious of something going on.

Without asking leave Martin Scott went out, and unclasping the chain, brought in the dog.

Fielding Day looked across at the shadow of a man, sullen, ashen, at whose feet the dog had settled.

The two pairs of eyes met.

Volcanic fire smouldered in the depths of both.

"Sort o' free an' easy like," sneered Day. "Lettin' th' dog in without leave. We allus keeps it on th' chain."

The hollow man laughed.

"There's things can be chained an' things can't be chained," he said, in his husky voice.

"Shut up your gabble," cried the old man.

He was drawn between two ecstasies—the ecstasy that a storm was brewing between the two men, and that Helen might hear it in that other room, and the ecstasy of waiting for that cry which Andry's wife said all flesh and blood gave.

He was listening, listening with an intensity that gave him a burning look.

"What does ta mean by that?" asked Fielding Day of the hollow man.

Martin merely smiled.

"Get out o' here," said the boss suddenly, in a white fury.

"I were here afore thee," laughed Martin.

"I won't ha' my wife upset wi' hearing thee," said Fielding.

They were grinning at each other, now, like two animals, the man who had tossed away a human soul, and the man who had picked up the empty shell that had held it.

"I shan't shift off this chair till I'm ready," said Martin. His hand was caressing the dog.

The thing was crooning with an old delight—crooning and sniffing rapturously at him, at his dripping old coat, and the thin shoes that let the water in.

"Come under, Nero," commanded the boss.

The dog slunk a few inches from the feet of the broken man. Passion of an old worship and fear of punishment were clashing.

"Nero!"

Martin's husky whisper brought it back to his feet.

Fielding Day crossed to the corner, and took the ivy stick.

"Not wi' my stick," said the hollow man, in that monotonous voice. He had risen to his feet. The dog had risen to follow him, thinking he was departing.

"Why didn't ta tak' th' dog wi' thee?" jeered the boss.

Whilst all the time each knew that the reference was not to the dog at all.

"Shut up!" cried the old man.

From that room whose wall-corner came to his ingle-nook, he had heard a muffled cry.

"'Twould follow me a' the same," boasted Martin Scott.

Fielding grinned again. He had a fiendish look.

175

He had reached the stick.

The dog slunk away under the settle.

Fielding Day approached and tried to poke it out. But a growl, mingled with a whine of fear, was all the answer.

Martin Scott stood watching him.

The old look of iron control was on him.

But when Day had moved the settle and clutched the dog by its collar he crossed the kitchen.

"Touch that beast wi' my stick—" he began.

Fielding Day threw back his head and laughed. The next moment the ghost of a man had rushed at him. They closed, two jealous savages, swaying together, and the table with the red-globed lamp crashed over.

"Hell!" laughed the old man.

He trailed himself across the kitchen, and with a spurt of his old agility, inspired by the joy in his mind, he picked up the flaming lamp and, opening the door, flung it out into the wet garden.

There was only the light of the fire over the chaotic scene in the kitchen as he came back, walked carefully past the wreckage and the struggling men, to his chair.

"Now, fight, if you like, you devils!" he gibed at them.

Like the god of Hate himself, he sat back in his chair, listening to the music of those moans torn from the woman in that other room, listening to the broken panting of the man who had deserted her, and to the inarticulate curses of the man who had picked her up. He wondered if Helen had heard and recognised Martin's voice.

"Let go—"

It was Day's voice.

Martin's thin hand was at his throat. Then they had staggered, and rolled together on the floor.

Martin was on top.

The firelight made a bright patch of blood-red beside them. The black shadows danced over them.

"I'll—gouge thy e'en out," gasped Day. Martin laughed.
Day shook himself a little away from that hand.

They had forgotten the woman, now, as dogs forget a bone they quarrel about in the ancient lust of battle. Only the desire to hurt was there.

"Went away, an' came back," he laughed.

"Think she cares now? Tha'll be dead, man—dead, next spring. I've kissed her, man, I've beat her—I've done as I liked. She's bin mine, all mine, every cell o' her body—"

The taunting of his rival made Martin's hand slacken. His grip left the other's throat.

But he still knelt on Day.

"She's bin mine," he said, looking into the other's eyes.

Fielding Day was cunningly getting his leg around Martin's. From under the settle came the growl of the dog.

"I don't care a hang for thy metaphysical possessions," sneered the boss.

"A thing I've hold on, is mine. If I—"

With a subtle twist he half got from under Martin. Despite his words, there was demonic spite in his face. A swift moment and he was on top.

"Now, Scott," he said, in a voice of suppressed rage. "I'm a savage, an' tha's turned me into one."

He was pummelling into Martin's head.

The latter had his teeth gripped. No sound escaped them.

"Tha'rt not worth killin'," he said. "Tha'll soon be worm-fodder, wi'out my help. I've Helen. She's mine, just like a share's mine. I've got th' deeds. But just to teach thee for comin' here, an' orderin' th' dog in or out—"

His blows fell again.

Then, when he had spent himself, he got up. Martin Scott lay still.

"Tha's noan killed him, Field?" asked the old man.

He had realised that Day must have been very angry. Why? The old fear was back.

"I took care o' that," answered the other.

Martin got up from the floor.

The dog came creeping towards him, and began to lick his boots. He sat down again.

"Here, let's ha' thee out—" began Day, crossing to the grey man. Martin's face was bleeding badly.

Then the words died away.

Old Mason sat with a look of ecstasy on his face.

From that room stole a woman's cry of anguish, escaped from teeth bared in agony.

The three men were silent.

At the sound the dog walked to the door of the room, scratched, and whined at what it did not understand.

"Hell! If sh—sh—she should die," gasped the old man.

Divided in motives he had expressed what all three felt. Fielding Day's ambition limited, Mason's revenge to burn out without fuel, Martin—to die in an empty world of ashes, if one woman died.

They heard Andry's wife give a startled "Oh!" and the doctor's "Hush!" of warning.

Then into the silence that had seemed an eternity rang a piercing cry of blind appeal.

"Martin!"

The stranded woman had cried out to the dying man.

He had sprung to his feet at the call. Fielding Day sprang before him with a look of deadly hatred.

"She has just harked back," he said. "That's a'."

Martin leapt towards the door leading out of the farm.

When he had closed it after him to within a few inches, he said, "All thine, is she?" His husky laughter was shaking with joy.

Fielding Day's curse followed him.

The old man had risen as soon as Martin was gone.

"Tha'rt not i' love wi' her?" he asked, with a gimlet-like look.

Day pushed his hands into his pockets.

"If any man makes out he has claims on summat 'at's mine," he said, "I could kill him—like a rat. She's my property. An' for that cry o' hers—"

He cast a murderous look towards that closed door.

"Tha needn't fear," said Mason. "Tha needn't fear. She'll never leave thee for him. She'd pluck her heart out by th' roots first."

"How do yo' know?" queried Day.

"Because i' some things she fashions after me," said the old man. "That's why. An' that's why it's so sweet a cup."

He laughed that horrible silent laughter. Then they heard Andry's wife coming.

Both men turned towards her.

"Is't over?"

It was old Mason's voice. "Ay," said the woman.

The firelight leaping up showed her moved face. She had not been a midwife long.

"Dead?" asked Fielding Day.

There was dull horror in his tone.

She nodded her head.

"Dead. Helen dead!" gasped the old man, staring at her. There was a magnitude of anguish in the cry.

"No," said the woman. "Th' child, I mean. A little lad, too. Still-born."

"Th' child," he breathed. "I thowt—"

He sat him down again.

He had thought his life's work blown down, before the roof was on it.

"There's bin a rumpus, hasn't there?" asked the woman curiously.

"A bit o' bother about some wages Martin thinks he should have," said the old man.

"She heard him," said the woman. "Quick ears she have."

She eyed the two men narrowly.

"There's your pay," said Day's voice.

The curiosity went from her eyes.

"She mun be kept quiet," she said. "I'll stay an hour—then I mun see to 'em at home. I'll be back i' th' mornin'."

She filled a vessel with water to wash the dead child.

"It's a bonnie bairn," she said. "Perfect, too. But just—no soul in it."

Fielding Day was pacing backwards and forwards.

The doctor came out.

"These things will happen," he said. "It's a pity. Better luck next time."

He hurried away.

At the foot of the hillside a dark figure rose out of the wet grass.

"How is—Mrs. Day?" asked a man's voice. An'—"

"She'll come through," said the doctor. "The child was born dead. A great pity." He hurried on.

Martin Scott stared back at the farm. Then he went on through the darkness.

He had forgotten the dripping of the rain, and Day's blows. A deeper insult than he could deal had been dealt at the boss. He was the father to a dead child, and in her agony the wife of Brungerly's scourge and pride had called on the dying failure. His broken boots, letting the rain through, Teddy's telling him not to let Lizzie see that sixpence, his cough—all were forgotten. He was a man. A woman cared about him.

CHAPTER XIII

WOMEN AND DOGS—GO BACK

THE milk kits, scalded for the next day, were piled outside, with the lids off. A hundred eggs were ready for washing on the table, just gathered up. Abel Mason's bed had been changed and made.

"Are yo' better?"

Helen stood, cup in hand, looking down on the old man. He was coming from one of his intolerable attacks of neuralgia. He glared back at the look on her face. It was scarcely pity, and her query had been put as to any other human being in pain.

"Tak' thy face away fro' me," he hissed. Then the pain came on again, and she was dabbing the soft heat of the sponge against the nerves, whilst he was tortured with the resemblance to the other Helen—when she had looked softly at him. He repaid her by upsetting the cup over the bed, so that the bedclothes were stained with the vinegar. She was slaving night and day now to keep him clean and comfortable. He had half suspected once that Day gave her money to send some of the washing out. A bundle had come in, but Day swore it was old newspapers. Always his suspicions were on the scent now. Almost helpless, she attended him as if he were a baby—he, with the heart of a fiend. He had taken to telling Day obscene tales in her presence, to torture her that way.

She had an understanding of him lately, that maddened him. Her face never showed the disgust of the Pharisee. She tended him, pale and quiet and unemotional, treating his assumed vulgarity as part of his disease. She never spoke of her mother now, to torture him. She bore with him, greatest torture of all.

"I want to go to sleep now," he said.

She shaded the light by pulling the sheet to throw a shadow on his face. Her hands were bleeding with much washing and the cold winds. His latest torment had been to order Day to crumple clean collars up and trample them, to give her more to do. Her voice was trailingly weak at times. She had not quite recovered from the birth of that dead child. He had told Day another child would be a fine plan, but Day had put into him a fear of the death of their victim—with a half suspicion that Day was in love with her. It had become his torment, that thought. He was always watching, fearing, then finding he was wrong.

He awoke from a short sleep to see little Aggie Trip within the cottage.

"Mr. Scott's got pneumonia. He's deein.' Mother says will yo' come?" she was repeating. "An', please, I've to go back on Jerry's cart—if yo' don't come. Mr. Scott keeps sayin' 'Helen!'"

Then she turned to Helen.

"What's hurt your face?" she asked.

"I tumbled, Aggie," Helen said, something palpitating in her voice. It was harder to lie to Aggie than to Four Gates. Abel Mason's fist had done that. It was the greatest insult she had known—because Four Gates could see she had that mysterious thing, a black eye. Day would be suspected of it. To receive a black eye was to lose caste. But what had racked her most was the crushing coil of Day's tenderness. She felt sometimes that she must run away screaming from his very presence. She was alive, now.

"Mr. Scott kissed me better when I fell," said Aggie. "Mother says he's goin' to heaven. Is he?"

"I shouldn't wonder. He'll be th' fittest there," said Helen. "Isn't heaven a nice place, then?" asked Aggie.

"I want you to say this after me—and tell Mr. Scott," said Helen, passing this query. "Mrs. Day is very sorry, but she's too busy to come."

Aggie piped the callous answer to that dying plea.

"Ay, tha can say it, Aggie," laughed the old man.

She started back.

"Fleyed of a poor harmless old man like me?" he said, in a soft voice. But Aggie still shrank.

"He's just a poor old man that's poorly, Aggie," said Helen. "Give him a kiss."

There was gentle malice in the words. Flesh and blood could not resist some antagonism to the old man, at times.

Influenced by Helen, whom Aggie held a very gospel of truth, the child pursed her lips and neared the bed, shutting her blue eyes as she went. A devil in hell threatened with a lash of fire could not have looked more evil. Aggie recoiled.

"No," said Abel Mason, "I don't like kisses, Aggie. There are sweeter things. Keep thine, an' do thy best an' worst wi' 'em, some day."

Helen was putting on cloak and veil.

Twilight was falling, but the black eye was prominent. She had not been down in the village for days.

"Field'll kill thee if tha goes," said Mason. He was purple with helpless rage.

"You'll bring another stroke on one o' these days," she warned him dutifully. "You needn't fear. I'm not goin' to Martin. There's one stronger nor Field'll stop me. Mysel'!"

He heard her getting the hens in. They had piled all the farm work on her too, save for a little help from Amos Trip, who milked and herded.

When she had gone, Mason cursed at Day for his tardiness in coming from Brungerly. It was Stocktaking Day. Then he consoled himself by planning other tortures for Helen. Whilst all the time he was counting the steps Helen made down to the village to put Aggie on Jerry's cart. A step sounded.

"Where is she?" he roared.

Then his neuralgia came on.

"Martin's—" he began, shouting it out in his agony.

"She's gone to that sucking—" began the other.

There was savage passion in his voice, there was feeling—beyond mere power of possession. But when Mason looked at him he was grinning in the old way. Only the ghost of that fear clutched at the old man again. He spoke of Aggie and Jerry's cart.

"There were a child on by hersel'," breathed Day in relief. "Hell! I didn't want that traunch—after the day I've had." The fear died down again in the old man's heart. He knew Day liked comfort.

"She took Nero, so she'll not ha' gone far," said Day. "Not wi' yon eye. She's proud as a hell-cat. She'd ne'er show Martin that, either." Mason laughed—and Day grinned. Then they heard Nero clawing the door.

"She's gone, then," said Day, in a still voice.

He stood looking at Mason.

"I'll get her before she lands," he vowed. "No man's got to trespass on my property."

He rushed out.

Mason was laughing.

He lay through the hours, between anguish of fear and rapture at Helen's punishment to come. In his attempts to reach a cup of barley water it spilled when near his lips. Then he raged that his hated cupbearer might be touching lips with Martin. He turned to plan again, afraid of madness, at the thought.

Nero's whine of welcome startled him.

It was Helen.

She entered and poked up firelight on the darkness. She stood by the fire, ashen about the mouth. She was twisting her wedding-ring round and round her finger. Day's step made her start. Her nerves were going, too, grinned the old man to himself, going as Martin's had gone, under the long strain.

She went to bed soon after.

"Got her goin' through the farm-gate," said Day.

"Did ta kick her?" asked Mason.

"I gave her a knock on th' other eye," Day told him, with his old brutality of look. "An' now I'm goin' to sleep th' sleep o' th' just. Martin'll be dead i' th' mornin'."

"He may give a bit more sport yet," said Mason anxiously. "But—I'm fleyed 'at he's nearly done."

Day took his candle.

He came downstairs soon afterwards.

"Locked out," he said, and put on his shoes to go to the tool-shed. Some minutes later the sound of the splintering of the wood of a door rang through the house.

Then all was silent.

In the grey dawn Day came down.

"Has she gone out?" he asked.

"Eh?"

Mason's voice was hoarse.

"She's not yon," jerked the boss.

As he spoke he was donning jacket and cap. Mason crawled out of bed and looked from the doorway to see him running down the hillside.

The trick of Helen to lock Day out and get the door smashed so that the key couldn't be hidden, had succeeded.

By hedge, dyke, and stone wall the boss went straight to Corple Stones Farm. The brightening landscape was a flash before his eyes. He stopped to regain breath and calmness by the white gate. A cock was crowing. He passed up the hill slope. The lamplight came under the white window blind as he neared the farm. He ought to have rushed into the place. But he wanted to know. A jealous crave was in his blood, a mad pulse. He peered under the window-blind, getting a full view of the interior.

She was there, veiled to hide that blackened flesh, sitting with the calm, hard attitude habitual to her. The lamp was on the table beside her. Martin was laid back on his couch pillow, his eyes closed.

From upstairs came Lizzie's sleepy voice:

"Shout if he worsens, Helen," she said. "An' mak' thysel' comfortable. Pu' thy cloes off, an' get a sup o' tay."

Helen had just arrived, Day guessed, and Lizzie, dead-beat, had gone to lie down for an hour, unless— Martin was seized by the death-struggle.

He was in time for the full scene.

It seemed an hour of waiting to him before Martin's eyes unclosed. There was a start as his gaze fell on the face of the veiled woman. Day realised that when last he had looked up it had been to see Lizzie's ruddy countenance.

"So—tha's come," said the hollow man.

He had *tha'd* her, as in the old days.

It was significant of the barrier he imagined her coming had broken down.

She nodded.

Martin's dark eyes were on her veiled face.

"Pu' that thing off," said the husky voice fretfully.

"It's a' reight," she answered.

There was something in her tone he could not understand. It was not coldness, or aloofness. It was a sound as of something that came, not from the heart, but the mind, something calculating, almost mathematical.

"How long can ta stop?" he asked. "Till th' finish?"

The woman turned her head, looking more fully at the ghastly man.

"If tha dees sharp," she said.

An agony shot into Martin's face.

She had come, but—

"I'll do my best," he said sullenly. Then his mood changed.

"Let's see thy face, Helen," he begged passionately. "I'll be a long time dead."

"Tha can't," she said, finality in her voice.

"Shake this pillow up," he asked.

The strategy of despair was in the plea.

Shaking his pillow she must come a little nearer to him, at least.

She placed her arm under the pillow, raised him, bending over him, but in such a manner that the helpless man did not even touch her garment, though a whiff of sad, sweet lavender came to him from her bodice. He closed his eyes, sniffing it.

Then he said pettishly, "What's ta ha' lavender amang thy cloes for?"

Perhaps, always, down in the dark of the tomb, that maddening smell of lavender would disturb his rest.

"Put me back," he asked wearily.

There was silence again.

"Is there aught tha wants?" asked Helen, with a nurse's interest.

"Ay," he answered.

"What?" she asked, her glance going towards the table, loaded with medicine and nourishment.

"A touch o' thy lips before th' coldness is on mine," he asked. There was sullen despair, mingled with a cry of hope, in the husky tones.

The man under the window made the slightest movement towards the door. Then as the window-stones obscured his vision, he moved back again.

"Why should I?" asked Helen. "Tha can't talk like that."

The chill respectability of a Four Gates matron was in her voice.

"Go away!" cried Martin.

There was fierce agony in his voice.

She rose, as to depart.

"No!" he cried. "No. Don't leave me. I—oh, this is hell." The last four words writhed themselves upon the silence.

"Let me sup," he asked presently. "That barley-water—"

She reached the cup to him, her arm under the pillow, and was placing it to his lips.

With a supreme effort of flesh and will, his finger, a burning stick of bone and skin, coiled itself round hers. She tried to withdraw it.

"Don't!" he begged.

She did not answer.

"I can hear thy heart beatin'," he said.

His eyes were trying to penetrate the veil now. Her face was whiter. He could see that. There were signs that she felt. He might gain that heaven—a kiss of hers, before going into the dark.

"Arta goin' to sup this stuff?" she asked in a steady voice. "An' let go—or I'll ca' Lizzie down an' say tha'rt ramblin'."

The two pairs of eyes met in conflict.

The fear in the man's eyes grew.

Helen, freeing her finger, set the cup on the table.

With a groan of fatigue, Martin's eyes closed. He lay back, very still. He was asleep, with the suddenness of weakness. The woman was watching the clock, and listening to his breathing. Now that Martin was asleep, she drew nearer to the lamp. Day could see her face— the agony on it, even through the veil. She held the lamp nearer to Martin, to observe changes in his face. Setting it down, he saw her hand pressing to still her heart-beats. She half rose. With her handkerchief she wiped the grey brow of sweat, listening again to the breathing. Then, looking round, fearful that the walls might see her, she pressed the damp handkerchief against her throat and nuddled against it, then slipped it within her bodice.

"Martin!"

The man at the window heard this, after a long silence.

The man she called did not move.

She bent nearer, listened to his breathing.

"Martin!' she said, somewhat louder.

There was only silence.

The wind rattled a back window somewhat. She was bending close to him now.

Day knew what was in her mind. It was in his mind also. Death might have come after that last futile struggle of Martin's to keep her finger within his.

"Martin—Martin Scott!"

Her lips were close to his ear now. There was a thin note of rising panic in the cry. Then, she had hold of him by the shoulders. She was shaking him, shaking him and calling in that low, quaking voice of fear, in that flood of absolute terror. He did not move.

Day heaved a breath of relief.

With a cry full of desolate remorse, she set her lips to Martin's.

Their warmth brought him back to consciousness, his eyes unclosed, their dark misery brightening into ecstasy. He saw her, palpitating, wild with passionate grief—surprised her at the moment of her terror.

"Tha'rt—tha'rt not—dead," she gasped, covered with shame.

He clutched at her as she was drawing away from him.

"Happen I—were," he said, breathing quickly. "Happen—tha steered me as I were goin'. I—Helen!"

The terror of her shamed pride, taken in its fortress, communicated itself to him. His cry on her name was grovelling.

"I shall soon be dead," he said. "Forgie me."

She had drawn herself free, a tall, black figure.

Low sobbing breaths came from her.

"Oh!" she cried. She burst into convulsive tears.

Sinking on her knees, she had drawn his head into the crook of her arm. Unveiled, and with eyes of generous tenderness, eyes that might be those of the old Helen's, she was looking down on him. She was kissing him like a wild thing. It was so torrential that Day stood dumbfounded. An avalanche had moved.

"I—can't stand—more joy, Helen," he heard Martin gasp. "It'll kill me—an'—I want to live."

Then the boss rushed at the door, and shook it in its socket.

"Who's there?" asked Helen.

"Thy husband," he said. "Open this door, or I'll batter it down."

"Wait a minute," she said.

He heard her footsteps draw towards Martin again. She had gone back, with her husband at the door. Wild with jealousy, after one desperate lunge at the heavy farm door with his fist, he rushed back to the window.

Helen had forgotten his existence.

She was rubbing her cheek against Martin's, as she knelt at his side.

"'Twere th' seet o' Jerry's cart—the tag-end o' it swingin' away to th' road led to thee, made me follow," she was saying. "But I didn't think to—"

Then, "Tha can't dee, now, Martin. Don't—go away—agen."

Then, with shuddering reproach, "How could ta leave me, Martin?"

They were kissing again, kissing like two children after a quarrel. Helen was sobbing, and smiling, and stroking Martin's face.

"What's that wi'?" asked Martin, noticing the blackened flesh, suddenly.

Then Day's fist crashed through the window.

"This is where I come in," said his voice, murderously still in tone.

"Now, open this door. Tell her to open it, Scott. If tha doesn't—I'll swing for her."

"Open it, Helen," said Martin's voice.

"Let him," she said. "What does it matter?"

She was thinking of Martin's soon having to die.

"Another kiss, then," she breathed, in answer to his look. Fielding's hand was ripping at the blind, now bare to his grasp.

"It's all reight," she said, opening the door suddenly. "Tha can come in."

He came in.

"I could tear thy pluck out, Scott," he said briefly. "But 't isn't worth th' trouble. Tha'll be worm-fodder inside twenty-four hours." Then he turned to the woman. "Now," he said, "arta ready?"

There was death in his glance for defiance.

Under the boss the outcast's carelessness of life was stirring—the recklessness that he had learnt in the tramp-hole, where life did not count.

"I'm comin'," said the woman who had defied him.

There was hidden satisfaction in her tone.

She backed towards the door, her eyes on Martin.

"Ay," he said, in answer to her look.

Day started.

No word had been spoken by Helen.

But Martin had caught the burning agony of her look lest he should die. He had smiled hopefully that he would get well, if possible.

"If ever she comes again, Scott," said Day, "if tha's only five minutes to live—I'll end thee."

It was his way of barring Helen, by fear for Martin.

Then Teddy Trip had thumped down the wooden staircase, one foot coming first all the time.

He regarded Day—and the window.

"What th' hell's up?" he asked. "Has ta smashed my window?"

Day tossed half a sovereign down on the table.

"Thee harbour my wife at your place till after Scott's stiff," he said. "An' thine hasn't a name to cover hersel' wi'."

"I'll let thee know I'm a respectable woman," shouted Lizzie. "Just wait till I've gotten my stays on." Then she gasped at mentioning her stays.

"Come on!" said Day brutally, and dragged at Helen.

It was full daylight as they got out.

The Corple Stones stuck up into the sky.

One stone, almost unnoticed at any other point, stood black and weird, by some strange effect of cloud and sun taking the curious look of a horned Mephisto, with rigid lines, the sharp chin protruding into and against the heavens, defiant even in death.

When the gate banged after them, and the hens fluttered within the cote at the sound, Day turned to Helen.

"Give us that rag tha stuffed inside thy bodice," he said.

She took it out and gave it to him.

Life had a sudden sweetness come into it. Martin still breathed. Who knew? It did not seem that he could die, now.

Then, across the morning upland rang Lizzie's voice, sharp with its message:

"Helen—Martin's goin'," she cried.

There were two swift opposing movements.

Day and Helen were struggling against each other. But the man's grasp was a vice.

"Cat!" he jerked. She had clawed his face.

Her throat was torn by jagged sobs.

Day forced her along.

Teddy Trip came running after them.

"Lizzie's mista'en, Helen," he panted. "'Twere just a bad bout. We'll let thee know—somehow."

He had turned round, and Day's fierce glance fell on his stolid, broad back.

"If he lives," said Day, "it's a' th' same to thee, Helen. If tha takes off wi' him, I'll find you, and he'll not boast o' it longer nor two minutes. An' 'twould be a' th' bitterer for thee to lose him then."

*

They went on in silence.

She knew he spoke the grim truth.

If Martin should die now, it would be harder than had he died before she had kissed him as she thought him gone. If they stole happiness from the altars of the grim gods of their unfortunate destiny, it would be harder still to have the cup shattered at their first draught.

When they reached the farm, Day gave a report to Mason, still holding Helen's elbow.

"She wants a hidin'," said Mason. "An' *I* can't gie it to her."

Fielding Day took the dog whip from the wall. The rage he had hidden from the farm near the Stones, all these silent miles, blazed out of him.

Time after time the lash coiled round her.

Like an unrepentant dog she took the punishment sullenly. Only when a faint cry broke from her lips Day hurled the whip away.

"That's it," applauded Mason.

Day hurled the whip away. If the stick had beaten himself at his own command, his face could not have been more dour. When Helen had crept away, and he fancied the old man asleep, he took something from a drawer, hurling it into the fire.

"What's that?" asked Mason, alert, from his bed.

"Pills," said Day laconically. Mason was dubious.

Day poked it out of the fire to show him, that wooden box, holding its charred emptiness to him. "Pills," he read on the blackened label.

"Ay," he said, his fear subsiding.

It was a pill-box.

But it had held a secret gift Day had bought for Helen, out of his own money, from that which he earned himself, the sum he had begun to set apart from the sums doled to him by the old man. It was a trinket, such as Four Gates lads would buy their lasses to wear about their necks. Sweat of his had purchased it.

CHAPTER XIV

AT THE ELEVENTH HOUR MARTIN DECIDES TO LIVE

THE red October sun, one of its curves flattened by a cloud that was trying to break itself on the heights of the Corple Stones, sent a crimson glow into Lizzie's kitchen. That always-busy woman was sorting out hard grubby apples such as grow wild in the neglected farm-orchards of the north, for no other purpose but to provide additional pig-fodder. Whenever she found what she termed a decent apple, bang it went into a tub under the table beside which she stood. The rest went into the fire, which was built half-way up the chimney, to dry a great heap of rushes and bracken for cattle-bedding.

The bang of the apples falling into the tub, the spluttering of those in the fire, mixed in with the tick of the clock and the pipe of a cricket in the warm ashes. Lizzie had put on her best Sunday apron; Aggie was wearing a new blue ribbon on her curls. All this was in honour of Martin Scott's recovery. Teddy was out taking the summer's growth from the hedges, making ditches for the winter rains. No one would buy his farm.

"Don't keep flackin' about," Lizzie scolded Martin. "Th' doctor said a chill might finish thee. Eh, dear, chaps are th' restlessest things God ever made."

Martin gave no answer. Swaddled in rugs and blankets on the couch that faced the farm window, he was staring into an ashen sky, where the sun would soon go down behind the Stones.

Lizzie sighed. Martin had not had a word to throw to the cat, all afternoon. The way he had tossed about had almost broken her heart.

"That'll be thy father," she told Aggie. Aggie ran out to look. She flew back.

"It's Helen," she announced, and was about to run off again, to meet her.

"Come thee back," commanded her mother; she turned towards Martin on finishing these words.

"Aggie an' me's goin' to gether moar apples," she told him, with a look that said he didn't deserve it.

"Thanks," he smiled.

"Keep out o' th' draughts," she warned him, and went off, to dodge into the orchard without Helen seeing them. She had a pleasure in leaving the two together. She had not forgiven Day his breaking of their window.

It seemed an eternity to Martin before the door-latch moved to Helen's hand. He had crawled from the couch, throwing aside the rugs, and trying to fix himself in Teddy's chair and appear at his best, with human shame at being so weak. Looking like two laths nailed together, as Lizzie said, his anxious, hungry gaze was glued to the doorway she would pass through.

The door opened, closed again.

She came straight towards him.

The sight of her face gave him a shock, hurt him like a physical blow. She sank on the rug near his chair, clutching at his hand like a wild thing.

"Get me out o' this, Martin," she breathed, rather than spoke. "Get me out o' it, somehow. It's drivin' me crazy—or maybe I'm crazy now. Let's get to th' end, no matter what it is. If it's th' grave, let's get into that, an' ha' done wi' it. Maybe they'll bury us together. No, no. Field wouldn't do that." She stared into the fire. There

196

was silence between them save for her reiterated plea to him to get her out of the misery he had brought upon her. Woman-like, she thought her broken god could perform miracles.

He had refused her the best.

His pride forbade the offering of the worst, a broken body, a mind embittered by those years in which he had drunk the dregs of life, and still been thirsty. The old habit of thinking came to him. He was trying, to defend her from this hungry, but unworthy self of his, as he had fenced to defend himself from her.

"Whear can we go? There's nowhere to run to," he said, chillily rational.

She rose, tall and straight, her head flung back, her face with that frantic look.

"Speak like that to me again," she said, "an' tha'll never see me again."

Staring into the fire, he crumpled up miserably.

"I can't work for thee," he jerked.

"Tha'll not need," she assured him significantly.

"I couldn't ha' thee work for me," he said calmly, as stating a chemical fact.

"Tha'll not need," she said, faintly smiling. Then, with desperate energy she sank on the rug again, clasping her knees with those thin hands of hers. Her chin was leaning on them. Her eyes stared wildly into the fire.

"Look here," she said fiercely, "I've had enough on it, Martin. Enough o' th' hypocrisy an' shame on it, enough of wantin' to be here an' stayin' yonder, an' wonderin' how much more to suffer yet. I can't bear th' crawl o' his fingers about me. I can't. I'm a honest woman. I wasn't cut out for it. An' I'm not goin' to slink here, like a guilty thing, to catch seet o' thee now an' then. Let's end it. Field'll kill us. But we'll not run away fro' him or Four Gates. We'll be together, as we were meant to be, an' pay th' price. Let's be what we were meant to be, an' then face Four Gates—an' him."

197

She was asking him to go and be killed, along with her. She was mad, must be mad. She was all his. They were equals, the mad woman, the one-lunged man. Besides—six years of life, pauperised, on another man's hearthstone! The Trips were kind. They wanted him to stay, poor as they were. That was a grimmer tragedy than to be killed. It appealed to his mood. To be kicked out by Day and have Helen tortured—No. To be killed along with her, and have the laugh at him that they went together—Yes.

"Lass!" he murmured, slipping a weak arm around her neck.

"Tha'll go back on me!" she whispered, unbelievingly.

He took her face between his hands, made her look at him. A relief at some end in sight was upon him. It took away that hopeless, trapped feeling. They were going to meet the gods who had laughed at them, to offer them the remains of the sacrifice.

"For better, for worse," he said. Then, "Seemingly we've curst one another, instead o' blessin', burnt one another instead o' healin'. There's nowt left but th' worst. But I'll take thy worst, an' thankful. I'm not much. An' there's things I ought to tell thee—" He stared into the fire, frowning, the horror of those nights when he had tried to choke her memory, reviving.

She laid her fingers across his lips. There was neither scorn nor pity in her look, but a weary, pagan disdain.

"I know," she said simply. He started. "I guessed. What's it matter, anyhow? It's all just as it happens. What's it to do wi' me? Am I a Christian? What's thy morals to do wi' me?"

There was fierce protest in her voice, now.

He looked at her. The distracted expression on her face was abating. He was beginning to realise that she was not mad, only desperate. He was beginning to realise the simple strength of her. The splendour of her rushed at him, dazzling him. The courage of her put him in awe. This was the woman whom he had argued to himself about, for five years. Physical weakness overcame him. He burst into tears.

"Christ!" he stuttered. "What a mad foo'l!"

It was his epigram on himself.

"Don't touch me. I'm not worth it," he said moodily.

She became a child, then, wiping his eyes as she had once done when he wept about his dead mother, on coming to the farm.

"Th' worst to offer," he said bitterly.

She was rubbing her cheek against his hand.

"This is th' best," she said, smiling. "It's what they've all to take i' Four Gates, those pairs that live quiet lives, an' dee quiet deaths. They've got to get down to one another's worst, an' be glad on it. But oh, Martin, if I could only live years an' years an' years, wi' th' smoke goin' up fro' our chimney, an' saying 'Good mornin'' to the other women as I bought in for dinner, as happy as them, an' as miserable when we'd had words—an' to grow owd together, an' see thee in th' nook, an' ax thee o' a mornin' how thy cough were, an' thee after my—rheumatics—"

She choked back childish tears, smiling wistfully.

"I never wanted anything up i' th' air," she confessed. "Just common things, an' a common life. But, ne'er mind—it's done wi', now. To-neet 'll finish it. I feel it—here!" She laid her hand on her breast.

Martin was staring at the ring on her hand.

"We'll leave it, i' some water, somewhear," she told him, following his glance.

"Let's go," said Martin, rising. "Help me into my coat—Teddy's coat, I mean."

He was without shame of his dependence, his having to be helped, now. He was her equal, at last.

They looked at each other by the light of the fire.

She went to him with the little croon in her voice. Then she laughed, softly.

"I feel clean to-neet," she said. "It isn't like there'd be any botherin' to-morrow, an' Four Gates gapin' at us. It'll all come out. It's th' only thing I've been fleyed on. It's because I've lived i' Four Gates. But—we'll be dead. An'—it's when I'm livin' I care about, most. I want to be happy—once. Tha'll kiss me, as we were meant to—an' it's finished. It's so simple."

"How?" he looked.

"If tha goes, I go," she said convincingly. He asked no further questions.

"I wonder," she began wistfully. Then, "It's hard not to hope, isn't it?" There were tears in her eyes again. A white passion swept over her, born of her indignities.

"I wish him dead!" she exclaimed, in that intense way. "I wish him dead."

"Don't let's waste time," said Martin.

They passed through the doorway into that red and grey world, with the ball of fire in the sky, and the crushing heights of the Corple Stones looming upon them.

Martin leaned upon Helen. They were holding hands—palm to palm. A mouthful of that mist might kill him, so the doctor had said. But there was nothing to be afraid of, since they were together, and so near bidding the world good-bye. Helen was happy. So was he. There was no condemnation of Four Gates to hide from. They would live, love, and pay the royal price of it. It wasn't the Petty Sessions, or the Divorce Court—or any of the sordid mix-ups of modern life. It was to snatch a mate—and die for it, the woman going into the unknown with the one she cared most for.

"Lass!"

The tender intonation stole to Helen's ears. He felt that she smiled, rather than saw it. The shadows were deepening, and the mist.

Some kind of old antagonism felt to have passed from the face of the earth to those two. Slowly, almost inch by inch, they crept up to the heights they had loved from childhood. On gaining the top they stood still, looking over the dark expanse of the moor. A few pools shone red, catching the glow of the sinking sun. Over the black ling the grouse screamed "ga-bak, ga-bak, ga-bak." The cry was borne away on the wet wind.

Hand in hand they went on, until they reached a forest of bracken on the slopes. It was almost dark by this. They could scarcely see each other's face. Amidst the bracken Helen spread her cloak, to check the rise of the dew.

"It's dry," she told Martin. "An' flesh an' blood's warm. Cuddle down, Martin." There was peace in her voice.

They crept together. The ghostly rustle of the dead bracken came to them, and at wide intervals the "ga-bak" of the grouse. Like two lost children they crept into each other's arms, and were comforted. The sun went down, the earth grew colder. Watery gleams came from the moon, shining through the vapours. Through the night they talked, or were silent, huddled together, Teddy's coat buttoned round them both, Helen's hair a muffler for Martin's neck. They spoke of all that had happened to them, the inevitableness of this end, the glory of having come together at last, though for such a little time. They watched the grey dawn creep up, the sky changing to opaline splendour, the valley showing itself through chinks in rolling clouds, a dream-world brightening into sunlight at their feet.

The curlew's weird call came to their ears.

They were both thinking the same thought, and read it in each other's eyes.

"Bonnie!" said Helen, and stretched out her arms to the world. Then she laughed, rather shakily.

The little pools lit up one by one; the wings of birds were mirrored in them.

"We'll go, now," said Helen. "If Field's set out after us, he'll ha' bin without bite an' sup, maybe, an' him so helpless."

201

She referred to her father.

"Martin," she murmured, as if remembering something non-important, "I forgot to tell thee—he isn't my father. I found it out one neet—comin' downstairs for a drink o' water. He were sat over th' fire, talkin'— tellin' it to his shadow on th' wall. It were just after I took Day. An'—It's made me able to bear wi' him."

"Then it were a' for nowt!" said Martin hollowly.

"But he told us—that time we came fro' th' fair—" he muttered again.

Helen explained in a few words.

"For nowt," he echoed, the irony of it sending him nearly out of his senses.

"There's somebody comin'," he said suddenly. "Look!"

Together they peered down into the film that half hid the hill slopes and the vale.

"It's him," said Helen. "An' he's forgotten to put his lantern out. It looks sickly, Martin. It looks like a death-candle at th' burn. Look how steady he comes on! I'm—I'm fleyed!" There was a shudder in her voice. The sweetness of life had turned her coward, for a moment.

Martin tightened his grip on her shoulders.

"I'd give two off my six years for a stick!" he said.

They moved further up the slope, crept through the bracken. Amidst their agony they kissed convulsively, holding each other's hands. By peering through the bracken and down the edge of the heights, they saw that steady figure coming on.

"It's no good fightin' him. He's got a revolver," said Helen. "I know."

"He's makin' straight for this bracken patch," he answered.

Helen was leaning against him.

"Let him come," she said. "I—I can't suffer any more, Martin. Will—will it hurt much?"

"No worse than havin' a tooth pulled, a soldier once told me," said Martin, staccato-fashion.

Then he said, "Curse th' lost years! Curses on me for a mad foo'! Gi'e us thy lips. Just when he gets ower th' edge, we'll kiss, an' shut our e'en—"

"I shan't be able to shut mine," said Helen hysterically. "I allus want to look—what's comin'."

Then she tore herself from his embrace like a mad thing. Standing up, her black hair blowing about her in the morning wind, her dress fluttering, her look went downwards to the approaching figure.

He saw her.

They caught his triumphant shout on the wind. He made a move towards his weapon. But the mist came down between.

Helen's voice came to Martin where he lay near the edge, unable to get nearer, a gust of coughing seizing him, tossing him about like a leaf, whilst he wept and clutched at the dead bracken in his humiliation of weakness.

"I'm not thine," she called, in an ecstasy of victory. "I'm Martin's, all Martin's. He's here wi' me. We've bin here a' neet."

A shout of rage came from the man in the mist.

"We're like quail o' th' moor," she called again, peering down through the mist. "An' when we're dead, we're mates still. Come an' kill us. We don't care. We've lived."

There was a report from the revolver—a blind shot into the mist.

"I'm here yet," she called. "Thinkin' o' Martin, yet."

A cry left her lips. Martin heard it. He gave a yell of fury between two bursts of coughing.

"I'm not hurt," she called to him. "Summat's happened. He's fallin—'"

They heard the clattering of stones down the track Day was climbing. Then there was a yell, and silence.

Helen looked over the edge and went back to Martin.

"He's fallen," she said. "No. I didn't push him. He fell. He were yards away. The mist lifted. Summat got up out o' th' grass."

Martin came to the edge and looked over.

"Th' lamp's fired," said Helen. She was speaking with difficulty. Then she said, "Could a man fall so far—and not be dead?" Martin shook his head.

"I mun be sure," she said.

"Look!" said Martin. The mist had lifted again.

A man was almost leaping down the hillside, crashing through the dead bracken in his hurry to get away.

"Somebody's done it," said Helen. "Let's get away from here."

There was an uneasiness in her tone. It was hard to believe Day was dead. She feared his getting up again.

"I want to look," she said, once.

"Better not," said Martin significantly. "Th' sooner we get away th' better."

She looked at him.

"Let's get back to Four Gates, then," she said. "Th' old man'll be hungry an' thirsty. But I couldn't go back—wi'out thee, Martin."

They passed away from the tops where the grouse feeding, feeding, as though they would never leave off, made the morning air astir with life. Sometimes, as they went down, they paused to touch hands, lips again. They alighted some hundreds of yards from where that figure lay, the lamp smouldering out.

"I've got to see," breathed Helen, and ran from Martin's hold.

She came back to where he waited.

"It's awful. He's dead," she said. "It's true, Martin. We—we're goin' on livin'. Oh!" She drew a deep breath of joy, looking at the sun—then gave a little shuddering sigh, drawing nearer to Martin.

"I wish we could just live quiet th' rest of our lives," she said. "I'm—tir't."

CHAPTER XV

LOVE TRIUMPHANT

THE little grey village was opening its doors to the sun, letting out breakfast smells. Many faces peered from the tiny-paned, shining windows, as Helen and Martin passed through the lanes. According to Teddy Trip's cousin, Margaret Trip, Martin looked as though he had "tumbled off a flittin'," whilst the woman who walked at his side seemed to have lost her e'en to all but him. It was a new Four Gates to Helen Mason. She was no longer afraid of it. She had Martin. With him she could live anywhere. She had discovered that Four Gates had just meant—Martin Scott. She was not afraid of it. But she was glad to get to the path leading up the hill to the farm. She could rest her hand within Martin's, then. They had all the fear joy brings to those long desolate.

Reaching the farm-gate, Martin paused. Momentary shame revived in him again. The broken man's humiliation shone in his eyes. In this moment of agony Helen's eyes caressed him. He smiled, and passed in after her.

They found the kitchen door ajar, swinging to and fro in the wind, just as Day had left it in his rush from the house.

Helen entered first.

She expected to find her father somewhat worse, but that glance at him as she entered the kitchen, shocked her into a little cry of self-condemnation. The wretched man was laid naked, save for his woollen shirt, on the bed in the corner. The ashes from the dead fire were strewn on his pillow, blown there by the cold wind. The bedclothes, tossed from him in some paroxysm of rage, lay upon the floor, the blind dog huddling into them, bleeding from a wound Mason had managed to inflict by calling it to him, to vent upon the beast his thwarted spirit of hatred. The old man's mouth was a black, parched cavern. His eyes glared like a savage animal's. Mumbles of incoherent curses tore themselves from his unslaked throat. But his eyes were the most terrible things to behold. They told the whole story. He was mad.

"Sup, father, sup," said Helen, rushing to him with a cup of barley-water. Then, to Martin, "Leet th' fire, sharp. Get him summat warm. Get them salt bags out o' th' cupboard. Stir, Martin, stir." She ordered him as in the old days.

With his gaze fastened upon her face, reading it as the drink gurgled into him, part of it dribbling back into the cup, Abel Mason's hand clutched at Helen's as she held the vessel, supporting him with her other arm under the pillow.

"Day'll m-murder thee," he gurgled, against the cup side. As he watched her face hope died in his, its wild light retaken by the wilder one of despair.

"Enough!" he said, motioning the drink away. With a superhuman spring he had clawed at her, those long, yellow nails of his ripping the white flesh of her arm. The cup clattered to the floor.

"Blood!" he ejaculated drunkenly, seeing the gash.

Helen threw herself between Martin and the bed.

"I'll not touch him," he assured her. "But—run down to th' village an' get two strong men. He'll get rough. He might hurt hissel'. An'—he's deein', anyway."

"No, no," said Helen, flinging her hands before her face. "He's waur—but not deein'."

The woman whom Abel Mason had reared only to torture, was conscious of a strange kinship with him. He had robbed her of all but the remnants of joy. But half her wild soul was of his nourishing.

"Deein'!"

The man on the bed half-roared the word.

"Deein'! Me?" he exclaimed, digging his nails into the sheets. "No. I'll n-not dee, I'll not! My work's not done." Then he said, alertly, forcing that brain of his to the task, breaking machine though it was, "W-where's he?" He was asking for Day, his weapon.

Helen Mason wavered.

She had lied often, but not to the dying. Her life with Day had been a lie. She was sick of lies.

"He's dead," she answered simply.

There was a sound that made her start back, dropping the rug she was trying to tuck around the leaden feet. He had twitched at the sheet, tearing it into ribbons. His passion-distorted features, the bulging, red-glowing eyes, with the tangle of white hair shaken over them, his mouth writhing twisted words that were snarls of obscenity, were a degradation to witness. He bore a resemblance to some white-haired giant ape, save for that spark of humanity that added loathsomeness to the display. It was the spirit of hatred starving in its den.

"Warm him some milk, Martin," said Helen, her momentary horror gone. "He's clay-cold."

"M-milk!" gasped Abel. "I w-want blood, th' blood o' every happy thing i' th' world. M-milk! I want th' blood o' thee, Hinson's spawn." He was chewing at the sheet, spattered with Nero's blood, smacking at it, as he finished.

Martin had got the fire roaring, and the salt-bags over it, on the shovel. Occasionally, as he turned them to get them evenly heated, he gave terse warnings that were commands to Helen, bidding her keep out of the reach of Mason's grip.

"Ay, keep away fro' me!" laughed the savage beast on the bed. Then in the impotency of his rage, he spat out his obscene snarls once more. White as alabaster, her lips bitten, Helen went on tucking the clothes round him, tending always that spark of humanity in him, submerged as it was in the beast. Whilst, with the cunning of the mad, he tried to drag her down with shame in Martin's sight.

The man approached with the salt-bags.

"Stick these to his feet," he said taciturnly.

He was telling himself the same thing as Helen—that Mason was dying, that they must be tender. He knelt down on the fender, raking at the fire to drown the sound of those awful words. Helen tucked the bags to the cold feet. Then she brought the warm milk, held him up again. She was too quick for that lightning clutch at her hair, and stood, pale and panting, leaning against the wall. There was no fear or horror in her look. She was merely protecting herself.

He spurted the drink from his mouth upon her, mingled with that trickling saliva. She wiped it calmly from her cheek.

"He's gettin' energy," murmured Martin. "Run an' fetch somebody. It isn't his own strength. He'll dee ragin'."

"Fetch p-parson," gasped the old man. "Get him to p-pray. He he!"

"Lie down," pleaded Helen. "You're shortenin' your life."

He raised himself on his elbow.

The compassion on the woman's face, the soft moved look of it, the sight of the tears trembling on her lashes, the tears of the happy weeping for the wretched, stung him into frenzy.

"Thy m-mother were a—"

He stopped suddenly. His gaze was glued to a space of wall where a ray of sunlight stole in through the chink of the blind.

"It's true," he defied something, hollowly.

"It's true. Take thy black hair from my throat, Helen Hinson. Take it to hell! Helen—look! What's that?"

He had turned to Helen with a note of human fear, addressing flesh and blood. But as she put her hand out to soothe him, the threat in his eyes, the infuriated look at finding himself appealing to her, made her draw it back. His yellow stumps of teeth crashed together, closing on air.

He fell back on his pillow.

After a few minutes, in which Helen had warmed a blanket, wrapping it round him whilst he looked the murder he could not effect, he muttered, "I want to eat. I'll be better to-morn. I—I'm not deein'! I can't dee." He lay back once more, speechless, but looking curses at them, at the two who had come together despite him.

"He'll get wild agen. Go for somebody to hold him down," said Martin.

The strange, primitive dignity of Helen asserted itself unreasonably.

"No. He shan't dee held down," she said irrationally. Then she shuddered. "Think o' deein' so full o' hate," she said. "Th' bitterness, th' emptiness—"

The eyes were unclosing again.

"K-keep thy damned p-pity!" mumbled Mason. "Lift th' dog on th' bed. It's my o-only friend."

Slinking and whining the poor beast was lifted up.

"Let m-me stroke it," pleaded the old man.

Then as it was placed within range he clawed at it, laughing shrilly till exhausted at its howls. Martin had snatched it away, and gave it warm milk to lap. Helen moved about, straightening the kitchen. Martin sat in his old chair. Something was bubbling in a saucepan.

From a slight stupor the old man awoke, opening his eyes. He screamed in agony. Helen rushed to the bed.

"G-go away!" he yelled to her, his glance including Martin. "Have I to see yo' so—sittin' so, happy, when I'm i' th' g-grave?"

"Let's go out," said Helen brokenly.

They stood together in the garden, looking down the hill, leaving him alone, but near enough to run if he should want them. His voice, rising higher, came to them at intervals. He was insisting on another life, telling himself it must be—because he craved it so, to complete his hate. He shouted, with curses, for life upon life, till his work was done.

The sun was shining on the hillside, bringing a hint of green to it.

"I never knew I cared—he brought me up," said Helen. Her hand was cold in Martin's clasp. Her eyes motioned his to the sunlight and the sky.

"Can it ever seem th' same agen?" she asked wearily. "A' that hate—!"

It was Martin's turn to comfort.

Then he said "Hush!"

There was a movement within the kitchen.

They entered.

Mason had crept out of bed, and was sitting on the edge of it. Some spurt of strength had entered the wasted frame, tottering on the brink of the grave.

"Lift me up," he begged. "Let me look at th' fire."

Helen ignored Martin's look.

Placing her hands firmly under his arm-pits she walked him over, step by step, towards the fire. He looked at it with a comforted expression, mumbling about the cold. The mighty brain, with its last spark of consciousness, was plotting.

"Are yo' warmer?" asked Helen's voice gently. "Maybe you'll get better—"

A cry from Martin arrested her attention.

With a backward movement of cunning Mason had grasped the thin, worn carving-knife from the table. The feeble body nerved itself in answer to that last command of the brain, yet to win its way.

"Let go of him," shouted Martin.

"I—can't," answered Helen, shutting her eyes.

The old, thin body would crash to the ground if she let go.

Martin rushed towards the old man, trying vainly to cover the space before that knife descended into the woman's breast.

Then—there was a snarl of savage lust, the mingled voices of man and beast. The old man's foot had touched the dog's bleeding side as Nero drank the milk. There was the thud of a heavy body crashing against the old man, the flash of teeth, and the blind dog had turned on his master, stung into treachery by the impulse of self-preservation, the hatred of pain.

"The stick!"

Martin rushed to it in answer to Helen's cry.

The two rolling forms were on the floor, now, snarling and yelling. Mason was biting at the dog—the dog at Mason. Before Martin reached Nero with the stick, all was over. Both lay very still, but the dog's side was throbbing, throbbing and bleeding, whilst low whines of fear and degradation broke from him. He had outraged great laws. He had bitten his master.

Helen sat with the old man's head on her lap. In her struggles to get Nero off him her hair had tumbled about her. It swept the distorted, grinning face of hate near her breast.

The eyes opened, to see Helen's face.

"Ten thousand eternities—to h-hate in!" he breathed painfully. "C-curse you both, an' your childer's childer. Ten thousand etern—"

He choked midway in the crave.

The battle was in his throat.

He clutched at air.

Helen leaned close down to him, her eyes staring into his, that kinship in her calling to him with a sob,

"You're all th' father I've known. I like yo'——" with a vain endeavour to give him love despite himself.

He stared back into those eyes, like Helen's, at the hair like his rival's.

He was fighting with Death.

"I—h-hate!" he said vehemently.

He spat at her. The glare of his eyes was furnace-fierce. Quite suddenly his head fell back, the repulsive grin of hate still living in the dying, becoming fixed. The light was fading from his eyes.

"M-Martin!" sobbed Helen.

Martin Scott bent down.

"It's over," he said. "Poor old devil!"

He wiped the spittle that had cost Mason his last breath from Helen's shuddering cheek.

"To dee—so!" she shivered.

"I'll ha' to fetch someone," he said.

"Don't leave me, Martin," shrilled Helen.

That dead face was too terrible to look on.

Together they went down to the village. They learnt there that a man named Jim Brett, a tramp, had given himself up to the local constable. He had pushed Day into eternity on the impulse of the minute. Sleeping at last in the wet bracken, after a shivering night, and dreaming of Sarah, he had been awakened to see Day. The sight of the tin-god had been too much for him.

When Martin and Helen got back with the doctor, the eyes of Abel Mason, closed gently by Martin, had half-unclosed again. They stared hate at all who looked, until the coffin-lid covered them. The old man's will left all to Day whilst he lived with Helen. The mortality of Day had, curiously enough, never entered either Mason's mind or Day's. The tin-god had left no will. Helen and Martin Scott would have a pot o' brass.

There were one or two people who specially went out of their way to Corple Stones Farm to ask how Helen

came to be away from home without her husband—
as she must have been not to be with him when he
was killed. But as Lizzie thought that "Lies were good
enough for busy-bodies" they went away as wise as
they came.

*

Spring!

The wind laughed in the green bracken. A million
heads tossed at once. A brook tumbled and laughed
with a gurgle of clear joy. And mixing in with it was a
woman's laugh—as clear and happy.

Away ahead she could see Martin. He had left her,
parting the bracken to make her a path through it. She
could just see the top of his head and the movement his
hands made tossing the bracken on each side. He had
left her. She had vowed she could manage that steep
ascend through the bracken all by herself. It was a
challenge. Her feet went into sploshes of diamond-clear
water left by the tumbling of the stream. They stuck
into the clean dirt. She stopped sometimes to look at
the sky peeping back at her through the bracken.

"Hush!" called Martin suddenly.

She stopped.

"What is it?" she breathed.

"A sandpiper," he told her. "Sh—sh!"

The sweet, sad thread of sound palpitated on the air.

"Th' first I've heard," he confided to her, as she
reached him. She stood looking at him, whilst he stared
in the direction of the sandpiper's cry. In his eyes was
the reflection of her own face.

"Th' eggs are bad to find," he ruminated, then gave a
muted cry of delight.

She followed his gaze into the sky that made her
dizzy. Round and round it, in anxious parental care,
went a couple of peewits.

"There's a nest somewhere near," he whispered.
He went stealthily, watching at times the tricks of the

213

parents to divert his attention, catching all the notes of those voices away up in the sky. Then, as he gained the moor-top, he stalked along right to the nest.

In a hollow of the rushy ground were three baby plovers. They were three bunches of soft brown with bright eyes. Martin handed one to Helen. She rubbed her cheek against it, crooning. Then she glanced with quick sympathy at the birds above. Their voices were insane with terrified passion now. Anger, grief, lament floated down to them. Helen touched Martin on the arm, dragged him away, hastened his putting the birds back into the nest in the ground.

"It's a wonderful thing to hold in your hand what'll travel round and round the sky," he said. He took her hand in his, and they swung across the moor-top, through the rushes that glistened in the sunshine like thousands of knitting-needles, and the shining grass, and over the soppy mosses and the bents.

When they could see the Corple Stones (they had climbed the Heights from the opposite side) he stopped.

"Whilst th' rocks shall stand—" he said suddenly, speaking from some depths within himself. The woman understood and smiled. They sat down to eat, resting on a springy couch of heather. Below them unrolled to view the splendour of a springtime vale, where a thousand daisies were staring at the sun in golden-eyed joy of life.

"I believe," said Martin, in a voice of faith, "I shall live to be eighty, an' hobble on a stick."

There was no answer but a quiet smile from the woman at his side.

"Teddy's farm needn't be a failure," he went on thoughtfully. "This year I shall sow—"

Swish!

A cloud of grouse flew across near to them, and Martin forgot to complete his sentence.

From perfect hour to perfect hour they went over the moor, or rested, till the dusk crept down, and a lonely dog that guarded the sheep followed them back for company, until dismissed by Martin. Then through the mist they saw the twinkling light of their nest, Corple Stones Farm, and went down towards it, hand in hand, following the same star.

THE END

Lightning Source UK Ltd.
Milton Keynes UK
UKHW040255300919
350673UK00017B/167/P